Tempt Me
If You Can

JANET CHAPMAN

Tempt Me
If You Can

Pocket **Star** Books

New York   London   Toronto   Sydney

Pocket Star Books
A Division of Simon & Schuster, Inc.
1230 Avenue of the Americas
New York, NY 10020

Cover design by Min Choi
Cover illustration by Gene Mollica

Manufactured in the United States of America

ISBN-13: 978-1-61664-043-9

To Benjamin Chapman

This one is all yours, even though you have always been the hero of your own story!

(So now will you stop sending me those anonymous fan letters, asking when I am going to give my smart, handsome, eldest son his very own book?)

Prologue

Benjamin Sinclair stared up at his two brothers standing across the desk from him, presenting an imposing, united front. They hadn't uttered a word since walking in, and they didn't have to. Sinclair men never bluffed, and once committed, they never backed down.

Knowing he wasn't leaving the office until he explained his ongoing black mood, Ben silently pulled a card from an envelope on the desk, slid it toward them, then fixed his gaze on the opposite wall as they read the short, succinct note written on a plain white card.

Sam Sinclair picked up the envelope, read the postmark, then looked at Ben. "You got this over three weeks ago."

"It's taken me that long to find out if it's true."

"And is it?" Jesse asked.

Ben dropped his gaze to the unsigned note that had sent him into a tailspin.

> You have a son, Mr. Sinclair. He's fifteen years old, and his name is Michael. It's time you came and met him.

The envelope was postmarked Medicine Gore, Maine.

"The investigators I hired believe that it's true," Ben returned softly, his gunmetal gaze once again fixed on his brothers. "His name is Michael Sands, he lives with his aunt in Medicine Gore, and the timing is right." He slid a thick folder toward them. "The investigators included a photo. You tell me if you think it's true."

Sam opened the folder and he and Jesse stared down at the eight-by-ten photograph.

"My God," Jesse said hoarsely, looking at Ben. "This could be a picture of you nineteen years ago." He looked back at Ben. "He has your eyes."

Sam, the oldest of the three Sinclair men, collapsed with a sigh into a chair facing the desk. Jesse, the youngest, picked up the photo before sitting in the other chair.

"All these years of enduring Bram's petitions for us to get married and have children." Sam shook his head. "And he had a great-grandson living in Maine all this time."

"How the hell could you not know you'd fathered a

child?" Jesse asked. "It had to have happened that summer you spent protesting some logging practice in the Maine mountains. We suspected you fell in love with a girl up there, but you were in such a foul mood when you came back, you refused to tell us what in hell was wrong."

"I was protesting the building of a hydroelectric dam," Ben clarified. "And the girl was Kelly Sands. I asked her to come back to New York with me, but she just laughed and told me to get lost. There wasn't even a hint that she might be pregnant."

"Did she know who you were?" Sam asked. "Who your grandfather was?"

"I didn't hide the fact that I came from money, but I didn't exactly flaunt it, either." He shrugged. "I don't think she ever equated me with wealth."

Jesse snorted. "If she had, you can be damn sure she'd have come knocking on your door once she discovered she was pregnant."

"The question is, why is she suddenly knocking now?" Sam asked. "Fifteen years is a long time to wait to tell a man he has a son."

"The note isn't from her," Ben said. "According to the investigators, Kelly Sands vanished ten years ago. Emma, her younger sister, has been raising Michael all by herself."

Silence settled between the brothers. Ben curled his hands into fists as his vision turned inward, narrowing on that long-ago summer when youthful idealism had pulled him north . . . into the arms of a beautiful and ultimately cruel young woman. Long-buried pain rose to the surface; remorse, grief, and anger warred inside Ben as he once again tried to wrap his mind around the fact that he had a fifteen-year-old son.

"So what do you plan to do about this?" Sam asked.

Dragged back to the present, Ben gave his brothers a tight smile. "I'm planning to go meet my son, just as the note suggests."

"And?" Jesse asked.

"And, while my investigators find out where Kelly Sands has run off to, I plan to make *Emma* Sands very sorry for not contacting me the moment her sister left Michael in her care. Once they find Kelly, I intend to make *her* even sorrier—not only for not telling me I had a son, but for abandoning him to a nineteen-year-old girl."

Sam was shaking his head before Ben even finished. "You can't," he said, leaning forward to rest his elbows on his knees. "I'm sure the boy loves his mother and aunt. You go after them for revenge, and you'll destroy any chance of having a relationship with Michael."

"He's right, Ben." Jesse stood up and tossed the photo on the desk. "For all you know, they told Michael his father is dead. Instead of letting anger cloud your judgment, you need to decide how you're going to approach the boy."

Ben also stood. "I've already got that part figured out. I leave tomorrow for a two-week bird hunt at Emma Sands's sporting camps. I'm booked at Medicine Creek Camps as Tom Jenkins."

Sam also stood, clearly alarmed. "You can't just show up there using an alias. The aunt will know who you are the moment she sees you."

Ben rubbed the neatly trimmed beard he'd been growing for a week. "I've changed quite a bit in sixteen years. Emma was only fourteen the summer I was in Maine, and she always disappeared into the forest whenever I visited Kelly. There's no way she'll know who I am. Then, once I get comfortable being around Michael, I'll find a way to introduce myself."

"I don't like it," Sam growled. "Somebody in town is bound to recognize you. Are you forgetting what happened the day you left Medicine Gore? The FBI might have concluded you didn't have anything to do with blowing up that dam, but they never caught the bastards. The townspeople probably still think you're responsible for Charlie Sands's death." He stepped up to the desk. "At least take Jesse with you."

"Jesse will be running Tidewater International while I'm gone. We're right in the middle of purchasing five new cargo ships, and the details still have to be worked out."

"Dammit, Ben," Sam snapped. "You need to think this through."

"It's the only thing I *have* been thinking about for three weeks." Ben slid the note back in its envelope, set it and the photo back in the folder, then tucked the folder under his arm. "If you'll excuse me, I have to finish packing."

Sam stepped around the desk to head him off. "At least take Ronald with you."

Ben gave a sharp laugh. "Showing up with a driver who looks like a hit man will certainly give the right impression. No, this is my problem, and I'll deal with it my way." He touched Sam's arm. "Don't worry, big brother, I can take care of myself."

Ben headed for the door, but stopped and looked back to Sam. "Oh, and that little wager the three of us had going, that you could persuade Willa to marry you and get her pregnant within two months of the wedding? Even though you succeeded on both counts, I believe your and Jesse's millions should go into a trust for Michael, seeing how Bram's *first* great-grandson won by fifteen years."

With that, Ben walked into the hall and up the stairs, his smile fading as his thoughts turned to tomorrow's journey into the northern Maine woods.

Chapter One

Just as surely as it would snow this winter, Tom Jenkins would be trouble. Most of her guests from big cities were trouble, but usually they had the decency to actually *arrive* before they sent her business into chaos. Tom Jenkins hadn't even made it to Medicine Creek Camps, and already he was causing her fits.

The man was lost.

Emma was sorely tempted to leave him that way.

But here she was, walking down yet another one of the tote roads that spiderwebbed through her neck of the woods, trying to remember why she loved this business so much. Emma sighed, resigned to the fact that she would smile nicely when she found Tom Jenkins, tell him it was her fault he was lost, and get him tucked into his cabin.

When she rounded a curve in the logging road, though, she stopped in disbelief. Four men, supposedly her friends, were beating up her missing guest.

The brawl had been mighty, if the torn clothes and bloody faces and churned gravel were any indication. It must have been raging quite a while, too, from the looks of the hard-breathing men. But with the odds so uneven, the outcome was inevitable. Her lost guest was now being held between two burly loggers while another tried to pound him senseless.

Only the man was *not* Tom Jenkins. Emma immediately realized that hiding behind all that blood, beard, and a mask of pain was the one man on earth she had sworn to kill should she ever get the chance.

He shouldn't be here, in her woods, turning this beautiful October afternoon into yet another black day of her life. Even the sun had suddenly gone behind a cloud, sending a chill down her spine that had nothing to do with the temperature.

He was sixteen years older than the last time she'd seen him, but she would have recognized him in the middle of a blinding blizzard. He'd grown taller and his shoulders had widened, but it was him. And even held captive by two burly loggers, the man of her nightmares looked more dangerous than a cornered wolf.

Benjamin Sinclair was back.

Another blow landed on his defenseless torso, and Emma winced at his grunt of pain.

Damn. She should be cheering, not saving his rotten hide.

Emma shouldered her shotgun, clicked off the safety, and pulled the trigger.

The echoing boom and avalanche of pelting bird-shot got everyone's attention. Three men dropped to the ground, letting their victim fall to his knees. The man with the punishing fists spun around, his eyes wide with horror. Emma saw the moment he recognized her, because his face darkened and his shock turned to a ferocious scowl.

"Dammit, Emma. What in hell are you shooting at us for!"

"I'm postponing your war a bit, Durham."

Durham Bragg spit on the ground in front of Benjamin Sinclair, who was dazedly staring at her, his own look of horror barely masked by his bloodied features. His other three attackers were strewn around him like fallen bowling pins, widened eyes peeking out from under their arms covering their heads. Emma looked back at Durham and waited with the patience of a hunter.

Her old friend snarled a curse she hadn't heard since her father had died. "Dammit, Emma Jean! If you want to stay neutral, then stay the hell out of this! We're having a little talk with this tree hugger before we send him back to his buddies." Durham turned back to his victim.

Emma jacked a new shell into the chamber and raised the barrel of her shotgun again as the three other men started to rise. They immediately dropped back down.

"He's not an environmentalist, Durham. He's one of my guests. He's signed up for two weeks of partridge hunting."

Durham spun back to face her. "Emma! Look at him—his clothes all but shout tree hugger. And I swear I've seen his face before, probably on some damn Greenpeace poster." Durham pointed at the man weaving on his knees. "For chrissakes, the guy could be a model for the L.L.Bean catalog!"

"His name is Tom Jenkins," Emma said. "Stanley Bates dropped him off at the painted rock and gave him directions to Medicine Creek Camps."

Durham shot a hesitant look at his kneeling victim. "Bates couldn't give directions to a goddamn homing pigeon," he said with a frustrated growl. He rubbed his forehead and let out a sigh. "Dammit. I *know* this guy from someplace." He gave Emma a speculative look. "He could be registered as your guest and still be a tree hugger. Hunting partridge could be a cover."

"Environmental soldiers don't get lost in the woods."

"Dammit, Emma Jean. Your daddy wouldn't be pointing no shotgun at me."

"Damn yourself," Emma countered. "You beat up one of my guests. Go home, and leave this man alone in the coming weeks. I *won't* have my sports harassed."

Benjamin Sinclair, the lowlife snake, finally stirred.

Emma ignored him until Durham grudgingly nodded agreement. Then she looked at the other three men, who were once more making their way to their feet, brushing the dirt from themselves as they glared at her.

She moved the barrel of her shotgun in their direction. "I'll have your agreement also, gentlemen."

They looked at her shotgun, at Durham, and then back at her. Finally, they nodded. Emma clicked on the safety, lowered her gun barrel, and looked at Benjamin Sinclair.

His right eye was swollen shut, his left one barely visible. His lip was split and blood was trailing down into the dark tangle of his beard. And now he was trying to stand while cradling his ribs. Durham finally helped him up with all the empathy of a hungry bear grabbing its dinner. Benjamin Sinclair groaned in agony and then glared at Durham with his one open eye.

"Happy hunting, sport," Durham muttered, slapping his victim on the shoulder, sending him forward several faltering steps. Durham motioned to his buddies and started up the tote road. When he got beside Emma, he stopped.

"You just be careful, missy. That man don't hit like any sport I've ever met," he growled, rubbing his own swollen jaw.

Emma widened her eyes in feigned surprise. "You mean he actually tried to defend himself?"

Durham ignored that. "Emma Jean Sands, you know

better than to go around pointing that gun at people, much less shooting the damn thing."

"And you know violence won't stop this war. Remember last time? People got killed."

All signs of anger left Durham's face. His eyes turned pained as he reached out one large hand and set it gently on her shoulder. "I remember, kiddo." He turned and looked back at Benjamin Sinclair. "You could be right about this one. He does look more lost than threatening, now doesn't he?" he added with a satisfied smile.

Durham and his band of bullies walked to his battered pickup without looking back. The truck started with a violent rev of the engine and its tires spun on the gravel, filling the air with a cloud of dust and debris.

Emma eyed their victim. Durham couldn't be more wrong. No matter how beaten and battered he was, Benjamin Sinclair was the greatest threat alive.

She finally gathered her courage and slowly walked up to him. "You are Tom Jenkins, I hope."

The lying snake looked her right in the eye and nodded.

"Well, Mr. Jenkins, Medicine Creek Camps is about six miles back."

"Is there a reason you weren't at the airfield this morning to pick me up?" he asked in an obviously pained growl, glaring at her from his one open eye.

"I was thirty miles north of town this morning, rescuing two lost canoeists who are staying at my camps."

"And when you found them, were they also being beat up?"

"No, they were only half-drowned. I found them on a small island at the north end of Medicine Lake, huddled together to keep warm after they'd capsized their canoe." Emma gave him a tight smile. "But then, they weren't dressed like a sporting catalog model."

Judging by his intensified glare, he didn't care for that observation. Time to get Benjamin Sinclair patched up and away from Medicine Gore—and Michael—as fast as the next truck out of town could take him. Emma tucked her shotgun under her arm and stepped closer. "You need a doctor. Come on, Mr. Jenkins. My truck is up the road."

"Go get it."

His words were still more growled than spoken, and Emma instantly felt contrite. Benjamin Sinclair—or Tom Jenkins until she was ready to call him a liar to his face—was in immense pain. "It's not far, Mr. Jenkins. And I don't think I should leave you alone."

Even slumped in pain, he was a good half foot taller than her. She didn't want to get within ten feet of the man. Wounded animals were dangerous, and right now Benjamin Sinclair looked like he ate kittens for breakfast.

Emma picked up his backpack and fancy gun case, wrinkling her nose at the metallic smell of blood mixed with dirt. The sun was shining again and the birds were back to singing, but the temperature had permanently dropped in her heart.

Michael's father was *here*.

"How far's the truck?"

"It's a good mile, at least," she told him, hefting his pack onto her shoulder. "I'm sorry, but there will be more loggers driving these roads home from work. I think we should stick together."

He reached for his gun case and grasped it like a cane. "Friendly town you've got here. Lead on, Miss . . . ?"

The man was obviously going to play out his charade. But he was badly beaten, he didn't realize she knew who he was, and she had one very powerful trump card. All she had to do was tell someone in town who her guest was, and every living, breathing person would descend on him like a nuclear bomb.

Benjamin Sinclair hadn't left any friends behind when he'd stolen out of town sixteen years ago—only a pregnant young girl, a town full of vigilantes, and a dead man.

Emma gave him a deceptively friendly smile. "I'm Emma Sands from Medicine Creek Camps. Um . . . welcome to Maine, Mr. Jenkins."

Benjamin Sinclair started up the tote road, but he didn't make it ten steps before his legs buckled and he fell to one knee.

Dammit. She would have to physically help him to the truck.

She expected him to feel like the snake he was; cold and slimy and disgusting. But what Emma felt as she set her shoulder under his was solid male muscle. The electric spark that shot through her nearly made her jump back.

Apparently he felt it, too. He shot upright and stiffened and glared at her again. Emma felt like a deer trapped in the light of molten gray eyes the exact same color of Michael's.

Did he remember her?

Of course he did. The man wouldn't have booked a stay at Medicine Creek if he didn't know where his son was living.

The idealistic young man she remembered from sixteen years ago had been dangerously intelligent, if somewhat misguided. He'd been bold and handsome and charismatic, and Emma, only fourteen at the time, had idolized him. Her older sister had naively jumped into his bed, and Michael was the result of that recklessness. And now, after all these years, the boy was going to meet the man who had abandoned him and his mother without a backward glance.

"Are you planted here, Miss Sands, or are you waiting for me to bleed to death to save yourself the trouble of a lawsuit?"

Emma grabbed the back of his belt and started off down the dirt road. "It's not my fault you were beaten up, Mr. Jenkins. My liability doesn't start until you actually check in." She snorted. "When out-of-staters wander these woods dressed like tree huggers, they have no one to blame but themselves for being mistaken for trouble."

Emma watched him frown down at his clothes before looking back up the tote road they were hobbling along. His arm around her tightened and she shifted his pack on her shoulder, making him loosen his grip.

"They beat me up because they didn't like my clothes?"

"There's tension in these parts right now. Environmentalists, mostly out-of-staters, are trying to get clear-cutting banned in our forests. Everyone's worried about losing their jobs as well as their way of life."

Good Lord. She was explaining this to the biggest tree hugger of them all! Last time he'd come here, Benjamin Sinclair had had the backing of the Sierra Club to fight damming the river for hydropower. He'd been quiet in his crusade, but nonetheless effective. The nearly finished dam hadn't been rebuilt after it had been blown up—along with her father.

"Damn. They let the air out of my tires."

Ben looked up to see a dusty red pickup with roof racks, a canoe on top, and four flat tires. Hell. Now he remembered why he hated this town. "Nice friends you've got," he muttered through gritted teeth.

The woman beside him sighed. "Payback for spraying them with birdshot."

His obviously reluctant rescuer opened the passenger door, and Ben eased into the seat with a groan. It was a relief to be sitting, and an even greater relief to be free of the disturbing touch of Emma Sands. He watched in silence as she tossed his pack and shotgun case in the truck bed, walked around to open the driver's door, and carefully placed her shotgun on the rack behind his head. Then she started rummaging around under the seat.

Soda cans and empty chip bags came out, followed by candy wrappers and a flashlight, then a pair of gloves, a dirty towel, empty shotgun casings, live shotgun shells, binoculars, and a first-aid kit. Ignoring the kit, she made a sound of relief when she pulled out an unopened bottle of whiskey. She tossed it to him and grabbed up the towel. Then, without saying a word, she slammed the door shut and started walking down the road.

She was definitely pissed about something. Ben hoped it was the fact that her tires were flat, and not that she knew who he was. He watched her stop at a nearby bog and dip the scruffy rag into it.

A feather could have knocked him over when Durham had called her Emma. The Emma Sands he remembered had been a quiet, shy little waif who liked to spend more time in the forest than around people.

This woman—this gun-toting, fire-breathing virago—was a far cry from the young girl he remembered. But what unbalanced Ben the most was his reaction to her.

When she had tucked herself under his shoulder, he had felt a jolt of electricity that had nearly knocked him over.

Emma Sands had grown up real nice, and had done well for herself. According to the investigators, she'd never married, and had been single-handedly raising Michael ever since Kelly had run off with a man ten years ago.

Ben knew Emma was a bush pilot, a licensed Maine Guide, and the owner of Medicine Creek Camps. He also knew Michael's name was on the deed with hers, and that their guiding and camping business was very successful. Emma clearly believed in investing in good equipment; the Cessna Stationair she owned wasn't cheap, the truck he was sitting in was this year's model, and the camps themselves sat on a thousand acres of prime woodland.

Only the investigators hadn't told Ben exactly where Medicine Creek Camps was located. They'd also neglected to include a photo of Emma, or mention that her legs came up to her armpits, that her blond hair formed a braid as thick as his wrist, and her tanned, flawless complexion framed startling green eyes.

Had she written him the letter?

And if she had, why now?

Ben didn't think she recognized him. He'd filled out, grown hard, and his beard should help insure that no one in town would recognize him.

Ben watched her rise from the stream, expecting he
would soon be getting his face washed like a four-year-
old. But she just stood there, staring out over the water
and then looking up at the sky. Finally she turned.

And damn if she didn't look even madder than
before.

Ben watched her walk back to the truck, her mind
obviously wrestling with some decision. She hesitated
at the driver's door, looking back at the bog as she ab-
sently wrung the life out of the towel she was holding.

She seemed to suddenly come to a decision.

Whatever it was, Ben could see she was not pleased
with what she had decided, just determined. She slid
into the seat beside him and picked up the mike of the
two-way radio bolted beneath the dash.

"Come on, Mikey. Talk to me," she said into the
mike. "I need a ride home."

"Where's your truck?" soon came a male voice over
the radio. "Did you total this one, too, Nemmy?"

Mikey? Could that deep masculine voice be Michael's?

Ben nearly stopped breathing.

"No. I've got four flat tires and my portable com-
pressor is in the shed. Come get Mr. Jenkins and me.
We're over by Smokey Bog."

"Holy cow! The sport made it that far? Walking?"

"It seems so, Mikey. Just come get us, will you? Mr.
Jenkins needs to see a doctor." She kept the mike

depressed as she hesitated, shooting Ben a dark look. "You're going to have to fly over, so we can leave for the hospital directly from here."

"He's hurt that bad?"

She continued to look at Ben, her eyes a dark, disturbed jade that made him think of glacial ice. "Bad enough, but he'll live. You can land on the bog."

"No way, bossy lady. Crazy Larry is home, and if he sees me flying he'll call the FAA again. And I can't land on that bog. It's too small."

Ben stiffened. She was asking the boy to do something dangerous?

And illegal?

"Michael, you can land here with your eyes closed. Just put Alice in the driver's seat. Larry won't know it's not me."

"Can't I drive over and get you, then you can fly Mr. Jenkins to Millinocket?"

Emma reached out and pressed the wet rag to Ben's forehead as she shook her head. "No. Just get in the damn plane and get over here."

"Shit."

"And, Mikey?"

"Yeah?"

"If I see the water rudders down as you approach, I'm gonna make you wax every inch of that plane tomorrow."

"Aw, Nem. I only forgot them once."

"And it cost you a month's wages, if I remember correctly. Now get going before our sport passes out and we have to carry him to the plane."

"Roger, bossy lady. I'm climbing in now."

Emma Sands hung the mike on its cradle and leaned back with a frustrated sigh. "It won't be long now, Mr. Jenkins. Michael will come get us, and then we'll get you to a doctor." She looked over and saw the bottle of whiskey, the cover still on, in his lap. "That whiskey will do you good, Mr. Jenkins."

"My hands won't work. I can't open it."

She reached out and twisted off the cap. He tried to take a drink, but he couldn't even grasp the bottle. Hell, yes, he'd defended himself. And he had the swollen knuckles to prove it.

"You're going to have to get some new clothes, if you still plan to hunt these roads," she said as he stared down at his useless hands.

Ben snapped his gaze up at the amusement in her voice, but he only had time to open his mouth before she held the bottle to his lips. The potent whiskey burned his bleeding mouth, and ran all the way down his throat to pool like liquid heat in his stomach. Damn, it felt good. And she was a generous savior, despite her crude care. She patiently let him have his fill, until he leaned his head against the headrest and closed his eyes. Lord, he could feel the whiskey already spreading to every aching muscle in his body. He'd been so sore and numb he hadn't realized how cold he was.

Ben cracked his eyes enough to see the sun was setting behind the nearest mountain, casting long shadows over the forest, making the bog an unreadable tangle of still water, stumps, and ripples.

His son was going to land *here*? In a floatplane?

Ben stiffened at the sudden roar of a plane buzzing overhead. Dammit. He'd crawl to the hospital before he'd put Michael in danger. He was just about to tell Emma that when he heard the radio crackle again.

"Help me, Nem."

"Figure it out yourself, Mikey."

Ben made a grab for the mike to tell the boy to abort the landing and go home, but Emma pulled it out of his reach and glared at him. "He can do this," she snapped. "Michael's a better bush pilot than anyone around here. The bog's big enough and he's talented enough to land here in his sleep."

"If he gets hurt, Miss Sands, I'm going to use that radio cord to strangle you."

She stared at him for a good long minute, and then she suddenly gave him a strange smile. "You have my permission to try."

"Guide him in."

"No."

"Guide me in, Nem," Michael echoed over the radio.

"If you want to solo on your sixteenth birthday, you better know how, Mikey. I won't be on the radio then."

Ben heard an exasperated sigh come over the speaker. "I've been flying solo for two years."

"And I've only had to replace the pontoons once," she shot back. "Don't make it twice. Watch the rocks."

She tossed the mike on the dash and got out, and Ben realized that every muscle in her body was primed for action. Her shoulders were squared and her eyes were trained like lasers on the fast-descending plane, which appeared to be brushing the treetops. Her hands were balled into fists and her feet were planted, and she looked like she intended to guide her nephew down by force of will alone.

So the tough-talking lady was worried, was she?

Ben was going to kill her before this was over.

He could see two heads through the windshield of the plane, but Alice was either a very brave or a very dumb passenger. Michael was doing the flying, and he seemed to be doing it very well. He had throttled back but he was still coming in fast, looking like a hawk diving for prey. He wasn't hesitating or asking for help now, by God. And his water rudders were up.

Michael Sands set the Stationair down on Smokey Bog softly enough to make an eagle weep. Ben brushed the blood trailing down his cheek, only to find his shaking hand came away more wet than red.

Damn, he was proud of the boy. Michael was doing

a job most men couldn't, and he was doing it magnificently. Emma might be justified in her boast, if this was an example of the boy's maturity and self-confidence.

Ignoring his protesting body, Ben climbed out of the truck and shuffled toward the bog, determined to be standing eye level and proud when he finally met his son for the first time.

Chapter Two

*E*mma watched with pride as her nephew carefully nudged the Cessna up against the muddy bank of Smokey Bog. She hadn't doubted for a minute he could land here; Mikey was the most capable young man she'd ever known.

He killed the engine and gave her a cocky smile through the windshield, then reached over, adjusted Alice's cap, and pushed her dark glasses up her nose. He was clearly proud of himself. He climbed out of the plane and walked forward on the pontoon, jumping onto the shore with the litheness of a cat. Not even sixteen yet, Mikey was already pushing six feet.

Suddenly he stopped and stared at the bloody man limping toward them.

This was not good. Michael Sands was far too intelligent not to recognize the father he'd never met but probably knew everything about. The boy did own a computer; what were the chances his curiosity hadn't led him through the internet to Benjamin Sinclair?

Her sister had never talked about Michael's father to him, but that hadn't stopped the boy from asking questions. And after Kelly had left, when Michael was five, Emma had answered every one of those questions with all the care and courage she could. She hadn't made Benjamin Sinclair out to be an ogre; she'd simply told Michael that his father had been young and confused. And yes, he was handsome; yes, he was tall; and yes, he was just as intelligent as Mikey was.

This should prove interesting, Emma decided as she watched them stare at each other. Knowing Mikey, he wouldn't reveal that he knew who Tom Jenkins really was. And their guest seemed just as determined to keep up the charade.

His eyes intent, Mikey reached out a hand. "Welcome to Maine, Mr. Jenkins."

Benjamin Sinclair seemed completely floored by the gesture, and took an unsteady step back, looking as if he were facing a ghost.

What? The man who could tear her family to shreds was suddenly scared?

Mikey was still holding his hand out, and what Emma saw when she looked at his face would forever stay etched in her memory. Mikey wasn't hurt, or angry, or even surprised. He simply stepped forward, picked up Ben's hand, and moved it over his shoulder as he reached around his father's waist to give him support.

"You're a bit of a mess, Mr. Jenkins. And my aunt is right about your needing to see a doctor. Come on. I'll help you into the plane. Go get his stuff from the truck, Nem. I've got him now."

Emma realized she had also taken a step back, her mind numb and her heart breaking at the sight of the only person in the world she loved gently coming to the aid of the one person who could destroy her.

They were finally back at Medicine Creek Camps, with their guest tucked into one of the downstairs bedrooms of her home, drugged to his eyeballs with painkillers. Michael was in the Cessna cleaning up after their bloody passenger, and Emma was stretched out in her recliner with a frosted bottle of beer in her hand and a hot washcloth draped over her eyes.

For a man of few words, her battered guest sure could find choice ones when he wanted—which they had learned when Michael had removed Alice from the plane. Benjamin had cursed their ears red upon discovering that Mikey's copilot was an old store mannequin with a hat and wig and aviator glasses. He'd then demanded to know what kind of person put a kid in the unthinkable position of landing on a spit of water so small it made aircraft carrier decks huge by comparison.

Michael, bless the boy's heart, had calmly told Ben

that Crazy Larry kept trying to report him to the FAA before he could turn sixteen and get his license. To that Ben had said—quite colorfully—they should both be turned in to Child Welfare. Emma had finally ended his little snit by poking the angry man in the back with her shotgun. He had gotten into the passenger seat, silent but fiercely glaring.

Alice was now floating facedown in Smokey Bog, where Ben had thrown her.

So much for her reputation. Not that the sporting camps couldn't weather a few critics, but Emma took pride in their business, which she and Mikey had pulled out of drowning red ink. Though still very young herself, Emma had talked her sister into buying Medicine Creek Lodge with the insurance money from their father's death. She and Kelly had run the lodge and camps together until Kelly had suddenly left Emma with the sizable mortgage and a five-year-old boy to raise.

Michael had been born an ancient in a baby's body, looking wiser than God. Thankfully he had been a good baby—sleeping when he should, walking when he should, and talking their ears off with precocious babble. By the time Mikey was five, Emma had wondered if he would be going to school or teaching it.

There wasn't anything the boy couldn't do. Emma figured he'd be ruling the world by the time he was thirty. There was such a calmness about Michael, a gift of understanding and insight so deep, she was in awe—when she wasn't intimidated.

She had finally stopped being amazed by the time Michael turned ten, and had learned to accept the fact that she was living with an old man. If she had somehow become the head of the family, Michael had become the godfather.

Now fifteen, Mikey was only allowing her to hold on to the fantasy that she was in charge. He had picked up the habit of giving her orders every now and then—usually when she was tired or frustrated or at loose ends. And like a good aunt, she always listened to him, allowing herself to be bullied or taken care of, whichever she needed at the time.

Emma pulled the washcloth off her eyes and took another sip of her beer when she heard the back door slam shut.

"He finally sleeping?" Mikey asked as he walked into the living room.

Emma carefully folded the washcloth as she watched him silently pad across the room to loom over her, his six-foot frame lanky yet graceful. "Our patient's sleeping like a lamb."

Michael snorted. "A lamb with fangs. I thought you were going to wash his mouth out back on Smokey Bog."

"Get his claw marks out of the dashboard?"

"Jeez, Nem. You'd think a grown man could handle

a little excitement without sweating bullets. It was close, but you got us airborne in one piece."

"He had just survived a savage beating, and didn't want to find himself decorating a pine tree forty feet up."

Michael grinned. "You only clipped a small branch." He suddenly frowned at her washcloth. "Another headache?"

"No. Just relaxing. Is everyone settled in their cabins for the night?"

He nodded. "Cabin three wants to head out again at first light. Apparently their little swim today didn't discourage them." He gave her a deceptively innocent, expectant look. "I could take the day off from school to guide our bird hunters in cabin five. Someone should stay around and keep an eye on Mr. Jenkins, and since I might be corrupted by his vocabulary, you should probably play nursemaid."

Emma shook her head. "No skipping school. And if I stay in this house with that wounded . . . bear, I'm liable to kill him. Besides, I just called and arranged for Durham to guide cabin five tomorrow. Maybe working for me will keep him out of trouble."

"I can't believe this clear-cutting thing has escalated to violence. There are better ways to resolve the issue. Those men could have really hurt Mr. Jenkins."

"Three cracked ribs, a concussion, and a wrenched knee is not fun."

Michael started putting together a fire in the hearth.

His back to her, he asked, "Does Mr. Jenkins look familiar to you, Nem?"

"Why?"

The boy shrugged and struck a match to his work. "No reason. I just wondered if maybe he's been here before."

"I can safely say that Medicine Creek Camps has never had the pleasure of his company."

"You gonna keep him here in the lodge?"

"For a while. Any problem with that?"

He added logs to the crackling pine. "No problem. But you're too busy as it is. And with me in school, you're all alone, running in every direction and trying to please every sport who wants to shoot a few birds." He searched her face, concern in his eyes. "Moose season starts next week."

Emma threw her washcloth at him and stood up. "Then it's time you helped me get an orange ribbon around Pitiful's neck."

He caught the cloth with ease and also stood up. "I am not going near that stupid beast. A well-placed bullet would be a blessing. He'll never make it through the winter, Nem."

"Sure he will. Pitiful's not stupid."

"No? That fool is in love with you. A two-year-old moose should know the difference between a woman and a cow moose. He's missing some rooms upstairs, Nemmy."

"I think he was grazed by a hunter's bullet last fall. That's why his right antler hasn't grown back this year," she explained in defense of her pet.

"I think he walked into the side of a logging truck. Face it, Nem, he's becoming a pest. He trashes the garbage cans and keeps trying to get in the kitchen."

"He likes my cooking."

"And he swamped one of the boats yesterday. He was trying to climb in it!"

"We have to look out for the dumb ones, Mikey. I'll make him a cake of oats and molasses, and you can tie the ribbon around his neck while he's eating it."

Emma left her nephew contemplating that delightful chore, and went to check on her guest before she turned in for the night. Benjamin Sinclair had made a tangle of his blankets and kicked them to the side, barely keeping himself decent.

For a city-sport, the man was amazingly fit. His deep-barreled chest was darkened with bruises that would have killed a lesser man. Emma quietly leaned over and pulled the covers up to his chin. She carefully brushed his hair back from his forehead, feeling for fever as she exposed a bandage over his left brow.

Welcome to Medicine Creek, Sinclair. Have we given you all the adventure we promised?

She straightened and turned to crack the window beside his bed, letting in the pine-scented autumn air, hoping the slight chill would help keep his covers in place. The full moon was shining starkly, drawing a runway on the lake, just like when they had landed two hours ago. That had been another first for her guest, and one he'd argued against. But again, Michael had calmly told him not to worry, that his aunt had been making night landings on moonlit lakes for years.

The lights in cabin three winked out. Emma leaned her head on the glass, breathed in the smell of what had been her personal heaven for the last fifteen years, and wondered how heavenly Medicine Creek Camps would be without Michael.

Even if Ben didn't take him away to start the new life he was entitled to, Mikey would be going to college, and then on to bigger and better things. And she would be right here, ready to push him or pull him in the right direction—waiting for him to return a grown man.

The wheels of change had begun turning today.

"Why does the boy call you Nemmy?"

Emma didn't turn around, unwilling to let him see her tears. "Because when he was a two-year-old he found Aunt Emma too big of a mouthful. He shortened it to Nemmy and it stuck. I hope that's what he writes on my tombstone."

"Where's his mother?"

"Gone."

"And his father?"

"I hope he's dead."

There was a moment's silence. "You're raising him all by yourself?"

She turned to face the bed. "No, Mr. Jenkins. Michael has been raising me."

"He's a remarkable boy."

"There is nothing boylike about Michael, Mr. Jenkins. He's older than all of us put together, most of the time. Don't ever make the mistake of underestimating my nephew, if you want his respect."

"You clearly have it."

Emma nodded. "Yes, and it took me many frustrating years to get it. Have you ever tried urging an infant to crawl when he's determined to walk instead? Or tried to explain to a five-year-old why he has to go to school to learn finger painting when he wants to learn how airplanes stay up? Or tried to tell a seven-year-old with a genius IQ that being a tree in a school play is a noble pursuit?"

"No."

"Then you should try telling a fourteen-year-old that he can't drive to town for supplies, or fly sports up from Bangor when we're shorthanded. Or try to comfort a grieving child when his mother leaves when he's too busy trying to comfort you instead. I gained Michael's respect by never, ever underestimating him."

"I'll remember that, Miss Sands."

Emma walked to the door of the bedroom and

looked back at the bed. "Be sure that you do, Mr. Jenkins."

Ben sat at the expansive kitchen table and watched Michael move around the kitchen until the boy eventually came to sit across from him. "Where did Medicine Creek Camps get its name?" Ben asked into the silence.

"From the mist that sometimes rises off the creek in winter, when it should be frozen tighter than Pluto."

"There are hot springs here?"

"There might have been at one time. Now the creek just runs unusually warm, fed by springs deep in the granite. Medicine Gore was settled by some Swedes back in the early eighteen hundreds. Apparently the creek ran even warmer back then."

"Ever see these springs?"

Michael took a bear-size bite of his sandwich, chewed slowly, then washed it down with half a glass of milk. "They're contrary wonders, only active when the mood strikes them. Nemmy took me to the headwaters of Medicine Creek once." He looked at Ben with unreadable, assessing gray eyes. "I was about eight." He shrugged again and raised his sandwich back to his mouth. "Maine doesn't really have any geothermal activity," he said just before he took another bite.

Ben waited until the whole sandwich was gone before he asked his next question. "Who built the lodge?"

Michael got up and went to the fridge, pulled out a bucket of ice cream, and put it on the counter. Then he got down two bowls from the cupboard and began to spoon a mountain of ice cream into each of them.

"Local tribes would come here and soak in the creek in winter, believing the mist held great medicine. That's probably why the settlers built this old lodge here." He gave Ben a cocky grin. "To lure city folks with tales of healing powers."

Michael returned to the table with the two heaping bowls, spoons stuck in them like chimneys. He slid one in front of Ben and sat down with the other one. "Eat, Mr. Jenkins. The ice cream will feel good on your mouth. It'll help the swelling."

Ben stared at the bowl in front of him, wondering what small nation he could hire to help him eat it. "So your aunt bought the lodge and built the new cabins?"

"My aunt and my mother."

The boy filled his mouth with a huge spoonful of ice cream. Ben wasn't ready to go down the path of Michael's mother yet, so he picked up his spoon and dug into his own monstrous bowl. And it did feel good rolling around in his mouth and sliding down his throat.

Between silent bites, Ben looked around the huge kitchen. Everything was aging but as neat as a hospital. There was a polished old wood-burning cookstove backing the great room, its pipe going into a massive wall of stone separating the rooms. There were yards and yards of countertops, worn patternless in places and chipped in others. A sink big enough to bathe a cow in sat under a bank of windows that looked out on Medicine Lake, making the water and nearest mountains appear almost touchable. And on the windowsill over the sink, running in each direction, was an eclectic assortment of rocks, moss, gnarled twigs, and Mason jars full of sand and broken glass and pebbles.

The old but obviously well-maintained lodge was more of a home than an inn, and a child's gifts brought in from the wild had been lovingly kept and displayed.

Michael had arrived home from school less than an hour ago. He had built a small fire in the cookstove, and then he had begun the task of filling his tall growing frame with food. He hadn't stopped eating since Ben had limped in and sat down.

"Your aunt doesn't make dinner?"

He had to wait for Michael to swallow. "Sometimes. Usually I cook supper." The boy suddenly smiled, as if he were comforting a worried child. "We'll eat in about an hour, Mr. Jenkins. Nem usually forgets to have lunch, so she'll be as hungry as a bear. I hope you like venison."

Ben didn't know which bothered him more—that Michael was expected to look after himself or that the boy took it upon himself to look after Emma. He should be playing football after school, not cooking dinner. Or he should be on the phone making plans with friends, not making meaningless small talk with a stranger.

"You got many friends around here?"

Michael gave Ben a look that said he was nearing a no-trespassing line. He pushed himself away from the table, unbuttoned his cuffs and rolled up his sleeves, then picked up his empty bowl and Ben's half-full one. He took them to the sink and started filling it with warm soapy water.

"I've made friends of sports from all over the world," he finally said, his back to Ben. "I still write to many of them. I've been invited to Germany next summer to stay with a family that vacationed here this past summer."

"You going?"

"No. Not without Nemmy." He turned and pierced Ben with serious eyes. "My aunt is all that's important to me, Mr. Jenkins. I would give my life to protect her, and my soul to see her happy."

Where in hell had that come from?

"Is this your standard warning to all male . . . sports?"

Michael shot him another serious look, then turned back to the sink and shut off the water. "Not all of them. Just the potentially dangerous ones."

"You think I'm a danger to your aunt?" Ben couldn't believe this. He might be a danger, all right, though not in the way Michael was suggesting. But how had the boy sensed anything at all?

"Yeah, I think you are, Mr. Jenkins. But I don't think you realize just how much."

Ben stood up, limped to the woodstove, and held his hands over the firebox. It had suddenly grown downright chilly in the kitchen.

Emma Sands was a beautiful woman, if a man liked glowing health and energy. And if he liked straightforwardness and courage, well, she fit that bill, too. The woman possessed nerves of steel. Hadn't she pulled a loaded plane off a puddle of water last night only to land it on a darkened lake? A person wasn't born knowing how to fly like that. Ben might have been scared as hell, but he had also been damned impressed.

So, how was he a threat to Emma Sands?

A sexual threat?

She had fit rather nicely under his arm for their trek to the truck yesterday. She had smelled like the forest, and gunpowder, and some animal he couldn't identify. But that hadn't stopped him from wondering what she would do if he took that shotgun out of her hand and kissed her.

Ben had marked the bizarre thought down to distracting himself from the pain. But he hadn't been in much pain last night, when she'd come to his room and set her gentle hand on his forehead. She'd smelled all fresh and delicious when she'd leaned over and touched him, awakening more than just his mind.

Which is why he'd silently watched her, and wondered at the strange mood she seemed to be in. She had appeared almost . . . sad.

Though he'd intended to hate the woman, Ben's instinct last night had been to comfort her, to make the sadness go away. He'd also wanted her to realize she was in a nearly naked man's room, and that it was dark and cold outside, and warm and welcoming in his bed.

Dammit. He didn't want to be attracted to someone who had stolen so much from him. To someone who, in her own words, hoped he was dead. But Michael was his son, and he wasn't about to let a foolish bit of lust mess things up.

"You two didn't cross swords today, did you?" Michael asked from beside Ben, his eyes nearly level with his.

He must have been scowling rather fiercely, Ben realized, because the boy's stance was defensive. "No. It's hard to fight with a shadow. I heard the plane take off and return once, and a truck come and go several times, but I was left to my own devices today."

Michael continued to look at him thoughtfully. Suddenly he gave Ben a crooked grin. "I imagine that was wise of her. Wounded animals aren't always kind to their rescuer."

The boy then turned and walked out of the room, apparently no more worried than Emma about abandoning him. Not that Ben had minded being alone in the house all day. He had spent most of the time in Michael's room, just sitting and looking around, wondering about the boy-child who was a stranger to him in some ways and so much like him in others.

Emma Sands was right. Michael was very old for his age—an enigma of youth and confidence and calmness. He had an ability to see past a person's surface, and he had a teenager's appetite. The boy was tall for his age, with dark brown hair in need of a barber and a peach-fuzz beard lightly shadowing his face.

It had been Emma, not Ben, who had given Michael his first razor. It had been his aunt, not his father, who had probably already talked to Michael about girls and safe sex and the wonder of young relationships. And it was Emma who was in the boy's heart now.

It was hell, being so close to his son and not being able to touch him. Not being able to explain that he would have come for the boy the moment he'd known about him, or that he would have married his mother sixteen years ago. He would have made things different if he could have.

Ben shuffled back to his room, resolved to find a way to become part of Michael's life. He would have to stifle any urge to punish Emma, or to find Kelly and punish her. He realized now how foolish he'd been to think he could have both his son and revenge. Sam was right. A boy doesn't live with a woman for fifteen years and then walk away to a new life and new father, leaving that woman behind. Nor would he stop loving a mother just because she abandoned him. Michael had

been only five at the time, but he would remember
Kelly with the love of a child.

Which meant that Ben would have to be very careful how he went about claiming Michael without alienating him.

Over the next week, Ben had plenty of time to dwell
on his course of action. He was left alone to heal as
well as explore the grounds of Medicine Creek Camps.
Michael was in school by day, and studying or cooking
or repairing a contrary generator at night. Emma had
three of her six cabins rented, and when she wasn't
guiding sports she was busy getting ready for moose season, which started next Monday. Ben became a silent,
forgotten fixture as he slowly healed and, unsurpris-
ingly, fell in love with his son.

He also became uncomfortably aware of Emma's
multiple attractions. He actually found his pants getting tight whenever she strutted away from him, her
long legs clad in worn, form-fitting jeans that hugged a
decidedly luscious bottom. And he couldn't wait for
each night, when she came to his room and opened his
window, felt his forehead for fever, and covered him up
to his chin. He didn't speak to her again after that first
night, lying there with his eyes closed and his conscience wrestling between anger and lust.

It was a long week.

Chapter Three

"*Son of a bitch!*"

Emma heard an animal's loud snort, and knew Benjamin Sinclair had just met Pitiful. She shoved her homing pigeon back in the coop and started running for the front of the house. If Pitiful got playful Ben would be right back in bed, this time with more than just a few cracked ribs.

There was a loud crash, another curse, and the sound of pounding hooves just as Emma rounded the corner of the house and barreled straight into Benjamin Sinclair. The man didn't even break stride. He simply tucked her under his arm and ran for the closest cover, which turned out to be the toolshed.

Bouncing like a sack of grain, Emma began to understand what cracked ribs actually felt like. She lost her breath completely when she was tossed against the inside wall of the shed and suddenly plunged into darkness. Her rescuer's yelled curses were now just muttered expletives, no less colorful for their lack of volume.

Emma didn't ask if he had rehurt his ribs, figuring it was hard to pant and curse and talk at the same time. The toolshed suddenly shuddered as if a truck had rammed it, and loud panting came from the other side of the door.

"There is a deranged moose out there, Miss Sands. It only has one antler, and it's got a huge orange bow tied around its neck. It charged at me just as I was stepping off the back porch."

The shed door shuddered again. Ben stepped back and pinned her against a rusty old water tank, apparently trying to protect her from harm.

Emma felt like laughing, but didn't dare. Lord, he was big. And warm. He even smelled nice, too. Thank God it was dark in the shed. His broad shoulders blocked any light that might reach her blushing face. Medicine Creek was getting warmer by the minute.

"That's just Pitiful, Mr. Jenkins."

His eyes caught the light from the dusty window as he looked at her with consternation. "I know. I was just minding my business when this animal ran out of the woods like a maniac. It was bellowing at the top of its lungs, its eyes rolling back in its head, that orange bow flapping like a cape."

"It's Pitiful."

"I know that! It must have tick fever or something. We've got to shoot it."

Emma snorted in an attempt to stifle a laugh. "No, Mr. Jenkins. That's my pet moose, who's named Pitiful."

He looked at her as if she were the deranged one, then suddenly cursed again.

The shed vibrated with another bang and Ben snapped his head toward the door. The latch was failing. He looked around, then suddenly lifted her onto the water tank as if she were a sack of feathers.

"Crawl to the back of the shed," he said, reaching for a broken oar leaning against the wall. "If he gets in here, he could kill us with that antler."

Emma doubled over in laughter.

"Goddammit! Don't get hysterical on me! If that crazy beast gets in here, you crawl out the window. Emma!"

She instantly sobered when she saw he might try to shake some sense into her. She opened her mouth to explain, but the shed door finally caved in, splintering the casing and ripping the door off its hinges. Ben swung around with his weapon raised, putting himself between her and danger.

Emma jerked the oar from his hands and threw it to the back of the shed.

"What the—"

"Pitiful! You bad boy! Stop that!"

The startled moose cocked his head to the side,

looking at them from only one eye, then let out a bellow that shook the rafters.

Emma shoved at her rescuer's back and jumped off the water tank. "Pitiful! You stop that hollering this minute. Now get out of here, you silly bull. Go on. Get!"

If ever a moose could look contrite, with an orange bow around its neck and one heavy antler tilting its head, Pitiful looked sorrier than a kid caught raiding the cookie jar. Startled to have her scolding him, he took a step back, shook his head, then bolted for the forest. Clods of muddy earth spewed up behind him, showering the shed and slapping Ben smack in the middle of his heaving chest.

Emma silently peeled the dirt off his expensive canvas shirt. Darting a curious look at his face, she quickly snapped her eyes back down and industriously began to brush at the mud that was left, fighting to keep her shoulders from shaking and her giggles from bursting free.

She lost the battle. The picture of his wild tangle of dark brown hair, his cheeks crimson, and his eyes widened in shock was indelibly burned into her brain. A giggle erupted before she could catch it.

Then the broken door slammed shut and she found herself pressed between it and a hard, unyielding chest.

It seemed Benjamin Sinclair was not amused.

"I just lost ten years of my life, and you think it's funny?"

Emma frantically shook her head, not raising her eyes above his chest, which vibrated like a deep-rooted oak weathering a gale. Two large hands came to rest on her shoulders, their thumbs nearly touching across her throat.

"That's good. Because I don't see anything funny about nearly getting killed by a deranged moose." He used his thumbs to raise her chin. "Do you?"

Emma finally found the nerve to lift her gaze and immediately wished she hadn't. Benjamin Sinclair sure as hell wasn't in shock now. His eyes were narrowed, and his jaw could probably chisel stone.

The sound of crashing branches and a pitiful wail came from the forest.

A loud, exasperated sigh blew over her head, all but parting her hair.

"Look at me."

She didn't want to, but those two thumbs became insistent. Emma looked up again . . . into the eyes of a man whose agenda had suddenly changed.

"Don't, Mr. Jenkins."

His mouth descended as if she hadn't spoken. His lips, which had looked so hard a minute ago, softly touched hers. His hands shifted to cup her head, holding her just firmly enough to deepen the kiss. Then he tilted her head back and used those so-handy thumbs to open her mouth and invade it with his tongue.

Warmth. Unholy heat. Emma's knees went weak

and she grabbed his shirt, steadying herself against his salacious assault. Her world began spinning, a charge of sensuous energy suddenly filling the shed. Damn, the man could kiss. Every nerve touched by him, from her knees to her hair, crackled to life as Emma fought to contain the passion building inside her.

He came here to steal my nephew.

He is huge and scary and not the least bit nice.

She wrapped her arms around his waist, going on tiptoe, turning her head and touching her tongue to his.

Pitiful bellowed again, the mournful sound pulling Emma back to reality. She tore her mouth free and rested her forehead on Ben's throat, her eyes closed and her heart pounding so violently her ribs hurt. "Don't, Ben," she pleaded.

Every muscle in his body went rigid. His breathing suspended and Emma felt his own heart pounding with enough force to bruise her.

"What did you just call me?"

She looked up, meeting his gunmetal stare. "Ben. Michael's father. The man who's come to take my nephew away."

She was suddenly back up against the shed wall, all signs of passion completely gone. "How long have you known?"

"Since I found you on the logging road."

His hands went back to her shoulders, and those damn thumbs lifted her chin again. "Does Michael know?"

"Probably."

He slammed a fist into the wall over her head, shuddering the entire building. She closed her eyes when that hand returned, this time wrapping ever so securely around her throat.

"My son was stolen from me fifteen years ago—and you, Miss Sands, are directly responsible for the last ten of them. Tell me why I shouldn't hate you."

"Because that would take your son from you forever, Mr. Sinclair."

He pushed away from her, kicked the water tank, and spun back to face her. "Why didn't you try to find me when Kelly left?"

"Because Michael wasn't ready to know you yet. He was only five. Did you expect me to introduce a child to a father who had abandoned him before birth when he'd just been abandoned by his mother? Michael needed stability. He needed *me*."

"I didn't abandon him. I never knew about Michael! I never knew Kelly was pregnant! Why didn't you contact me later?"

Emma just stared at him.

"Dammit! Who the hell do you think you are, playing God with my life!"

"Your identity has never been kept from him. I expected Michael to look you up himself, once he was grown. The decision is his, not mine."

Emma turned and opened the door, then looked

back. "I don't know if I believe you. Kelly said she told you she was pregnant, and that you didn't seem all that concerned. But I do know you have a wonderful, very precious son, Mr. Sinclair. And if you ever do anything to hurt Michael, I will hunt you down and kill you."

It took every ounce of courage Ben possessed to walk into the kitchen that evening. He nearly faltered when he saw there were only two places set at the table, and that Michael was sitting at one of them.

The boy knew who he was. Maybe. *Probably*, Emma had said. Michael had probably known all along that the bastard who'd seduced his mother and then walked away sixteen years ago had sat across the table from him every day for the last seven days.

How had he done it? How did a fifteen-year-old boy look a father he had never seen before in the eye, and talk to him about the history of his home, his problems with a generator, his schoolwork, and the weather? Everyday things. Meaningless, casual conversation.

"Your aunt's not joining us tonight?"

"Nemmy's away."

Ben stood behind his chair and looked at his son. "But her truck's still here. So's the plane."

The boy stared back at him, his eyes a calm gray ocean of unreadable depth. "She's gone into the woods." He took Ben's plate to the stove and filled it.

Ben pulled out his chair and sat down. "What does that mean, she's gone into the woods?"

Michael set a plate of stew and dumplings in front of him. "It means she's troubled." He sat down and picked up his fork, resting his arms on the table, looking at Ben with still calm but questioning regard. "Do you happen to know what could be troubling her, Mr. Sinclair?"

Ben picked up his fork. "She told you who I am."

"No. I've known since you walked up to me at Smokey Bog."

Ben snapped his gaze to Michael's. "Then why the pretense all week? Why didn't you say something?"

"You chose to come here under another name. It was your move."

Ben took a deep breath and blew out a heavy sigh. "Only once I got here I couldn't decide how to make that move. I didn't know how to walk up to you and say, 'Hi, I'm your father.'" He shrugged. "I still don't know what to say to you."

A slight grin crept into the corners of Michael's mouth as he leaned back in his chair and crossed his arms over his chest. "You could have said how glad you were to finally meet me."

Well, hell. It seemed this boy—this man-child—didn't resent him, but simply was glad to meet his father. "*You* sent me that letter."

"What letter?"

Well, someone had sent that damn letter. "About a month ago a letter was sent to me, unsigned, from Medicine Gore. All it said was that I had a son, and that I should . . . I should come meet him."

"So you came."

"I'd have come sooner if I'd known about you." He leaned forward in his chair. "I never would have *left* if I'd known about you."

"I didn't send it."

"Would your aunt have?"

Michael drove his fork into his stew. "Nope. Not Nem. She hates your guts."

"So I gathered. Mike, do you believe me? That I didn't abandon you?"

The boy shrugged as he took another bite. "Probably, knowing Kelly. She could be . . . self-serving sometimes."

Which was why Ben had eventually been relieved when Kelly had turned him down sixteen years ago, when he'd asked her to come home to New York with him.

"Could Kelly have sent me the letter?"

The boy looked thoughtful, then shook his head. "Not likely. My mother hasn't been heard from in over ten years. And you said it was postmarked Medicine Gore." He looked toward the bank of windows over the sink, seeming to take stock of all the gifts adorning them. Ben saw a shadow of pain move over his face before he turned back. "Nem must have sent it."

"But why? She loves you. She wouldn't want to risk your leaving with me."

"Because she *does* love me. Because this clear-cutting war scares the hell out of her. She would do anything to make sure I'm safe."

Ben lowered his gaze. "I know about Emma's father." He looked back at his son. "Your grandfather was killed just before you were born."

Michael stared directly into Ben's eyes. "Someone blew up the dam the paper company was building. Grampy Sands got caught in the flood."

Ben nodded. "It happened the day I left."

"Yup. The very same day you disappeared."

As he stared into his own young eyes, Ben suddenly realized what Mike was implying. "You think I had something to do with that dam blowing up?" He closed his eyes and rubbed his hands over his face. "Jesus. You and Emma and Kelly believe I'm responsible for Charlie Sands's death?"

"The whole town thinks you're responsible."

"Good God."

"I'd keep the beard and a low profile if I were you."

"I didn't do it. I didn't blow up that dam!"

"Well, the loggers sure as heck didn't."

"Neither did the environmentalists. That would have been counterproductive. The flood would have damaged the very land we were trying to save."

Ben stood up and stalked to the counter, leaning his hands on the sink and looking out the window. There was nothing but darkness outside and the reflection of the kitchen staring back at him. He could see Michael sitting in his chair, his back to Ben, his arms resting on the table. He spoke again, not turning. "Mike. I swear to you, I didn't blow up that dam. And I would have known if anything like that was being planned."

"It's not me you have to convince. It's the people here. Sixteen years is a long time for a suspicion to take root."

Ben turned and looked at his son, who was now looking at him. "Charlie Sands was your grandfather. So more than anyone else, *you* have to be convinced."

"I already am."

"Just like that? You don't know a damn thing about me."

Michael stood up and approached Ben, his stride confident, and stopped one step shy of touching him. "I know all about Benjamin Sinclair," he said softly. "I can tell you how your grandfather, Abram, built his shipping company from nothing, and I can tell you what your personal net worth is. But most of all, I can tell you that my father never would have walked away sixteen years ago if he had been responsible for another man's death."

Ben could only stare back, frozen in awe.

Blind faith. Childhood loyalty. And a young man's confidence in what he could determine from facts and figures and history.

And maybe a little help from Emma Sands? Even hating him, for fifteen years she had apparently not held judgment on her nephew's father. She hadn't betrayed his identity when he arrived, and she hadn't interfered this past week. She had simply let them walk their own course to this moment—then disappeared into the woods to give them this time.

"Michael. What is it you want?"

"A father."

He was going to drown in a puddle of emotion. Ben forced himself rigid, but the tremors began anyway, starting deep inside and working their way outward.

This boy scared him to death. He wasn't ready to be a father. Hell, until now, he hadn't really believed it was possible. From the moment he'd read the letter, Ben had been sure it was all a dream—that he'd conjured up a long-lost child because he'd needed something to cling to after his grandfather's death.

Ben realized he was standing as still as a statue, sweating bullets, and staring at empty space. Michael was sitting at the table again, quietly eating his supper.

As quietly as his son, Ben walked back and sat down. "I never would have left, Mike, if I had known about you. My God. It never even entered my mind that Kelly might be pregnant. She seemed so . . . she

seemed like she knew what she was doing," he finished on a whisper, heat climbing up the back of his
neck. He shifted uncomfortably in his chair. "It's not
an excuse, but I was barely nineteen. I thought I had
the world by the ass and my whole life ahead of me."
He leaned forward. "I asked her to come away with
me, but she refused."

Michael finally looked up, a sad smile on his face. "I
love my mother very much, Mr. Sinclair, and I came to
terms with who she is many years ago. But Emma was
the anchor that held my world together."

"And you're worried that if you come to New York
with me, she'll be alone."

Michael nodded. "Yes. But that's not the only problem."

"Then what is?"

"Remember the guy who stopped in here Wednesday evening?"

Ben snorted. "Galen something. He's got the per-
sonality of Pitiful."

"Well, Galen Simms thinks he's courting my aunt,
which is why he was such a bastard to you. He didn't
like finding you staying in the lodge."

"So if Emma marries him, she won't be alone."

"He's not courting Nemmy as much as he's courting
Medicine Creek Camps and my aunt's reputation as a
guide," Michael said. "Simms has a set of camps on a
lake twelve miles north of here. But while our business

Chapter Four

*B*en gaped at his son.

"Once we get home, she can start a new life, like me. You have a big house, don't you?"

Home. The boy wanted to go *home*. Just hearing him say it made Ben break into a cold sweat. "Have you mentioned this little plan to your aunt, by any chance?"

Michael snorted.

"Then she won't be kicking and screaming. She'll be going for her shotgun." Ben stood up and planted his hands on the table. "Michael, you can't tell a grown woman what to do. I know you don't like being reminded of the fact, but you *are* only fifteen years old. Your sense of authority is all screwed up."

Michael also stood. "Come with me. I have something to show you."

Ben grabbed the edge of the table, wanting to upend

is booming, his is sinking in red ink. He's looking to marry himself a business manager."

"Your aunt is astute enough to see that. Besides, she didn't seem all that enamored with Simms."

"But Nem might think about marrying him anywa so I don't feel obligated to stay. What she doesn't kn is that if I leave here with you, I intend to take with me." He tossed a smile across the table. "Kick and screaming if I have to."

Ben blinked, then rubbed his hands over his several times, to wipe away his shock. "Excuse me

"You finally came, and it's time for me to leave icine Gore. But I'm not leaving here without and if I have to torch the Cessna, the cabins, one thousand acres, I will."

it, but closed his eyes and counted to ten. This was not at all going well.

He finally followed Michael through the great room and into what he knew was Emma's bedroom. He stopped in the doorway and watched Michael walk over to a window and reach up on the top of the casing, pushing the curtain aside to feel along the molding. When his hand returned, it held a key. He walked over to a long, scarred, unadorned chest and unlocked it.

"Michael—"

"Come here. You need to see this."

Ben took a guilty look back at the great room, then stepped into Emma's private domain as the boy lifted the lid on the chest.

It appeared to be full of . . . frilly things. Woman stuff—doilies, fancy bedsheets, a handmade quilt. And household goods—a teapot and matching sugar and creamer, a dark green candle, a sprig of dried flowers, a crystal vase.

"This is where my aunt keeps her dreams." Michael lifted the quilt and pulled out a silver picture frame. "She bought this in Portland when she and Kelly took me there for my fifth birthday. Nem said it was for her wedding picture."

Lovingly rubbing the frame, Michael smiled. "I told her she couldn't ever get married, that I wouldn't let any man take her away." He looked up, and Ben took a step back from the pain he saw in the boy's eyes. "She told me not to worry, that she'd only marry a man worth loving, and that he would be very hard to find."

He put the frame back under the quilt and ran his hand over the contents of the chest, touching everything, disturbing nothing. "She told me she's had this chest since she was ten. I was often with her when she would find something that caught her eye, and she would buy it, bring it home, and it would disappear. It was a long time before I discovered she was squirreling her purchases away in this chest."

"Why are you showing me this, Michael? A lot of young girls start a hope chest. All of them plan for the day they'll set up their own home."

"Nemmy stopped buying things after Kelly left. Once, when we were in a store and I caught her looking at some china, I asked her why she didn't buy it. She told me there was no more reason to."

The boy slowly closed the lid and stood to face Ben, his eyes clouded with emotion. "It took me several years to figure out what she meant. Now, I intend to see she gets her dream."

"Does she blame herself for your mother leaving?"

"In some ways, Nem feels responsible for everything. If a sport comes here and expects to catch a boatload of fish and it rains all week, she feels responsible. If I get caught driving to town, it's Nem's fault, not mine. If I run the plane up on a rocky shore and tear the pontoons all to hell, it's because she didn't teach me well enough." Michael lifted his arms and let them fall back. "So she probably thinks she could have done something to prevent Kelly from leaving."

"So as penance she's given up her dream of having a home of her own? But this is her home." Ben pointed to the chest. "Those things should be out, being used."

Michael shook his head. "No. Nem's dream wasn't some unfocused hope. I believe it was aimed at one man in particular. And I realize now that she's probably loved him since before I was born."

"Who is he?"

The boy cocked his head and looked directly at Ben. He was silent so long, Ben didn't think he would answer.

"If I draw you a map, do you think you could find my aunt without getting lost?"

That wasn't an answer!

And he wasn't going to get one, Ben realized. This boy was going to dump the problem of his aunt right in his lap, and he wasn't going to give him a clue.

It was a test. Michael wanted to see if he had a son's right to ask for help from his parent. He wanted to know if his father intended to take up his battles—not for him, but with him.

So Ben was going to have to find Emma Sands, discover who the woman was in love with, and get her married to the guy. Then he could have his son.

Damn if the boy couldn't give lessons to Solomon.

"I guess that would depend. Did your aunt take her shotgun?"

"Yup."

"And that addled moose of hers?"

"Probably."

It was a diabolical test. A gauntlet of heroic proportions. "You got a compass I can borrow? And a sleeping bag?"

The smile Ben received could have blinded the sun.

The cold, wet forest floor seeping through her wool pants made her uncomfortable, but it was nothing compared to the anger Emma felt as she watched the deliberate desecration of the woods she loved.

Tree huggers were driving spikes into the trees. There were six men, and they didn't at all look like the fancy environmentalists who had been hounding the state house and the nightly news for the last two months. These men were grubby, disgusting jackals with their own agenda for gaining their objective.

She'd heard about the terrorist act of spiking trees, but that problem had been a distant one, usually in the northwestern forests of the country. Loggers, most of them friends of hers, would come here to harvest these trees, and be ripped to shreds when their chain saws hit those spikes. The saws would disintegrate on contact, sending missiles of sharp, jagged chain into unprotected flesh. Innocent, hardworking men would be maimed and possibly killed.

Emma owned a thousand acres of prime forest herself, and had spent the last ten years adding to the acreage surrounding Medicine Creek Camps. It was to be Michael's heritage. Whatever decisions the state government made would ultimately affect her, but she couldn't take sides in this issue. She sold stumpage off her land to the paper and lumber mills, but she was careful what was cut.

That wasn't enough for the environmentalists. They wouldn't be happy until all the forested land was rendered untouchable. They were targeting clear-cutting this time, but Emma feared it was just the first of several calculated steps aimed at turning millions of acres of woodland into another forest reserve or national park.

She'd been minding her business this morning, headed for a crystal spring she knew had the sweetest drinking water in the area, when she'd heard the echo of metal thunking against live wood. It was a distinct sound that had rattled around in the forest, and it had taken her a good twenty minutes to find the source.

Now she was wet, and cold, and getting madder and madder the longer she watched. But she couldn't go charging in, like when she'd rescued Ben. These men were out-of-staters, not neighbors, and they didn't look as if they would like being discovered.

Yet she couldn't walk away, either. There was no way she could point out all the vandalized trees, and no way the loggers could take metal detectors to all these trees.

She could scare them off. Stay hidden and blast the air with birdshot, making them think the calvary had arrived. Maybe even find Pitiful and get him to introduce himself, the way he had to Ben yesterday.

Emma checked her shotgun, making sure both the chamber and the magazine were full, then patted her pocket to make sure she had more shells so she could quickly reload. She raised the butt of the gun to her shoulder, aimed it ten feet above the men's heads, and clicked off the safety.

A large, powerful hand suddenly covered hers, muffling the click of the safety being replaced. Another large hand covered her mouth as a crushing weight landed on top of her, pinning her on the wet forest floor.

She usually wasn't one to panic, but Emma wildly struggled to dislodge her heavy assailant. Her shotgun was ripped from her hand and pushed away, and she was roughly grabbed by the shoulder and rolled over. Still pinned and her mouth still covered, Emma stopped struggling when she looked up into the iron gray eyes of a very angry Benjamin Sinclair.

He didn't speak. He didn't even offer a curse word.

She didn't even squeak, she was so stunned. The

face less than a foot from hers didn't belong to a city sport or corporate executive. She was looking at a man ready for battle, who didn't intend to let her win it.

He lifted off her and grabbed her shotgun and pack. He kept his other hand latched on her jacket and pulled her to her feet with one swift, powerful jerk, then started dragging her down the hill.

Unable to do anything else, Emma stumbled after him. She tried to dislodge his grip on her jacket, but Ben Sinclair didn't break stride, turn around, or even acknowledge that she had to run to keep up. He did start with his infamous cursing again, once they were far enough away they couldn't be heard.

Emma gave him a few choice words in return. When he stopped, she stumbled into the fist shackling her.

"Lady, if you don't shut up and quit struggling, I promise you won't be able to sit down for a week."

Emma snapped her mouth shut and glared back at him. He turned and started along a brook, once more dragging her behind him.

"How you and my son have survived this long is the eighth wonder of the world."

"What are you doing here?"

He stopped again and turned to her, his scowl darkening even more. "I'm on a fool's mission." That information given, he pushed her ahead of him and then prodded her back. "Keep going until I tell you to stop."

Emma thought about planting her feet, but he was a

head taller, sixty pounds heavier, and definitely stronger than she was. So she walked.

"You were going to go charging right in there, weren't you? You were going to take on six men with a four-shot gun and not a soul to help within twenty miles. You're more insane than your moose."

The lecture continued and Emma learned that she was impulsive, irresponsible, and lacking the brains of a chipmunk. She discovered she was too brave to rush in where even fools wouldn't go, and that she needed a keeper. And then he asked her again how she'd managed to raise his son to manhood without getting either of them killed.

Emma suddenly sat down on a rock beside the brook, put her chin in her fists, and scowled at the water.

Ben loomed over her.

"Are you through yet?" she asked, still not looking at him.

"Not by half."

"Should I be taking notes?"

Her pack and shotgun fell to the ground with a heavy thud, and the legs standing beside her bent at the knee, bringing an even angrier face within an inch of hers. "You could have gotten killed."

Emma smiled at him. "That would have solved a lot of your problems."

He lunged for her and Emma pulled back. He caught

her shoulders and followed her down off the rock. Ben was back on top of her, and Emma was starting to get more than a little angry herself. "If you don't quit manhandling me, I'm gonna make sure you never father another son."

Completely ignoring her threat, he grabbed her hands pushing against his chest and pinned them over her head with one of his own. Then he took his other hand and gently brushed the hair from her face.

"Emma Sands. Such bravado you show the world. Such a scam artist you are."

"Get off me."

He used his knees to spread her legs, and Emma sucked in a surprised breath when she felt him nestle far too intimately between her thighs.

"That was the wrong direction!"

"But the safest, if I want more children."

"How did you find me?"

"Michael drew me a map."

"You're supposed to be getting to know your son, not interfering in my business."

The gentleness left his face as suddenly as it had appeared. "Someone had to interfere. You were about to let your cannon loose on those men, weren't you?"

"They were spiking the trees."

He growled a nasty word.

"If I ever get you near a bar of soap, I'm going to use it to wash out your mouth."

He suddenly grinned. "You have my permission to try."

"Are you planning to get off me any time soon?"

He wiggled, settling himself even deeper against her. "I'm rather comfortable." His grin turned sinister. "You're nicely padded in all the right places."

"Get off—"

Emma didn't finish. His hand was at her mouth again as Ben's head snapped up and he cocked it to the side, listening.

"They're walking down the back side of the ridge," he whispered, his head lowered beside hers as every muscle in his body seemed to double in size.

He didn't uncover her mouth. Did he think she was going to scream hello to the terrorists? Emma bit down. She was rewarded with a ferocious glare as he rubbed the abused hand on her jacket.

"I'm beginning to pity the poor bastard who ends up marrying you."

Emma tried to punch him, but he caught her fist, brought it up to his lips, and kissed it. "Don't spar with me, Emma. I'm bigger and stronger and meaner than you."

"You also have a bigger ego than God."

"I need a big one if I want to hold my own against the Sands clan."

"I'm surprised Michael didn't draw you a map that would take you to Canada."

Ben frowned darkly. "Michael's got his own agenda,

and I don't think either of us will ever fully know what it is. Are you sure Kelly gave birth to him? You didn't just find him in one of Medicine Creek's hot springs, bubbled up from hell?"

"I know he's looking more and more like his father every—"

He shut her up again, but with his mouth this time. Emma gasped at the bolt of heat that suddenly shot through her. She was wet and cold and she couldn't breathe, but she was also hot and tingly and so very confused.

Fire, of the delicious, feminine kind, flared deep in the pit of her belly. And Emma couldn't stop herself from kissing him back any more.

This was so dangerous. Her nephew's father was seducing her, and she hoped he wouldn't stop. She was setting herself up for a world of heartache, but all she could do was curse the clothes that separated them.

"Slap my face, Emma."

She took her freed hands and pulled his growling mouth back down to hers.

He kissed her again, opening her mouth with his tongue and taking in the taste of her, giving back his own sweet essence. His weight was no longer crushing, it was welcome. One of his hands began roaming her body, and Emma wiggled to give him easier access.

"Stop me, Em."

She started doing a little exploring herself. He was

so muscled and firm, and the canvas shirt under his jacket unbuttoned easily. The hair covering his chest sprang to life against her fingers, and Emma felt Ben take a deep, shuddering breath.

"Last chance, Emma. Stop me now."

The bellow of a huge bull moose came echoing down over the ridge, followed by the cracking of branches. Ben threw his head up in surprise. Her own breath suspended, Emma watched as he slowly looked down at her, his expression turning to horror.

Emma pushed him away. "Get off me!"

He scrambled to his feet and turned his back, his hands tugging at the front of his pants.

For a stunned second, Emma lay motionless. Lord, what an idiot she was—she'd nearly let Ben Sinclair seduce her!

Was this what Kelly had felt sixteen years ago? Was this how quickly, how insanely, it had happened?

"I'm . . . Emma, I'm sorry."

She didn't look up at those softly spoken words. "Forget it, Mr. Sinclair."

He lifted her chin with two gentle but insistent fingers. His face was drawn, but flags of color darkened his cheeks. Leftover passion? Embarrassment? Anger?

"This shouldn't have happened."

"Damn right it shouldn't have."

"I wasn't thinking," he said through gritted teeth.

"Certainly not with your upper brain."

His eyes widened in shock, then he suddenly threw back his head and burst out laughing. He sat down on the ground beside her. "My God. What am I supposed to do with you, Emma Sands?"

"You can go back and get Michael and take him home."

He instantly sobered. "Now? You want me to take him away right now?"

Her throat closed tight, Emma nodded.

"While you stay out here and hide?"

She lifted her chin. "I am not hiding. Michael can call me once he gets settled."

He muttered something as he picked up her pack and shotgun and his own pack.

Then, just to make the day even more delightful, it started to rain.

"Damn. We've got to find shelter," Ben growled.

"Medicine Creek Camps is sixteen miles that way," she said, pointing behind him. "If you start walking now, you'll be there before dark."

He stood looking at her, her gun in his fist, his hands on his hips, both packs slung over his shoulders, and his eyes squinted against the rain. His jacket was open and his shirt was buttoned crooked.

L.L.Bean should be here with their camera now.

"I think I'll stick around a while, if you don't mind."

"I do mind. Go away, Mr. Sinclair."

He lifted her chin again, washing her face—and cooling her blush—she hoped—with rain.

"Let me rephrase that. I am going to help you set up a shelter and then we are going to put on some dry clothes."

"Michael didn't pack you a tent?"

He shook his head, his face thoughtful. "Do you think it was an oversight?"

Emma grabbed her backpack off his shoulder and started up the brook. "Knowing Michael, it wasn't."

Ben seemed startled she was leaving, and ran to catch up. "What's that supposed to mean?"

"It means he's paying me back for not letting him skip school for the moose hunt." She looked over her shoulder and gave him a nasty grin. "Either that, or he thinks a cold, wet night outdoors would do you good."

"He hauled me out of bed at four this morning and stuck a map in my hand. Your nephew comes by his sadistic nature quite naturally, I see."

"I'm not the one going around threatening to throttle somebody." Emma stopped and turned fully to face him. "If you ever threaten to lay a hand on me again, Mr. Sinclair, you won't live long enough to gloat about it."

He nodded, his expression serious—but for his laughing eyes.

Chapter Five

Well, that had been brilliant. Attack the woman. In the dirt, no less.

Very brilliant, Sinclair.

How in hell could he have known she'd go off like a keg of gunpowder? She was supposed to be in love with another man!

On his cold, dark trek through the woods this morning, Ben had devised a plan to find out who the love of Emma's life was. He'd intended to kiss her so that she'd slap his face and tell him that her heart was already taken. She was supposed to yell the bastard's name and threatened to have him kill Ben for making advances.

Instead, the little minx had blindsided him.

Thank God that rutting bull moose had made all that noise. For one short second, Ben had known exactly how the horny beast felt.

Now Emma was mad enough to kill him. On top of nearly taking her right there on the ground, he could have gotten her pregnant. He hoped like hell there were no more Sands sisters. At this rate, he was liable to found a dynasty on them.

Ben balled up his L.L.Bean shirt and threw it across the shelter Little Miss Wonder Guide had erected from a tarp and tree branches. It kept out the wet, but not the wind.

"Dammit, it's snowing!"

"It does that in Maine sometimes," came an equally disgruntled voice from the other side of the tarp.

He tore into his pack and pulled out another shirt, this one flannel. He scowled at the logo stitched on the pocket, a deer leaping for joy. Ben crammed his arms in the sleeves before his shivering made the task impossible. "Are you sitting out there trying to get pneumonia, or is your stubbornness keeping you warm?"

A green rubberized cape with a head poking out of it popped into his line of sight. "It will be a lot warmer with hot tea in our stomachs. You want to come out here and watch for the water to boil?"

She disappeared before Ben could answer. Fine. Let the fool woman catch her death. What did he care?

That brought Ben back to his problem, and his backfired plan.

He'd seen the disgust in her eyes. If looks could kill,

he'd be dead. "Couldn't we have pitched this tarp near one of your hot springs? *Damn* it's cold."

Two steaming cups preceded two small hands into the shelter, followed by a billowing green poncho sporting huge flakes of snow. The flakes weren't melting because Emma's smile could freeze a penguin.

"You're welcome to move on, if you like. The nearest hot spring is about three thousand miles west." As angry as she obviously was, she was careful when she handed him the hot cup of tea.

Ben sighed as he blew on his tea. "Let's call a truce. This shelter is too small for a battlefield."

"I'm sure Mikey packed you a poncho, Mr. Sinclair. And if you turn that map upside down, you should be able to follow it back the way you came."

"I thought you had six cabins of moose hunters arriving today. Shouldn't you be seeing to your business?"

"Mikey will settle them in. And I'll be there early tomorrow to take them out."

"Why do you call him Mikey? It doesn't quite fit."

Although it was small, Ben finally got a smile from her. "To remind him that he's not a grown-up yet, and that I'm older and hopefully a bit smarter than he is."

"He calls you 'bossy lady' sometimes."

"Just when he's pissed about something."

"He called you that the night you found me."

She held her tea up near her face, letting the steam warm her. "Every so often, his confidence slips. He had never landed on anything like Smokey Bog without me being in the seat beside him."

Ben suddenly didn't need the tea for warmth, as his blood began to boil. "You put my son in a situation that could have killed him?"

"No, Mr. Sinclair. Michael is an excellent pilot. I didn't have any doubts; he did." She shot him a grin. "And he forgot them once he got down to business."

"You were nervous. I saw how tense you were."

"I was worried about my plane," she shot back. "Pontoons are expensive."

He was sorely tempted to kiss her again.

Ben realized she was scowling at him and remembered he should be scowling back. "Plane floats are more precious than a boy's life?"

She looked immensely satisfied with herself; apparently convinced she was keeping the battle lines drawn. No cold war for this woman. She would go down fighting to the bitter end.

It was a survivor's defense, one Ben imagined she had developed to survive all that she'd lost. She and Kelly had lost their mother when they were very young; then at fourteen she'd lost her father rather violently. And at just nineteen, she had suddenly found herself alone to raise a five-year-old boy. Oh yes. Emma Sands was definitely a survivor.

He was going to have to sneak up on her tonight.

While she slept.

While her shotgun was out of reach.

And he would not lose control this time. He would kiss her once, just to prove to himself that he could. He wouldn't jump all over her, or get lost in that luscious body that could drive a man to insanity.

Ben felt himself get hard just remembering the feel of her beneath him.

"I'm turning in for the night, Miss Sands. I'm not used to getting up at four in the morning and then walking half the day over half the mountains in the state. Good night."

He crawled into the sleeping bag Michael had packed him and zipped it up to his neck, hiding the evidence of his lustful thoughts.

The soft glow of the battery lantern cast Emma in a halo of deceptive warmth. Shadows danced beside her on the tarp, which was beginning to sag with the weight of wet snow. The forest had grown eerily quiet, and Ben imagined their little shelter looked like a cocoon of peace in these woods his son called home.

Through half-closed eyes, he watched the woman who had raised Michael. She sat motionless as she contemplated the snowflakes pooling at the entrance of their temporary lodge. Emma Sands also called this place home. She was as comfortable here in a crude shelter in the middle of a snowstorm as a squirrel was nestled in a tree of leaves and downy fur. This beautiful woman, with long, wavy blond hair and a face angels would envy, was the most remarkable woman Ben had ever known.

She held strong convictions toward many things. If she found men driving spikes into trees, she'd try to stop it. If she found men beating up another man, she would step in with her shotgun blazing. When she loved a boy like a son, she would do anything to protect him. And if she gave herself to a man, she would give herself fully.

Would she have let him make love to her today if he hadn't stopped?

Maybe. But why? Because of her nephew? Because Ben held the power to take the boy away from her?

He would bet his business that Emma hadn't been thinking of Michael when she'd exploded with a passion so strong Ben had been blinded to everything else, too.

It seemed an eternity before the cause of his lust finally crawled into her sleeping bag two feet away and turned out the lantern. Then she set her shotgun between them, rolled over, and rested one hand on the stock—not at all worried about sharing a tent with him.

Which was the first mistake he had seen Emma Sands make.

There was a very sensuous woman behind the prickly manner she showed the world. All she had to do was give a little sigh, and the throbbing ache of his groin went from fully aroused to solid stone.

It amazed Ben how erotic waiting could be. And how horny the sound of a carefully lowered sleeping bag zipper could make him. And how anticipation had turned into a whole new form of foreplay.

He had to remember he was on a mission—that what he accomplished here could mean the difference between having his son or alienating him forever.

She was an abandoned sleeper, and it made him imagine her being abandoned in other ways. Carefully, knowing the longer he kept her sleeping the more manageable she'd be, he brought her hands together and slowly lifted them over her head. She stirred, but merely mumbled in her sleep and tried to turn over.

Ben moved closer as he pinned her hands over her head and eased his leg over her thighs. She arched against him. He thought she was awake and trying to throw him off, but when he moved more fully on top of her, she mewled deep in her throat.

This isn't smart, Sinclair.

Ben felt a moment's hesitation as he softly touched his lips to her cheek. He'd never forced a woman in his life, but his actions were drawing close to that invisible line. What he was doing was dirty pool. It was also erotic as hell, a challenge to his ego, and a means to an end.

Emma came awake with a start just as his lips settled over her mouth.

"Easy, Em. It's me, Ben."

"Get . . . off."

It was a weak command at best, lacking conviction because she was confused. Ben brushed the hair from her face even as he tightened his grip on her hands. "I want to show you that I'm not an animal, Em. Let me make my mistakes up to you. Come on, pretty lady. Kiss me back."

With no light to see her face, all he could rely on was what her body told him. And when she sighed and relaxed her muscles, he knew he was nearly home free.

"This isn't a good idea. It wasn't smart earlier today, and it still isn't."

"We're two mature adults—and I would very much like to show you how civilized I really am. Just a kiss, and then we'll stop." He let go of one of her hands, testing his luck.

That was a mistake.

Her free hand connected with the side of his head with enough force that he actually saw stars. Then she gave him an impressively strong shove, knocking him over and scrambling from the prison of her sleeping bag.

She snapped a light on, and Ben found himself staring down the barrel of her shotgun.

"Get dressed, Mr. Sinclair. We're heading home."

Ben squinted at his watch. "It's not even five in the morning!"

"Which will put us there in time for me to take out my sports. Move."

She lowered her shotgun to find her boots, and Ben jumped her, covering her mouth with his hand as he pinned her down.

Her eyes widened just before he turned out the lantern—although her shock might have had something to do with the Smith & Wesson revolver in his hand.

"Sshhh. Someone's out there."

She quieted her breathing to listen. A truck engine died, and several voices carried down the hill to their shelter.

Emma started to struggle. "That's the loggers! I've got to warn them about the spikes."

"You can't know that. We can barely hear them, much less tell who they are."

She turned the light back on and frantically started making a tangle of her sleeping bag. "Ohmigod. I don't want them to find me here like this. Someone will surely tell Galen—" She snapped her mouth shut as Ben set the revolver on his sleeping bag. "Where did you get that?"

"I brought it with me." He grinned at her astonishment. "Don't look so shocked. I may be a city sport to you, but I'm not a defenseless one."

"You need a permit to carry a gun."

"I have one."

Her eyes narrowed. "Where was it when Durham was beating you senseless?"

"In its holster, tucked deep into the back of my belt."

"Why didn't you use it?"

It was Ben's turn to be astonished. "I sure as hell wasn't going to escalate things by drawing a weapon."

At the sound of a large diesel engine starting, she once again scrambled for her clothes.

Ben decided he'd better get dressed as well. "For the wilderness, it sure is damn busy around here."

"You stay and pack up camp while I go tell them about the spikes."

"I'll come with you."

"No! I mean, no thank you, that's okay."

Ben narrowed his eyes at her. "You aren't marrying Galen Simms, Emma."

"What?"

"Michael's worried you're going to marry Simms so he'll be free to go away with me. You're *not* marrying the man."

"You've got no right to tell me what I can and can't do."

Ben dropped his gaze to the sleeping bags and then back up to her. "Maybe not"—he moved his nose to within an inch from hers—"yet."

She reached up and grabbed the pole holding the tarp and gave it a yank, pulling the canvas and heavy snow down on his head while she scooted out the open end. By the time Ben was able to toss the entrapping canvas aside, all he could see of Emma were puffs of steam coming out of her nostrils as she disappeared up the hill to the loggers.

Ben looked around in the dim light of the slow-breaking dawn, expecting to see scorched earth in all directions from their shelter. The heat from that woman should have melted the snow all the way to Canada.

"It's not going to work, Mikey."

"What won't work?"

Emma stopped packing her gear, walked around her bed to her nephew, and touched his arm. "I know this isn't easy for you, having your father suddenly show up out of the blue. And I also know you've always dreamed of this day. But he's the proverbial rolling stone, Mikey, who never gathers moss."

He just looked at her. Since she and Ben had returned this morning, the boy had been watching her like a hawk, silently but expectantly. Emma knew he was concocting something in that overintelligent brain of his, and was waiting to see what had come of his manipulations so far.

"Mikey. It's very possible Benjamin Sinclair really didn't know Kelly was pregnant. And I truly believe he didn't have anything to do with your grandfather's death. He wouldn't be here now if I thought he did. But no matter how wonderful you might think he is, that doesn't change *what* he is."

"And just what is he?"

"A rolling stone," she repeated, continuing to pack her gear. "Think about it. The man's thirty-four years old, he's not married and never has been. No children other than you—that we *know* of—and no commitments."

"He's been running Tidewater International for the last five months, Nem."

"Well, bully for him. But he doesn't even own a house, Mikey. He lives with his two bachelor brothers and grandfather."

"Abram Sinclair died five months ago," Michael told her, causing Emma to stop packing and look up again. "And his older brother, Sam Sinclair, just got married, and he's thirty-six." He grinned. "Ben will settle down when he finds the right woman."

Emma gave him a good scowl. "How do you know all this?"

"It was in all the New York papers last spring, when Abram Sinclair died. My great-grandfather left his entire estate, including his shares in Tidewater International, to some woman he met on the Maine coast just six weeks before he died. She's the woman Sam Sinclair married."

Emma snorted. "That's one way to get back your inheritance. Which only proves that just because biology makes Benjamin Sinclair your father, that doesn't mean we can trust him."

"So what are you getting at, Nem?"

Emma threw her pack on the bed and grabbed her nephew by the arms. "You're not the only one who knows how to use the internet around here. I've read a few articles about the Sinclair men myself." She sighed. "I just don't want you concocting any dreams about the three of us, Mikey. There is our relationship, and there will be one between you and your dad, but there will never be one between the three of us. Understand?"

"You don't like him? Not even a little bit?"

"That's not the issue here. It doesn't matter if I like him or not."

Giving up any hope of making him understand, she turned and picked up her gear, then turned back to him. "You sent him after me on purpose, Mikey, hoping something would . . . evolve between us." She poked him in the shoulder. "It's not going to happen, little man."

What she got for that declaration was a kiss on her forehead. "If anything needs to happen around here, it needs to happen to *you*. I love you, Nem. I want to see you happy."

"D-don't do this to me, Mikey," she whispered. "Don't make me cry. I've got sports to take out." She reached up and touched his cheek. "Get to know your dad, Michael. But leave me out of it. Please."

Before he could respond, she pulled free and ran out the door.

Chapter Six

"*Women like flowers*. How about you call down to Greenville and have a big bouquet sent up?"

"It would cost a small fortune to have flowers delivered way out here."

"You've got a fortune." Michael gave Ben a calculating look. "Which is good. The way I figure it, you owe Nem several hundred thousand dollars."

Ben stopped walking down yet another damn tote road and stared at his son. "What makes you think I owe her a dime? And where in hell did you come up with that figure?"

The boy rested his shotgun on his shoulder and grinned. "Child support for the last fifteen years."

"What!"

"I haven't been cheap to raise, you know. Nem tried to see that I didn't do without. My computer cost as much as a new boat and motor. And I broke my leg when I was eight. And I've been outgrowing my clothes faster than she can buy them. Then there were the floats on the plane."

Ben started walking again, forgetting he was supposed to be hunting partridge, and darted a look at the boy walking beside him.

Michael hadn't even blinked at the idea of missing school today. Ben wasn't sure what Miss Flaming-Mad Emma would have to say on the matter, but they'd gotten back to Medicine Creek just before sunrise, and the woman had showered, changed clothes, and taken out her moose hunters. It was probably as much a perverse notion as a selfish one that had made Ben ask Mike to spend the day with him. After all, he *was* the boy's father. He should be able to let the kid skip school.

"How did you damage the floats?"

Michael suddenly looked uncomfortable. "I . . . well, I sort of hit Crazy Larry's dock at full power. But that didn't damage them as much as when I bounced off it and hit the rocky shoreline." He grinned at Ben. "Nemmy was mad enough to drown me."

"How old were you?"

"Thirteen."

"She wasn't in the plane with you?"

"No. I was supposed to be practicing high-speed taxiing."

"What happened?"

"Crazy Larry's niece was visiting."

That certainly explained things. Ben slapped Mike on the shoulder, then left his hand there.

And it felt damn good.

Ben chuckled. "Hell, Mike. Show me any disaster, and I'll show you a woman standing nearby, watching."

"Yeah. Well. Nem wasn't quite as understanding. I chopped enough firewood to keep Medicine Creek Camps heated into the next century."

Two partridge suddenly flew up from the side of the road, startling them into nearly dropping their guns. Neither male took aim at the departing birds, instead stopping to face each other.

"Nem's going to be mad you let me skip school."

"She can't possibly get any madder than she already is."

"Did you . . . have you really come here to claim me as your son?"

"Damn right. Are you ready for a father? For *me* to be your father?"

Gray eyes, so innocent yet so old, shined back at him. "I believe I am, Mr. Sinclair. I love my aunt with all my heart, but it's definitely time I had a father." The corners of his mouth suddenly turned up. "I probably know more about you than you know about yourself."

"How?"

"Nem kept a scrapbook. She gave it to me on my tenth birthday."

"Emma kept a scrapbook?"

"She started it before we ever got internet out here. I suppose she thought I should be able to decide if I eventually wanted to contact you or not. After all, you could have been a jerk."

"And just having this scrapbook, and whatever you could find on the internet, made you want to meet me?"

"That, and other things. Nem always answered any questions I had about you while I was growing up. When I was eight, she gave me a picture of you she'd found in a business magazine. But it was seeing everything pieced together that made me want to meet you: what kind of businessmen you, your brothers, and your grandfather are; what charities you support; even what sort of women you date." He gave Ben a sidelong glance and a crooked grin. "I noticed you don't date any one woman for very long."

Ben switched his gun to his other shoulder and started walking again. He couldn't believe this. His son knew all about him, and he hadn't even known the boy existed.

"I'm sorry you didn't know about me," Michael said softly, as if reading his mind. "And I'm sorry Abram Sinclair died before I could meet him. We . . . I probably should have contacted you sooner."

"Bram would have ransomed his kingdom to have met you."

"I know how he rose from poverty to build a multi-million-dollar shipping business," Mike said with awe.

"And that you're Tidewater International's new CEO."

Ben nodded. "My younger brother, Jesse, works with me. I can't wait for you to meet him. And our older brother, Sam. They're both very eager to meet you. Um . . . we should find something for to call me. 'Mr. Sinclair' is too formal, don't you think?"

"What would you like me to call you?"

Ben felt the back of his neck heat up. *Dad. Call me dad.* "What would you be comfortable with?"

The boy obviously didn't like his question answered with another question. Mike's neck colored all the way up to his cheeks. "Well, how does 'Dad' feel to you?"

"I'd like that."

"Okay then, Dad—if we don't turn around and start back, Nem's going to come home to a dark kitchen and no supper on the table." He gave Ben an inquiring look. "You don't happen to know how to cook, do you?"

"I've been known to burn a barbecue. You got a grill at Medicine Creek?"

"Yup. Now, about those flowers. I hear they can take the anger right out of a woman. And since you and Nem are both being tight-lipped about what caused this particular feud, maybe you should give them a try."

"Maybe *she* should be sending *me* flowers."

Mike cuffed Ben's arm. "Jeez, Dad. Even I know it's a man's place to cave in first." He got that calculating look again. "No one—not even Galen Simms—ever sent Nemmy flowers."

Ben was beginning to suspect he could take lessons from this boy. "Is that so?"

"And would you like to *really* make my aunt melt?"

Now there was a thought. He was almost afraid to ask his next question. "How would I do that?"

"Elmer Fudge cookies."

"Excuse me?"

"Nem loves them. Have a whole case of them delivered with the flowers, and your any wish will be her command."

Emma Sands at his command. Lord, he was loving this boy! "Can I get the cookies in Greenville?"

Michael wrapped his arm around Ben's shoulders and steered him back toward Medicine Creek. "Just leave it to me, Dad."

Within the embrace of his new lease on life, Ben couldn't even feel the ground under his feet. *Dad.* As casual and natural as could be, Michael was touching him and calling him Dad. Well, damn if he didn't suddenly feel like one.

Her hands too numb to work the knob, Emma rattled the door with kicks until Michael finally opened it.

"Jeez, Nem. What happened to you?"

"Where were you today?"

He took a step back as he shot a frantic look over his shoulder.

Emma followed his gaze. "I should have guessed

when I realized Mr. Man of the Mountain here was missing, too. You played hooky, didn't you?"

She directed her question to Mikey, but she was looking at Benjamin Sinclair, whose eyes were also wide with shock, moving up and down her wet, shivering body.

"Uh . . . yeah," Mikey said. "Nem, what happened?"

She turned her glare on her nephew. "I've been swimming in Beaver Pond."

"In your clothes?"

That question came from Sinclair, who stepped up—rather protectively—beside Michael.

"Get in here by the stove, Nem. You're freezing," Michael instructed, grabbing her sleeve and giving it a tug.

"No kidding, Sherlock." She pulled free and waggled her finger in his face. "I called the school to get you out to help me. They said you weren't there."

"I . . . we . . . Dad and I went partridge hunting."

Emma's finger froze. He was calling Ben "Dad"? "I see."

"Nem. Come on." He grabbed her by the sleeve again and pulled her over to the woodstove. "Why did you need my help? Oh, God. Is Pitiful okay?"

"I have no idea where Pitiful is hiding," she told him, fumbling with her coat buttons, finally snapping two off to get it open. She let it drop to the floor with a soggy plop. "One of our great white hunters saw a moose feeding in Beaver Pond and shot the damn thing. Right there—in five feet of water, over a hundred yards out!"

"Jeez."

She glowered at her astonished audience as she held her hands over the firebox. "The damn moose sank right to the bottom. I wanted to tie a rock around that guy's neck and sink *him* beside his trophy bull."

"Jeez, Nem," Michael said again. He softly touched the frozen ends of her hair. "But you were guiding Martha Perry today. She shot the moose?"

"No. Martha's husband was the brilliant one. I *knew* better than to agree to let him come along. I should have followed my rule about not guiding men. But it was Martha's hunt, and she wanted him there."

"You didn't try to get it out by yourself, did you?" Mikey asked.

"Oh no. I had the gracious help of Mr. Perry. How in hell do you think I got soaked? At least he's as soaked as I am. And so is Martha." Emma grinned nastily. "My only satisfaction is that she's madder at her husband than I am."

"Where's the moose now?" Ben asked.

Emma shivered. "With any luck, it will surface tomorrow."

"You left it there?" Michael asked, sounding outraged.

"It's a thousand-pound bull, Mikey. And it's stuck on a sunken stump." With squishing feet, Emma started out of the kitchen. "I'm going to change, and then you and I are going to pull it out with the truck. Dress warm. And grab some rope on your way to the truck."

"Wait."

Emma turned to face Ben, her eyes telling him to butt out. "Yes?"

"You're not going out again tonight." Apparently immune to her icy glare, he continued talking. "It's dark, it's below freezing, and you're hypothermic. You need a hot bath, food, and then bed."

"What I need, Mr. Sinclair, is for you to mind your own damn business while I mind mine. Get going, Mikey."

Michael looked back and forth between her and his dad, his expression uncertain, his eyes filled with indecision.

So this was it. She had already lost him. Emma closed her eyes and turned for the bedroom, her shoulders drooping beneath the weight of her wet clothes and heavy heart. "Never mind, Michael. It's time I learned to rely on myself anyway."

"Nem?"

She didn't stop at his hoarse plea. She squished her way to her room and softly closed the door, leaning back against it and lifting her face to the ceiling to keep her tears from falling down her cheeks.

Oh God, she had known this day would come. She'd been preparing herself for it forever, but there was no way she could *ever* have been prepared for the wrenching pain she felt.

The only person she loved would be leaving her life in just weeks, maybe even days. Michael would write and call and come to visit, but in between she'd be more alone than Jonah had been in his whale.

Standing by the door, with hands shaking either from the cold or the force of her heart shattering, Emma shed her clothes. She stepped out of the water that quickly pooled around them, then padded into her bathroom and turned on the shower. Not until she was under the hot, driving spray did her tears break free, washing down the drain with the mud and the last of her hopes.

She stood there until the shivering stopped and the tears ran out, then dried herself off and opened the bathroom door with a sigh of resignation. She wasn't leaving that damn moose to rot all night. Even if Mr. Perry had been more enamored with the trophy than the meat, Emma refused to let it go to waste.

With her truck, a long rope, and her wits, she could drag the moose out of the bog and field dress it. Tomorrow she'd get it loaded and down to the tagging station—even if she had to camp out all night to guard the damn thing.

It was only a matter of logistics.

Emma was wrapping the towel around herself when she exited the bathroom, mentally making a list of the equipment she would need, when she suddenly stopped at the sight of two stockinged feet at the foot of her bed.

She snapped her head up and met Ben's scowl.

"Get out of my room. Now."

"I'll get out just as soon as you get in bed."

"I have work to do. And bed will be the front seat of my truck tonight."

"What? Why?"

"I've got to stand guard over that moose, or every coyote within fifty miles will be filling its belly."

He slowly shook his head, and Emma finally noticed what he was holding. His hands were on his hips, his legs were spread for battle, and in his right fist was a rope.

"If that's the best rope Mikey could find, he's regressing. It needs to be a lot longer and thicker. It's a thousand-pound bull."

"This rope is plenty big enough. I'm guessing you're not a pound over one twenty."

She frowned at him. "What in hell are you talking about?"

He stepped up to her and Emma stepped back, bumping into the bathroom door as she clutched her towel more securely. She had to tilt her head up in order to keep eye contact, and from this angle, the guy looked way too tall and determined.

"It means I'm going to tie you to that bed if I have to, Emma."

He was bluffing. She lifted her chin in some semblance of authority. "You wouldn't dare."

His eyes ignited like silver moonbeams.

"Michael wouldn't let you."

"I'm bigger than Michael, too."

"I *have* to go get that moose. It'll bloat up like a balloon if I don't field dress it tonight."

"Mike and I will go get your precious moose. You're in no condition to haul it out, much less sleep in your truck. I won't tie you up if you crawl into bed and give me your word to stay there."

"Medicine Creek Camps is my responsibility, not yours. And it's not Michael's anymore, either. Get out of my room."

"Give over, Em."

He wouldn't *dare* tie her to the bed. Would he?

"Fine. I hope you fall in Beaver Pond and get frozen there until spring!"

"You know it's for your own good, Em. You're dead on your feet."

She swept past him to her bureau. "If there's one thing a woman always loves to hear from a man, it's that he's being a jackass for her own good." She grabbed some long johns and an insulated T-shirt and marched into the bathroom. "Make sure you don't wear one of your nice shirts, Mr. Sinclair. Bloodstains don't come out of expensive material any easier than good old flannel. And don't forget a pillow."

With that parting shot, she slammed the door in his face.

When she opened it again, her hair dry and her body decently covered, there were two sets of stockinged feet in her room.

Emma walked right past them and pulled back the covers and plopped into bed. She fluffed her pillows, straightened her blankets, folded her hands on her lap, then finally looked up. One set of gray eyes was laughing at her and the other set was studying her with concern.

"I heated some soup for you, Nem. You didn't have any supper."

Michael placed a tray on her lap. Emma looked down at the bowl of steaming chicken noodle soup, a sandwich big enough to choke a horse, crackers, hot tea, and a whole package of Elmer Fudge cookies.

A peace offering. Michael had seen her stiffen when he'd called Ben "Dad," and taking sides with him now was making the boy feel like a traitor.

Emma wanted to throw the entire tray against the wall, bury herself under her blankets, and cry for a week. But she didn't want Mikey pulled in two directions by two people he cared for.

She looked up at the young man she'd taken into her heart the moment he'd taken his first breath. Knowing her eyes were swimming in unshed tears, she smiled at him. "Thanks, Mikey. I'm starved."

"We'll go get the moose and bring it back here tonight. You just rest and stay warm, Nem. Please don't worry about anything. Da—Mr. Sinclair and I can handle it."

"Just be careful. The moose is near the south shore."

"We'll find it. Eat. I'm gonna go get the equipment together now. Eat," he repeated, giving her one last hesitant look before silently striding out of the room.

Emma picked up the spoon and slowly swirled it around in the soup, watching the steam waft into the air. The bed beside her dipped with Ben's weight, and a hand settled on the blankets beside her as he leaned across her legs. When she lifted her gaze, intense gunmetal gray pierced her.

"This isn't going to work, Emma. We have to stop clashing every time we get within ten feet of each other. It's tearing Mike apart. He shouldn't have to choose between us."

"I'm not asking him to." She looked back down at her dinner. "I was a little . . . angry when I came in. And hearing him call you 'Dad' caught me off guard." She looked back at Ben. "I'm glad he likes you. I'm glad you had today together. Now you can take him home."

He shook his head, his gaze never leaving hers. "No, I can't. Mike's not ready to walk away yet. Can't you see that?"

Emma sighed, picked up one of the cookies and pulled it apart, exposing the chocolate. "Then I've got to give him a push," she said, then raked the creamy center with her teeth.

"You push him, and he's liable to push right back. Just give him some time." He stole one of her cookies and popped it into his mouth.

The guy had no idea how to eat an Elmer Fudge.

"Give me some time, too, Em. Michael's not the only one trying to feel his way through this mess."

"Let me ask you something, Mr. Sinclair."

"You could start making things easier for Mike if you called me Ben," he suggested.

"Okay. Ben. Did you ever question that Michael might not even be your son?"

"Damn right I did. The moment I put down your letter."

Emma ignored the fact that he still thought she had sent the letter. "But you don't have any doubts now?"

"I didn't have any before I came here. It's like looking in a mirror twenty years ago."

Emma smiled. "Yes. Michael's the spitting image of you when you came here that summer. But how come you were sure before you even saw him? You must have known you weren't the first man to be with Kelly. Michael could have belonged to someone else."

Ben shook his head. "I had my lawyers check. And a private detective firm. I knew before I made my reservation here that Mike was mine."

"I see."

"I had you checked out quite thoroughly, too."

"Me!"

"You haven't had a very easy life, have you?"

Emma raised her chin. "I've had a wonderful life. Other than losing my parents and Kelly's leaving, this has been heaven. Don't you dare pity me."

"Pity you! Good Lord, woman. I'm in awe of you."

Emma snorted and grabbed another cookie. Ben plucked it out of her hand and replaced it with her spoon. "Soup first," he ordered. He picked up the bowl of cookies, stood up, and put them on her nightstand.

Even in his stocking feet, the man had a tendency to loom. He stood there silently and patiently, and Emma knew that if she didn't start eating he'd still be planted there come spring. She ate several spoonfuls laden with noodles, then pointed her spoon at the door.

"Enjoy yourself tonight, Ben. Consider field dressing that moose by headlight a rite of passage for father and son. I just wish I could be there to watch." She gave him a brilliant smile as she got in the last salvo. "Mikey's allergic to moose hair. So make sure you take your own knife."

Her chin was suddenly lifted and her gasp muffled by warm, wickedly delicious lips—which were just as suddenly gone.

Chapter Seven

"Quit rubbing your eyes. You're making it worse."

"I can't help it. They itch."

"Why in hell didn't you let me dress the moose by myself?"

His son looked over at him with red, swollen eyes. "Because we were only trying to get the guts out, not butcher it. You were hacking off some of the best meat."

"Yeah. Well. It'll be a cold day in hell before I look at hamburger again."

"Jeez, Dad. Beef isn't born in plastic wrap."

"Mine is." He was so tired, Ben nearly dropped his head into the steering wheel. He rubbed his own eyes and peered out the windshield to see Medicine Creek Camps finally come into view. The sun was up, but blocked by mountains.

"Shit," Mike said.

"Now what? Did that damn moose fall out of the truck?"

"Simms is here. That's his truck."

Ben saw a dirty black pickup parked next to the house. "It's barely daybreak. What in hell is he doing here this early?"

"Or this late?" Mike asked softly. "Nem caved in awful easy last night. I never thought she'd really stay in bed."

Ben remembered Emma saying she was going to give Michael a push, if that's what the boy needed. Was Simms that push? Had she called him as soon as they'd left last night? If that man had spent the night with Emma, there was going to be more than just moose blood on his hands.

"I tried to warn you. You should have sent her those flowers."

Ben halted the truck beside the black pickup, then grabbed Mike's arm to stop him from jumping out. Not taking his eyes off the lighted kitchen windows, Ben spoke softly. "Let me handle this, Mike."

"You won't do anything . . . crazy?"

Ben smiled and let go of his arm. "I'm not making any promises."

"Nem wouldn't . . . she didn't . . . she doesn't even like the guy."

"Then that makes three of us. Don't worry—Simms wasn't here all night."

He hoped. But hell, who knew women? He certainly couldn't figure this one out. She was supposedly in love with some unknown guy, yet she had exploded in passion yesterday in the woods. She loved Michael like a son, yet she had sent a letter that would ultimately take him away. She just might be crazy enough to think that Galen Simms would be a good way to give Mike the push he needed to leave the nest.

He should have tied her to the bed last night, out of reach of the phone. Hell, he shouldn't even have brought her back home yesterday morning. He should have kept Emma in the woods for a week, and made love to her until she agreed to marry him.

Whoa! Married?

Where the hell had that come from?

Yeah, Mr. Brain-dead. The woman is in love with another man. You want to live with that the rest of your life?

Damn right he would, if it would gain him his son. He didn't love Emma Sands, but that shouldn't be an issue. Love and lust were two different things completely. He could see himself married to Emma without bringing love into the equation. He would simply offer marriage as a solution to their problem.

And she just might accept—for Michael.

"You going in, or are you waiting for the preacher to arrive?"

Ben turned his head and stared at his son in disbelief.

"Simms," Mike clarified. "You going to kick him out, or throw rice at their wedding?"

Ben sighed in relief. "It would help if you would at least give me a hint. Who's the guy she's suppose to be in love with?"

"You haven't figured it out yet?" Mike narrowed his eyes, making them barely visible inside all the swelling. "Exactly what happened when you found her in the woods?"

"I'll write you a letter explaining what happened and leave it in my will."

"You tried to seduce her, didn't you?"

"Goddammit! Your aunt tried to knock my head off. I couldn't get close enough to seduce her!"

"Well, Jeez."

"If you even so much as whisper about this, I'll be all over you like road dust."

Michael vigorously nodded, smiling like a well-fed cat. Which immediately made Ben suspicious.

"It's a ruse, isn't it? You invented some dream guy, and put the idea in my head that Galen Simms wants to marry Emma. You're trying to manipulate your aunt and me into getting together so you don't have to give up either one of us."

The boy instantly sobered. "Nem's hope chest isn't invented. Neither is Simms. And I'm not being selfish. I can still have both of you even if we don't live to-gether." Michael sighed and rubbed his eyes again. "I should probably just go to college and not bother living with either one of you." He looked over at Ben with ancient, tired eyes. "I'll just act like you're both my parents, only divorced or something. Millions of kids live out of two households."

"College is still a long way off. You're only fifteen."

"But I get my high school diploma at the end of December. I accelerated my classes. I've even taken some college courses already. And I've been accepted at MIT with full scholarship as soon as I'm ready."

Ben fell back against the door of the truck as if he'd taken a blow to the chest. *Michael Sands is a genius.*

"Mike."

"It's okay, Dad. The chances of you coming here after fifteen years and picking up a relationship with me was far-fetched anyway." He smiled sadly. "And no one knows my aunt better than I do. She can be more stubborn than a mule when something's important to her." He rubbed his eyes again. "She sees you as somebody who wants to take her whole life away. Do you blame her for fighting back?"

"No. Put that way, I'd probably fight like hell myself. I'm not going to walk away from you, Mike. And I won't walk away from your aunt, either. We can work it out."

"Not if we don't get Simms out of the house. He really does plan to marry her. And he's getting desperate."

Ben whipped his head around and glared at the

kitchen window. "Hell. I forgot about him." He opened his door. "Give me some time. I can get your aunt to come around eventually."

The boy's grin was suddenly back. "Then you're a better man than I'll ever be. Nem has more defenses than a porcupine."

Ben stalked up to the house, determined to cause a scene that would become legend in Medicine Gore. If he had to—and he hoped he did—he was going to kick Galen's ass all the way home.

Assuming he found Simms sitting at the kitchen table. If he was in Emma's bed, he might drag the bastard across the lake once or twice first. Either way, the man was going to know Emma Sands was no longer available.

When Ben walked in the kitchen door and didn't find anyone, the blood drained from his face and he felt light-headed as he pictured Emma in bed with another man.

There was a sudden crash from the great room and the unmistakable sound of flesh being struck. Ben heard a pained gasp and another crash. Two strides brought him onto the scene of any woman's nightmare. Emma was being held down by an angry man while she struggled to protect herself.

Galen Simms's head snapped around as Ben roared in outrage. He was on the bastard before Simms could scramble to his feet. Ben pulled him up by the back of the neck and drove his knee into Simms's ribs, sending the man sprawling on his back, away from Emma.

Ben saw her scramble away into the corner as he went after Simms again. The man was trying to stand and Ben caught him in the torso this time, using his boot. Simms rolled with the blow and came up on his hands and knees, then rolled again to avoid Ben's third attack. He slammed into an end table, breaking it into splinters.

"Goddammit! What in hell are you doing!" the man yelled.

"Protecting what's mine, you son of a bitch." Ben caught the retreating bastard by the shoulder and turned him to plant a fist in Simms's angry face. The man went down again, but quickly scrambled to his feet and ran for the kitchen door. Ben started to chase him, but suddenly caught sight of Emma, and he froze.

She was standing in the corner of the great room, a broken lamp held up like a weapon, her eyes wide with fear. The moment she realized the threat was over, she dropped the lamp and covered her face with her hands.

Ben looked at the open back door and saw Michael standing there.

He looked back at the corner. Emma was now sitting on the floor, tucked up in a ball so tight it was a wonder she could breathe, looking like a frightened child trying to make herself invisible.

Ben hunched down beside her, swearing under his breath when she flinched. Not knowing what to do but unable to just do nothing, he reached out and cupped her face. She tried to scoot away, only to be stopped by the wall.

"Emma. Honey. It's just me." He inched closer. "Come on, honey. Let me help you up."

Hoping like hell he was doing the right thing, he carefully reached an arm under her knees and another around her shoulders, pulled her against his chest, and stood up. She buried her face in his shirt.

Ben kicked the broken table out of his way and sat down in her giant recliner, keeping her wrapped in a desperate embrace of fear and guilt. He'd been sitting outside in the truck thinking the worst, and she'd been in here trying to fight off a brutal attack.

"Let me look at you, honey. Where are you hurt?"

He couldn't pry her loose of the protective fist she'd made of her body, and the last thing he wanted to do was force her. So he simply held her, rubbing her back.

As Mike rushed into the living room, he suddenly stopped and looked around at the destruction. Michael's face paled as he brought his gaze back to his aunt on Ben's lap.

"N . . . Nem? Nemmy? What happened?"

Ben motioned him over. "Simms attacked her. Come talk to her, Mike. I can't tell how badly she's hurt. She's too upset."

Three strides and Mike was kneeling beside the chair. He reached out and lightly touched Emma's head. She stirred, but didn't look up. It felt to Ben like she was trying to burrow under his shirt and hide.

"Oh, Nemmy. Did Galen do this to you?"

"Go away, Mikey," came a muffled, distant plea.

"Tell me where you're hurt."

"I'm fine. Go away."

"He won't leave until you prove it, Emma. Let us take a look at you," Ben urged, nudging his finger under her chin, which was like trying to wedge an elephant into a keyhole. Ben forced the issue and quietly sucked in his breath.

"Mike, go get us an ice pack."

The boy nearly tripped over himself rushing to the kitchen. Ben lifted her chin again. "You've got the makings of one hell of a shiner, Emma. You're going to have to sit up and let us take care of you."

Her eyes were scrunched tight and leaking tears, and her cheek was already turning colorful. He had to use his shoulder to push her upright, and then he suddenly had to use both his hands to keep her from bolting off his lap.

"Easy now. Don't get shy on me."

Her eyes finally made contact with his, and just as suddenly she looked down at his chest and her whole face turned scarlet.

"My God. You're embarrassed? Emma, look at me."

She darted a worried glance at the kitchen door. "I . . . I don't want Michael to see me like this," she whispered. She tried to scoot off his lap again. "Let me go to my room."

"So you can curl up in a ball in the closet?"

She shuddered. "I'm okay now. I just sort of . . . Galen surprised me. I . . . I never thought I could be overpowered like that. I thought only weak women were victims."

"Hell, Emma, the bastard weighs nearly twice what you do. You can't expect to stand up to a man the size of Simms, no matter how fit you are. You have nothing to be ashamed about."

She gave him an uncertain look, then shuddered. "You can let me up now."

"You might be calming down, but it's going to take me a little longer. Are you hurt anywhere else?"

She shook her head.

Ben didn't believe her. He'd felt her flinch when he'd stopped her from jumping off his lap. More than just her face and her confidence was bruised.

"Here's an ice pack," Michael said, returning to the room. "Shit! That bastard punched you!"

Emma covered the evidence of Simms's attack with her hand. "'Bastard' may be appropriate, Mikey, but its not a word I want to hear coming from you." She turned a one-eyed glare on Ben. "This is your fault."

"That Simms attacked you?"

"No. That Mikey has started swearing." She took the ice pack from her nephew and gingerly touched it to her cheek. "If this is an example of your fatherly influence on him, it's probably time you went back to New York."

"It won't work, Emma."

She blinked at him.

"The subject is not Mike's language, nor mine. Where else are you hurt?"

She blinked again.

"Then I guess I'll just take you to the bedroom, strip off your clothes, and find out for myself."

Emma darted a look at Mike, who was wholeheartedly nodding approval of Ben's threat. She brought her right hand up. "I hurt my hand when I punched him back. Are you satisfied now?"

Her knuckles were bright red and swelling.

"Nem? Why did Galen attack you?"

"I told him I wouldn't marry him. And that I was selling Medicine Creek Camps."

"What! Why did you say that?"

"Because I am."

"But you can't!"

"Sure I can. I may have already found a buyer."

Ben leaned back in the chair but kept his hands securely on her hips. The surprises just kept coming—from finding out he had a son to finding out he loved that son to discovering he was even willing to marry his son's aunt.

"When did you decide this?" Ben shot a worried look at Michael. Emma was going to push the boy, all right. Only it was a matter of who got pushed over the edge first—Mike or Ben.

"I've been thinking about it for a while now."

She was positioning the bag of ice over her hand with the attention of a scientist working on a complicated experiment.

Mike gave Ben an uncertain look, silently asking him if this was a good revelation or a major snag in their plans. Ben didn't know what to tell the boy, so he asked Emma, "And what do you plan to do then?"

She still refused to look up. "I thought I might go to college."

"What?" Michael asked.

Emma looked at her nephew. "I've always wanted to be a marine biologist. I love the ocean. And I want to go live by it."

"Well, Jeez, Nem. You could have said something a little sooner. You could have sold the camps years ago."

She tried to get off Ben's lap, and this time he let her go. She stood up and faced Mike. "You and I weren't ready years ago."

Ben rolled his eyes and also stood up. "Well, ready or not, here comes life, people." He crossed his arms over his chest and glared at them both. "You two have been spending all your time trying to outmaneuver each other—and me—instead of seeing the obvious. Now both of you are going to sit down on that couch while I tell you how things are going to be from now on."

"This isn't your boardroom, Mr. Sinclair. You can't order us around."

One small step brought Ben's face within inches of hers. "Sit."

Mike pulled her down on the couch beside him. Ben smiled at her glower.

"You, Emma Sands, are not going to sell anything. The *three* of us are going to stay right here at Medicine Creek Camps until Mike graduates from high school. There's no sense in uprooting him at this point."

"Then you're moving to your own cabin."

Ben still smiled. "That's fine. I'm going to have to bring in some office equipment, so a separate cabin would work better for me. Like you, I have a business to run. But I'll be taking my meals here."

She opened her mouth to protest, but Ben continued. "And you, Michael, will stop coming straight home after school. You'll stay and play some basketball. Or hang out with the guys. Flirt with the girls, and get into trouble if you have to. But you're going to get into *teenage* trouble—not confrontations with Crazy Larry, the FAA, or the Highway Patrol. Understood?"

Emma jumped up from the couch. "Are you implying that I've kept Michael away from his friends?"

Ben took hold of her shoulders and sat her back down, smiling with all the confidence of a man who knew he was finally in control of the situation. "No, I'm not saying any such thing. Michael has kept himself isolated because he's too old for his own good."

He straightened and looked at his son. "I don't care if you're smarter than Einstein, Mike. You're going to burn yourself out if you don't start learning to kick back a little. It's time you started being fifteen, not fifty."

Ben could tell that Mike wanted to say something, but his very intelligence kept him silent. And probably a little shock.

"And just what will you be doing while Mikey is getting into trouble and I'm not selling my camps?" Emma asked.

"I'm going to be running my business and dating you."

"What!" She stood again, her face red, her hands balled into fists.

"I think I'll start by taking you to the dance next Saturday night," he continued.

Ben ducked the suddenly airborne ice pack, winking at Mike as he headed for the kitchen. "Go clean yourself up, Em, while I make breakfast. Mike and I are hungry. We've been up all night doing your work."

"Hey, Dad?"

Ben stopped and turned. "What?"

"Is that a piece of moss I see sticking to your shirt?" the boy asked.

Emma gasped so hard, she started coughing.

Ben looked down at his shirt, but didn't see anything.

"Don't worry about it, Dad. A little moss never hurt anyone."

Chapter Eight

For the last four days, Mikey hadn't come home until after nine at night. God only knew what the boy was up to. Emma had fretted over Ben's revelation that her nephew didn't have friends his own age. But fifteen-year-old boys usually had more hormones than brains, and she was afraid Mikey's would awaken before she had The Talk with him.

"Something sure smells good in here. You got enough for one more, Nem?"

As if her thoughts had conjured him up, Mikey walked through the kitchen door with—Ohmigod—a girl in tow.

"Ah, sure. There's plenty."

"Nem, this is Jasmine. Jass, this is my aunt, Nemmy."

"Hello, Jasmine."

"Hi."

"Come on, Jass. I'll show you my computer," Mikey said, leading the girl through the kitchen.

Her spoon suspended over the stew, Emma stared at the retreating kids. Should she be letting Mikey take a girl to his bedroom?

This was Ben's fault! He should be here supervising the problem he'd created. Emma marched out of the house and up onto the porch of cabin six. She used the wooden spoon to knock on the door, then used it to point at Ben. "Your son brought something home that he wants to show you. He's in his room."

Ben plucked the spoon out of her hand and sniffed it. "That's not moose you're cooking, is it?"

"Hurry up. You've got to go see Mikey before . . . well, just get going."

"I'm right in the middle of a conference call to Singapore, Em. Can't it wait?"

Emma pushed past him and found the phone on a desk that took up the entire main room of the small cabin. She pushed the red button that was flashing.

"Hey!"

"Being a father takes priority, Ben. Go see Mikey. Now."

"That was an important client you just hung up on, Emma. What's Mike got that won't keep a few more minutes?"

"A girl. And the blouse she has on is probably outlawed in all fifty states. Enough said?"

With a muttered curse, Ben was out the door and halfway to the house before she'd finished.

Since she was here and he was gone, and dinner was probably going to be postponed a bit, Emma decided to snoop. Her quaint little cabin now looked like the command center for the United Nations. A map of the world was tacked up on the back wall, over a table of office machines that could be on a spaceship headed to Mars. One of them was whirring and spitting out papers faster than Emma could read them. She looked more closely at the map.

There were little pins stuck in it all over the world, mostly in the water. Some were at coastal cities, some far out to sea. Some were red, some were green, and all of them were on little black lines running back and forth across both the Atlantic and Pacific Oceans. Purple pins were stuck inland, at what Emma realized were major airports.

Tidewater International was huge.

And Ben was trying to run it from Medicine Creek Camps?

Emma sat down in the big executive chair and stared at the map. Why hadn't Ben taken his son home already? Trying to work here couldn't be easy.

She wrapped her arms around herself. She'd made a mess of this whole thing—for everyone but Mikey, it seemed. For the last four days the boy had been walking on clouds—whenever he was home—and whistling his way through his chores. Whistling!

Well, she was glad for him. The poor kid had been so confused when his mother left, and Emma worried that he'd blamed himself. So she had spent the last ten years trying to make up for Kelly's treachery.

She had no idea how any mother could simply walk away from her child and not even bother to contact him again. A letter would have been nice, or a birthday card or even a postcard, from wherever she was.

But then, a postcard would give them a way to track her down, and Kelly obviously wasn't ready to be found. More than once, Emma had been tempted to hire a detective, just so she could walk up to her sister and slap her face. She hated Kelly for what she'd done, and she was never, ever going to forgive her.

Emma jumped when the phone suddenly rang. She stared at its blinking lights and many buttons, and finally picked up the receiver. "Tidewater International. No, Mr. Sinclair is not available at this time. What? A check? For *how* much! No, I don't think that's correct. You're way too high . . . I don't care if you've already delivered it; you can just come take it back. I see. Well, then you'll have to accept a check for two thousand less. No . . . No . . . One thousand, then, and not a penny more. Thank you, Mr. Coffin."

"Me? Oh, I'm the . . . vice president in charge of acquisitions. Yes, Tidewater International will be sure to do business with you in the future. Good-bye."

Emma's smug grin suddenly disappeared when a tall, ominous shadow fell across the desk.

"Well, Miss Vice President. Make any good deals lately?"

"The phone rang, and you weren't here, so I answered it."

"Thank you. I think."

Emma started straightening the papers on the desk. "Money must grow on a tree in your backyard, Ben. You paid way too much for that sissified truck parked outside."

Two hands, palms flat, settled on the papers she was straightening. "Did I?"

"Well, not now. I got you a thousand dollars off. Remember that when you write out the check."

"I surely will, Miss Vice President. Take any other calls?"

Emma finally looked up into Ben's laughing eyes. "Singapore called back, but I told them your girlfriend had just gone into labor with twins, and that her father was coming through the door with a shotgun. They said they'd call back."

He was around the desk before she could scramble out from behind it. And before she could finish gasping, Emma was being lifted up and plopped down on the mahogany surface, scattering the papers—right along with her emotions. Muscular thighs spread her knees, and long arms wrapped around her as those laughing eyes suddenly changed.

It was a look Emma had seen before.

She tried to push him away. She knew it was impossible, but she didn't want to ever let this man realize the power he was gaining over her.

"That was a very nasty thing to do, Emma Sands."

"Will you have to turn all your big boats around in midocean now, Mr. Sinclair? Have you lost face with your Singapore clients?"

"Probably."

"Will that bankrupt Tidewater International?"

"Probably."

"So Michael won't have a company to inherit?"

"There's always Medicine Creek Camps."

Emma nodded. "That's true. It's a good thing I haven't sold it yet."

"If I promise to finally kiss you, will you stop kneading my chest?"

"Oh! I'm so—" His lips stopped her from flirting any further.

Flirting! Was she *flirting* with Ben Sinclair? Had that voice really been hers?

She would love to analyze this side of herself, but she was being kissed senseless by a man who knew exactly what he was doing.

He was beginning to smell like the woods he was spending so much time in, Emma discovered as Ben's tongue invaded her mouth. Thank God she was sitting on the desk; she could feel herself already turning into a blob of jelly. Her head spun. Her heart began to pound. And she had to move her hands away from his delightful chest and grab his shoulders so she could kiss him back.

He should come with a warning label.

"I want to make love to you."

Emma blinked up at Ben. Had she said those words or had he?

"But I can wait. A little while."

Emma sighed in relief. Of course he'd said them. If *she* had, Ben would have had her naked before she'd finished the sentence.

Now there was a thought. Why not just rip off her clothes and . . . and *do* it?

What was stopping her?

Maybe the bone-chilling fear that she would find herself in Kelly's position two months from now? The terrible fear that she was no better than her sister?

Another abandonment would kill her.

Michael would be graduating in two months, then he would be leaving to start his own life. And Tidewater International was run by a man who would need a special woman by his side—one who was intelligent, cultured, and worldly. Knowing how to skin fish and track a deer were not skills Ben's girlfriend would need to know.

A mighty sigh blew over her head and Emma realized she had wrapped her arms around Ben's waist and was hugging him, her face buried in his chest. With the gentleness of a concerned man, he was hugging her back, his chin resting on her head.

"I'm either making you mad or sad every time I touch you, Emma Sands."

"Dinner's going to burn."

He simply held her tighter. "It's okay. Mike and Jasmine are seeing to dinner."

"I still have to go."

"In a minute. Let me just hold you."

Said the spider to the fly. He was holding her close enough that Emma could still feel his desire.

She was so confused. Ben's lust for her certainly seemed real, but how could a man feel concern for the woman who had kept his son a secret from him?

He wasn't after her camps, or her skills as a guide. He had truly been angry that she'd placed herself in danger with the tree spikers. And he'd been determined she not go back out that night to retrieve the moose. And he would have killed Galen Simms had the jerk stayed around long enough.

Benjamin Sinclair wasn't acting like he hated her.

Emma snuggled closer against him. This was nice. Never in her life had she leaned on anyone else for support, but she was so damn tired of trying to figure things out.

She sighed. "If Mike's anything like you when there's a female around, dinner will be burnt to a crisp. I've got to go."

Ben finally stepped back and Emma regretted the sudden lack of contact. But she had to stop feeding her dream of happily ever after. She could enjoy what time she had left with Mikey and Ben; she only had to remember the joy was temporary. Two more months and it would end.

"Look at me, Em."

She finally looked up.

"Try as I might, I can't read your mind. But I do know mine. You belong to me, Emma Sands, just as much as Mike does." He cupped her face in his large hands and gave her a swift, forceful kiss. "Try to get used to the idea."

With that promise echoing in her ears, Emma ran out of the cabin with all the dignity of Pitiful.

"I hope to come to one of your camp sessions next summer. Mom does, too."

"That's great, Jasmine. You'll enjoy it immensely." Emma smiled at the girl sitting across the table. The poor darling seemed completely intimidated by Ben. Those were the first words the girl had spoken since they'd sat down to dinner.

"But you live right in town, Jasmine. Why would you want to come stay at one of Emma's cabins?" Ben asked, looking directly at the girl.

Mikey came to her rescue, for Jasmine was too busy choking on her dinner to answer. "Nem runs weeklong camps in the summer for women only," he explained.

Ben looked at Emma. "Really? How innovative."

Emma suddenly felt as self-conscious as Jasmine, only for different reasons. Lord, the man was handsome, with his hair nearly as long as Mikey's and his beard bristling with his smile.

"That's been the success of Medicine Creek Camps," Mikey said. "There are a lot of women who want to hunt and fish, but are put off by the whole macho image. Nem runs ads in all the national magazines, inviting women to come and explore the wilderness. She won't guide men at all."

"And the women come?"

"They sure do. Especially to the summer camps. We advertise them as a week's escape from the real world. One ad asks that if kids can be sent to summer camps, why not moms? We offer fishing and hiking and kayaking, wildlife safaris, and floatplane rides. We ran three weeklong camps last summer and four weekend camps. Some of the women are coming back for deer hunting this November."

"Interesting. And you don't guide men at all?" he asked, looking at Emma.

"Not if I can help it."

"Why not?"

"When some men book a guide for a week, they leave their manners at home. They shed all pretense of civilization and come here to play Rambo. Finding out their guide is a female kind of destroys the fantasy."

"They become jerks," Mikey added, drawing his father's attention again.

Ben's face suddenly lost its humor. "What kind of jerks?"

The boy shrugged. "Nem usually hires local guides to take them out."

"That's why I cater to women," she explained. "And because it's good business. I've discovered a niche that needed filling. The women of this world are just as interested in the wilderness as men are, or even more so. And they have fun."

"And this market is what Simms was after?" Ben asked.

"Yup. That and my acreage."

There was a knock on the kitchen door loud enough to rattle the windows. Emma saw Jasmine's eyes widen in horror.

"Oh, God. I'm dead," the girl said, sliding back her chair and standing up. "Thank you for dinner, Miss Sands. I've got to go."

Ben had reached the door and opened it. He must not have liked what he saw any more than Jasmine did, because he took a defensive stand between their visitor and the girl.

"Where's my daughter?" came a booming voice.

"She's just finishing her dinner. You're Mr. LeBlanc, I take it?" Ben answered.

Emma said quietly, "You don't have to run, Jasmine. We'll invite your dad in for some pie."

The girl turned her look of horror on Emma, then blushed. "I have to go."

"Jasmine! Come on, girl."

Emma stood up. She stepped in front of Mikey, who was headed for the door, and pulled him to a stop before pushing past Ben.

"Good evening, John. You didn't have to come all the way out here. I was going to bring your daughter home. Why don't you have some pie before you leave?"

John's demeanor suddenly changed, and his face turned as red as Mikey's.

"Good evening, Emma. I . . . we can't stay. I've got a Grange meeting tonight."

"Some other time then, John. Come on. I'll walk you to your truck while Jasmine gets her school pack."

As she closed the door behind her, she saw Ben staring at her through the glass. She smiled and led John away from the house and certain trouble.

"What was that all about?" Ben asked.

"Nothing," Emma answered as she sat down at the table to have her pie.

Mikey snorted.

Emma shot him a warning look, but the boy ignored it. "That was John LeBlanc. He doesn't particularly care for me. Nor you, either, if he learns you're Benjamin Sinclair," Mikey informed him.

"Why?"

"Something about the sins of the father," Mikey explained as he served himself a piece of pie, not sounding terribly concerned.

Ben shot Emma a questioning look. "Is it common knowledge that I'm Mike's father?"

"Yes. And John LeBlanc was on duty at the dam the morning it was blown up. He walks with a limp now, and like everyone else in town, he blames you and the environmentalists you came here with."

Ben stood up and paced to the woodstove. He turned to Emma and his son. "It's archaic to blame Mike for something they think I did. Does everyone else treat him like that?"

"No, just a few. Mostly those who were directly involved. Durham did for a while, but I set him straight years ago. He was Dad's closest friend and the one who found him. It's hard for some people to let go."

"LeBlanc certainly changed his attitude when you showed up. Why?"

"John used to date Nem," Mikey piped up.

Emma could see that Ben didn't like that news, either.

"His kid's your age, Mike. Which means . . ." He looked over at Emma. "That you were just a baby when you dated him."

"Jasmine's his stepdaughter," Emma explained. "And I was nineteen at the time and he was twenty-six. Any other questions?"

"No. But I think you should know that you're not dancing with anyone else tomorrow night."

"You don't really intend to go to that dance, do you?"

"Hell, yes. We have a date."

Emma looked at Mikey, who was nodding agreement. No help from that quarter. "Someone's bound to recognize you, Ben. There's sure to be trouble."

"I don't intend to hide out here for two more months. And it's probably time I cleared my name, don't you think?" He looked at his son. "And Mike's, too."

"A local dance is not the place for public vindication. Especially not when liquor's involved. Half the town will be drinking tomorrow night, and the other half will be carting them home and tucking them into bed."

"I won't start anything."

"You won't have to. Don't you see? These are hard-working, uncomplicated people, and they have long memories when they've been wronged. If just one person recognizes you, there's going to be trouble."

"John LeBlanc didn't recognize me."

Emma walked over to stand in front of him. "Wayne Poulin probably will."

He growled deep in his chest. "Is that bastard still

around? I would have thought someone had killed him years ago."

Emma remained silent.

He glanced at Michael, then back at her. "Who . . . who did Kelly run off with?" he asked in a suddenly subdued voice. "I thought she was in love with Poulin." He darted another look in Michael's direction. "That's what she told me that . . . that day."

Emma went back and started clearing the table. "We don't know. According to Wayne, it was some guy she'd been seeing in Bangor." Emma shrugged. "It's possible. She went shopping there often enough."

She took Mikey's untouched pie from him. "Kelly and Wayne fought more than they loved. Wayne would get crazy jealous if Kelly even looked at another man. She probably got tired of the roller-coaster relationship and took off with the first man who offered her a way out."

Michael pushed his chair back and stood up. "Be thankful, Dad," he told Ben. "I could have been living with Wayne Poulin all these years if Kelly had married him." The boy made a face and gave an exaggerated shiver. "But for the grace of God and my frightened mother, I could have been his stepson."

Ben blew out a tired sigh. "What a mess."

"Things have a way of working out for the best," Michael said. "Don't look back. Look at the present. And the future. I've had a good childhood; I've been loved, given security, and experienced life to the fullest so far." He gave his father a great big grin. "And I've still got a lot of living ahead of me, and it's going to be a wonderful adventure. Don't regret anything. If you hadn't come here sixteen years ago, I wouldn't exist."

With a gentle punch to his father's arm, Michael walked out of the kitchen, giving Emma a wink.

The silence he left behind was thoughtful. Emma didn't move. Neither did Ben.

"He's right, Ben," she said into the void. "I've been silently thanking you for Michael for the last fifteen years."

"I wish . . . I'm sorry I missed those years," he said, still not turning. "I would like to have known him."

"You can now."

Ben finally turned around, and Emma watched a play of emotions cross his face. Curiosity settled into place when he finally spoke again. "Where's Kelly now? Has she ever contacted Mike?"

Emma shook her head and went back to clearing the table. "I had taken Mikey with me to Portland for the weekend," she explained. "When we returned, all I found was a note from her saying she had to leave for a while. It also said she'd call once she got settled, and that she'd send for Mikey." She looked at him. "She never did either one."

Ben's face was unreadable.

Emma carried the dishes to the sink before she

turned to him again. "Wayne Poulin claims Kelly has written him two or three times over the years, but I don't know if I believe him. He was always a loud braggart, especially when he was drinking. He continues to claim she'll come back to him." Emma shook her head. "He's trying to save face, even after all these years. I actually feel sorry for him."

"Why didn't Kelly marry Wayne? She told me she intended to." He snorted. "Apparently I was just someone to pass the time with, because her *real* boyfriend was spending the summer at some logging camp in Canada. When he came home, she ran right back to him. It took me a week to get her alone again, so I could ask her to come to New York with me. "

"I don't think she was running *back* to Wayne as much as she was running *away* from you."

Ben stiffened. "What do you mean?"

"Kelly was afraid of you, Ben. You were so sophisticated and worldly, and so passionate about the dam not being built. I think Kelly was afraid that if she fell in love with you, you'd . . . you would overwhelm her."

"She told you this?"

"More or less. I tried to get her to contact you several times during her pregnancy, but she was afraid you'd insist she and the baby move to New York. Or worse, that you'd fight for custody." Emma walked over to him and touched his arm. "She was eighteen and scared, Ben. And we'd just lost our father. We were both scared. So we took the insurance money the lumber mill paid us for Dad's death, bought Medicine Creek Camps, and we clung to each other."

"She was nineteen and you were only fifteen."

"Friends helped out a lot. And Kelly was old enough to get custody of me, mostly thanks to the people in town."

"You still haven't said why Kelly didn't marry Poulin."

"That was the one smart thing Kelly did. Wayne went ballistic when he found out she was pregnant, and she knew he'd never accept Michael." She started washing the pots in the sink. "Wayne went to college that fall, and when he came back the next spring, Michael had been born. Kelly and Wayne got together and broke up at least a dozen times over the next five years. Until she suddenly vanished into thin air."

She stopped talking and silence settled over the kitchen, but for the sound of clanking pots as she scrubbed them. Emma had gotten over her adolescent crush on Benjamin Sinclair the day Kelly had left, blaming him for the whole damn mess. Instead of staying and fighting for Kelly's love, he had abandoned them all, and Kelly had only followed his example.

And on that long-ago night, Emma had decided the only person she could ultimately rely on was herself. She glanced at the man of her dreams—and her nightmares—and found him staring out the back door at nothing. It was then she suddenly realized she'd unknowingly been holding on to her hopes these past ten years. Ben had come for his son as soon as he'd known, and he'd grown into someone even more remarkable than her teenage mind could have imagined.

But it was too late for her. She had struggled too long and worked too hard to risk her heart.

"You should take Mikey down to Bangor tomorrow, to a hockey game at the university. He would probably like that."

He turned, his eyes dark with some unidentifiable emotion. "Tomorrow night?"

"Yeah. The hockey team's really good."

"But that would mean you and I would miss the dance in town."

"I guess so. But I would understand."

His approach reminded her of a stalking bobcat, and Emma took a cautious step back, holding a pot lid up like a shield.

He caught her by the shoulders and just stared at her, his hands warm and solid, his whole presence overwhelming.

"Are you afraid to be seen with me? Is that it? Are you afraid to go out with the man you think killed your father?"

Emma snorted and pulled free, her eyes narrowed as she planted her hands on her hips. "For an intelligent man, you sure can be dense sometimes. You wouldn't be standing here now if I thought you killed my father."

She pointed at him. "Your only sin was walking away from my sister without a fight."

She saw him flinch, and she continued. "It appears you leave your brain at home when you come here, Ben. Sixteen years ago, the result was Mikey. This time you could start an all-out war. The clear-cutting controversy is much more widespread than the dam was. More jobs are at stake and more men are desperate. There's also the question of *my* feelings. I don't intend to be your entertainment. I'm not dancing with you and I'm not hopping into your bed only to watch you walk away again, taking Mikey with you this time. Understand?"

He forced her back a step. "Nothing about my being here is entertaining. This has got to be the most difficult journey I've ever made. And the most important." Emma glared at him, but he just smiled back. "Thank you for sending me that letter."

"I didn't send the damn letter!"

He continued talking as if she hadn't spoken. "It might have been a little late in coming, but I'm grateful anyway."

"I did *not* send that damn letter," she repeated through gritted teeth.

He took hold of her shoulders and kissed her nose. "I forgive you for waiting so long, because I understand. And don't worry; I'll look out for Mike in this land-use war. I'll keep him safe."

She wiggled away and bolted for the great room. He called her name, and she stopped and turned. "What?"

"There's one more thing you're mistaken about."

"And that would be?"

"When I get you in my bed, entertainment will be the last thing on my mind."

Just then the dishes in the cupboard began to rattle and the floor started to vibrate. Emma knew it was just another one of the small tremors they'd been experiencing for the last couple of months, yet she was suddenly afraid Ben had commanded the very forces of nature to prove his power.

She fled to the safety of her bedroom.

Chapter Nine

Every so often the world seemed to close in around her, and Emma got the urge to escape. Usually she hiked a portion of the Appalachian Trail up to Mount Katahdin, and with every step deeper into the wilderness, things would somehow fall into perspective. Climbing mountains and wading across streams quickly reminded Emma that a single life was insignificant in the bigger scheme of things, and that whatever problem she was facing was usually minor when viewed through the eyes of Mother Nature.

But hiking wasn't going to help her today, so she went shopping instead.

She flew down to Bangor, landing on Pushaw Lake and bumming a car from someone at the seaplane base. Then she spent the morning wandering around the mall, eating fast food and trying on shoes that tortured her feet. And for the first time in over ten years, Emma entered a store that had nothing but home furnishings, and bought decorative towels.

Eventually she headed for a dress shop. It took her over an hour, and more nerve than she knew she possessed, but she finally purchased a dress she would probably have to burn after tonight.

The whole flight home, the bag from the boutique sat beside her. The salesgirl, and even some customers, had talked her into buying the dress, and the closer to home Emma got, the more her courage deserted her. What had she been thinking? Had some oversexed fairy suddenly taken over her brain? She couldn't actually wear the damn thing in public.

She would have to burn it *before* tonight.

Emma suddenly banked the Cessna, aborting her approach to Medicine Creek Camps and headed back down the lake. It was time to visit with Greta.

"Well, well. Look what my cat dragged in."

"This poor old thing couldn't catch a cricket. I carried him in."

"So now that you've done your good deed for the day, come have some tea with me, Emma Jean. I just made a carrot cake."

"No wonder Wayne Poulin and Sheriff Ramsey are looking so fat lately. You're feeding them too well, Greta."

Greta LaVoie brushed that aside and motioned to Emma to take a seat. The petite woman lifted the kettle from the stove and began filling it with water. Then, with motions that belied her seventy-five years, she bustled to her china cabinet and set up a tray for tea.

Emma did as she was told, dropping her bags on the floor beside her and sitting in comfortable silence, waiting for the only mother figure she had ever known to begin mothering her. This was exactly what she needed. In this ramshackle old boardinghouse, Emma had always been treated like a princess. Greta had been coddling and caring for her since Emma was six years old. Scraped knees, broken hearts, and one or two squirrel bites had been mended here by a woman who hadn't changed in twenty-four years. As timeless and as constant as Medicine Lake itself, Greta Lavoie had been Emma's sanctuary.

The caring and worry went both ways.

Six years ago Greta had lost her lifelong companion, and had leaned on Emma in her grief. Sable Jones had affectionately been known in town as Greta's sister, but everyone had known the truth. Same-sex living arrangements were nearly unheard-of forty years ago, when the women had arrived in Medicine Gore, but they had quickly become part of the close-knit community. The two women had bought this old house and opened up a boarding home, taking in mostly bachelor woodsmen who wanted to be cooked for and pampered. When Sable Jones had died, the entire town had come to her funeral and mourned their loss.

"How's things out at Medicine Creek?" Greta asked as she cut two large pieces of cake and set them on the tray.

"Fine. Greta, have you ever seen Wayne Poulin get any mail from away?"

Wayne had been boarding at Greta's for nearly fifteen years, and Emma had been thinking about Wayne, and Kelly, and Ben's letter.

"Sure. He gets lots of mail from away. He corresponds with other foresters all over the world. Why?"

"Would you have noticed if he ever got any mail that could have been from . . . from Kelly?"

Greta stopped fussing with her dishes and looked over at Emma, sorrow etching her aged face. "No, child. I know he's said Kelly has written him, but I haven't seen any letters like that."

Emma shrugged. "I was just wondering."

Greta walked over and set her hand on Emma's shoulder. "Kelly would have written you, not Wayne. I don't believe anything he's said about her. He was mighty upset when she left, and he's still telling people she'll come back to him. It's his pride speaking, Emma Jean."

Emma nodded agreement. "I thought so. But I wondered."

"Been shopping, I see," Greta said as her foot touched the bags Emma had brought in. "What'd ya get?"

With a grand flourish, Emma picked up one of the bags and plopped it on the table. "When have I ever gone to Bangor and not brought something back for you?" she asked, reaching into the bag and leaving her hand there.

"Don't tease me, Emma Jean. I'm too old for games."

Emma scowled and pulled her hand back out. "Then you're probably too old for what I brought you. I'll just to give it to Mikey."

Greta sat down and grabbed the bag. "That overgrown boy's not getting my gift," she scolded as she reached inside. She squealed when her hand came out gripping a book. "Stephen King's newest! Oh boy. I'm gonna be scared silly tonight!"

Emma shook her head. "I don't know how you can sleep in this creaky old house after reading his stuff."

Greta was hugging the book to her bosom and grinning from ear to ear. "I met him once, you know."

She'd heard this story a thousand times already, but Emma dutifully answered the unspoken request. "Really?"

"Sable and I were shopping in that bookstore in downtown Bangor. You know, the one that has *all* his books. And he was there! He autographed one for me and one for Sable." Greta was positively glowing, her eyes shining as she tried to look knowledgeable. "He's a regular person, you know. No airs about him. He walks around town as if he's nobody."

Emma reached for the pot of tea so she wouldn't roll her eyes. "I didn't sleep for a week when I read that book you lent me."

Greta reached back in the bag and found the rest of her surprise—linen towels with moose on them. "Oh, Emma Jean, you shouldn't have."

Emma had intended to keep them, but on the flight home she had given herself a good talking to, reminding herself that old dreams were better left unresurrected.

"Oh, Em, they're beautiful. They're too nice to use, though."

"You could cover your rising bread with them," Emma suggested. "Or just hang them here in the kitchen for looks."

Greta set the towels on the table and patted them as she leaned over and looked at the other bag on the floor. "What's in that one?" she asked, raising her brow.

Emma picked up the shiny black plastic bag and sat it on her lap. "Um, I bought a dress. For the dance tonight."

Silence stole across the table and Emma finally looked up to find Greta staring at her, utterly surprised. Then the old woman waved at Emma to show her the dress.

"By the color of your face, missy, I'd say this dress is not your usual style." She cocked her head at her. "Or is it your date that's got you blushing?"

Emma did roll her eyes then. Leave it to Greta to sink her teeth into the heart of the matter. "Mikey's been visiting you."

"With amazing tales about a long-lost father," Greta confirmed with a nod. "He's more excited than a cat stuck in a mouse hole." She picked up the teapot and poured herself a cup. "Go on, Emma Jean," she continued. "Show me the dress."

"I . . . I'm not going to wear it. I don't know what possessed me to buy it."

"A good-looking man possessed you, if I remember Benjamin Sinclair." She covered her cheeks with frail hands. "Land sakes, that boy was handsome."

"He's no longer a boy, Greta. He grew a foot taller and two feet wider, and he's got a beard Paul Bunyan would envy."

"You gonna pull that dress out, or are you trying to wrinkle it to death?"

Emma finally opened the bag and slowly pulled out the scarlet sheath she had purchased.

"Oh my."

Determined to show just how silly she was, Emma held the dress up to her chest. It wasn't all that long on the bottom, and not too tall on the top, either. It was cut low in the back and held up by two narrow straps.

"Stand up and show me," Greta demanded, motioning with her hand and standing herself. "Oh Lord, that's a sight I've waited years to see."

"What?"

Walking around the table and taking the dress to hold it up to Emma's shoulders, Greta smiled and shook her head. Emma stared at the woman who came up to her chin, and swore under her breath when she noticed the sheen in her friend's eyes.

"I've been waiting twenty-four years for you to come to your senses, Emma Jean. This is you. The real you. This dress was made for your beauty."

Emma snorted and sat back down. "I was temporarily insane when I bought it. That is *not* me. I'm flannel and denim and hiking boots."

Greta reached into the bag and pulled out the matching shoes. "These could have been a bit taller in the heel," she said with a sigh. "But I suppose anything sexier and you would have broken your neck."

"I'm not wearing the dress, Greta."

"Of course you are, child. And you'll put your hair up all nice and feminine-like, and you'll wear your mother's pearls."

Emma gave her a horrified look. "I'll be laughed right out of the dance hall!"

"Oh, posh. It's time the menfolk around here got woken up." Greta laid the dress over a chair and sat down. "It's about time *you* woke up."

"I'll look like I'm trying to impress . . . people."

"Not people, Emma Jean. Just one man."

"I sure as heck don't want to impress Ben." She sat her cup in the saucer with a clink. "Are you forgetting everything he's done?"

Greta stared at her. "What has he done, exactly?"

"He got my sister pregnant and then walked away."

"Did he? According to Michael, Ben Sinclair walked away from a confused young girl, not a pregnant one. He didn't know, Emma. That makes a mighty big difference in my book."

"Rumor has it he blew up the dam."

All Emma got for that unworthy statement was a good glare.

"He's going to cause trouble, Greta. And he's going to take Mikey away."

"Maybe not." The old woman smiled at her. "Once he sees you in that dress."

"Greta!"

"Oh, eat your cake, Emma Jean."

Emma picked up her fork and drove it rather forcefully into the huge piece of cake. But she didn't get the dessert halfway to her mouth before the back door slammed open and Mikey walked in.

"I'm here, Aunt Greta. What's to eat?" he hollered to the entire house. "Oh. Hi, Nem. Back from your pilgrimage already?"

"That's no way to come barging in here. And wipe your feet," Emma said.

With the negligence of a teenager, he made a showing of scuffing his feet on the rug before he sauntered up to the table and examined its contents. He reached to pull out a chair, but stopped when his hand landed on the dress.

"What's this?" He held it up. He looked from Greta to Emma, then back at Greta, and softly whistled. "Wow. Aunt Greta, you going to kick up some dust tonight?"

He winked at her as he held the dress by the straps, examining it again. "Ah, Grets, don't you think it's a little cold for this outfit?"

Emma grabbed the dress out of his hands and pushed it back in the bag. "Good point, Mikey. It's definitely too cold for this."

"That's your aunt's dress, Michael. And I'm lending her a pretty gold shawl to wear with it."

For one fleeting moment, Emma saw shock wash over Mikey's face. And then he just stared at her. Finally he nodded. "Take the shawl, Nem. And make sure those straps are good and secure."

Emma stood up. "Here. You can have my cake. I'm going home."

"Not yet, Emma Jean. I need you to take some laundry up to Wayne's room for me," Greta said, standing up as if to block her exit. She smiled up at Emma. "You don't mind, do you?"

"Mikey can do it."

"No. He's got to get out the Henry J. He's driving me into Greenville for a doctor's appointment."

Emma arched one brow at Mikey, but he was too busy stuffing his face to look back. His mouth full, all he could do was nod and shovel.

"Wayne Poulin is thirty-five years old. He should be doing his own laundry."

"Here's the key to his room. Just put the clothes in his drawers for me. Please?"

"Should I rotate his socks while I'm at it?" Emma drawled.

Greta shoved the basket at her. "That would be nice. And maybe you could dust a bit while you're up there."

Emma scowled at her.

"Oh, and make sure you don't knock down the key he's got hidden behind the picture on the dresser. It's to his desk, and I don't dust in there. It's where he keeps his private papers," Greta said, tossing a small ring of keys onto the laundry. "And while you're upstairs, that gold shawl is folded over a hanger in my closet. Take it. And wear it and the dress tonight. That's an order, Emma Jean."

Emma went upstairs to Wayne's room and set the basket down in the hall. She tried three keys before she found the right one. Silently scolding herself for what she was about to do, but determined nonetheless, she

opened the door and stepped into Wayne's private domain.

Emma sat the basket on the bed and looked around,
wondering if she would have gone to Wayne's rescue as
quickly as she had Ben's. She snorted. Not likely. She
had never had a teenage crush on Wayne Poulin. She'd
taken his measure the first night he had come to the
house to pick up Kelly. She hadn't liked what she had
seen then, and she still didn't.

There was something calculated about Wayne. His
beady little brown eyes ruined his otherwise handsome
face. He was short, with straight brown hair, and he
had a wiry body. He was a forester for one of the larger
mills just north of here, and he spent a great deal of his
time in the woods. He reminded Emma of a pit bull.

Wayne's room showed all the signs of a man who had
spent fifteen years living in a boardinghouse. It was clut-
tered with books and trade magazines and outdoor
equipment. There was a gun rack on one wall sporting a
shotgun, two high-powered rifles, and a compound bow.

The ring of keys bit into her hand, and Emma realized she had a death grip on them. Well, she was here,
Wayne was not, and she knew where the key to his
desk was. She was going to look for Kelly's letters.

She heard a garage door open and looked out the
window. Mikey was carefully backing out Greta's classic 1956 Henry J. Emma shook her head. That car was
the pride of both Greta and Mikey, and he was the only

one she would let drive it. For two years now, Mikey had been driving Greta to appointments, the grocery store, and the library in Greenville.

They had been stopped by a deputy once, and there had been quite a ruckus over there being a thirteen-year-old at the wheel. But Amos Ramsey, the county sheriff, also boarded at Greta's, and after a week of burnt meals and gritty bedsheets, all the deputies suddenly went blind when Mikey was driving the Henry J on the back roads of the county.

Greta and Mikey pulled out of the driveway and the house took on an eerie silence. Emma quickly found the key sitting behind the picture on the dresser, right where Greta had said it would be. She turned back to Wayne's desk. It was on old rolltop without a speck of dust on it—which meant Greta had all but told Emma to snoop.

Which she fully intended to do. And even if she didn't find Kelly's letters, she would see what Wayne used for stationery. Then she would ask Ben what his letter had looked like. Maybe Wayne was the one who had lured Ben here. Emma wouldn't put it past the man; he was bitter enough to want to stir up any trouble he could. Maybe he even thought that if Kelly found out Ben had come back, she would return also.

Yeah, that made sense. Wayne had never moved on from Kelly's abandonment. He had received pitying looks from people at first, but now he was the recipient of laughter. After ten years, he was starting to look more like a fool than a pining boyfriend.

Wayne blamed Ben for the whole mess. And it had been Wayne who had first suggested Ben and his group of environmentalists had blown up the dam and killed her dad.

The old desk creaked as she raised the top, and the inside was much more stark and far more organized than the room. In this one place, Wayne was a professional, it seemed. His paycheck stubs were all filed by date in one of the cubbyholes.

She found some writing paper and envelopes, and stole one of each. Then she searched all the drawers and every nook and cranny, finding no letters from Kelly. But under the blotter, written in bold, harsh lines, were some numbers. Studying them, Emma realized they were map coordinates in longitude and latitude. It wasn't a range of parallels or minutes, like a tract of land that Wayne's company might be planning to harvest, but one particular spot.

They could mean anything. With a Global Positioning System, Wayne could have marked any spot for future reference when he had been in the field. The coordinates could be a start-off point for cruising timber. It could be a logging camp. Or a freshwater spring he had found. She tucked the paper back under the blotter and sighed, looking around the room for anyplace else Wayne might hide a letter.

Emma was just closing the rolltop when she spotted the corner of the paper sticking out from under the blotter. She pushed it fully under the blotter to hide her snooping, but was drawn back to it for some reason. The coordinates made her curious. She had a GPS in the Cessna, as well as a handheld device, and she knew the exact coordinates of Medicine Creek Camps. These numbers were northwest of her camps, less than one day's walk.

She also knew there was nothing in that general area. The mills hadn't cut that land in nearly forty years.

She pulled out the stationery she'd stolen and quickly copied down the coordinates. Then she shoved the scrap of paper back under the blotter and closed the desk and locked it. She took the laundry out of the basket, and instead of putting it in his bureau, she set the clothes on Wayne's bed. The jerk could rotate his own socks.

She was going home, taking a long, relaxing bath, and then dressing up for an evening of certain disaster.

"What are you doing? We're going to be late."

Emma looked up at Ben and frowned. "I'm creating ammunition for the coming battle with Mikey. This is a game timer. Here. Take this string and tie it to that porch post over there."

"What in hell is a game timer?"

Emma straightened and made sure her coat was buttoned up to her chin. "It's a clock with a string attached. You stretch the string across a game trail and set it. When a deer comes walking along, it trips the string, stopping the clock. That way you know what time the deer are walking that particular area. Most animals are creatures of habit."

"And we are setting this up on your porch . . . why?"

"So I know exactly what time *your son* comes home. This gives me the ammunition to catch him in his lie."

"Why do you think Mike's going to lie to you?"

"It seems to be a newly acquired habit of his, ever since his father told him to go out and have a little fun."

"Now, Em, you know I was right."

"I know that it's dangerous to let an overintelligent teenager loose on society. Sheriff Ramsey drove out here yesterday to warn me that Michael was seen in town with an unsavory group of kids."

"How unsavory can kids get in Medicine Gore, Em?"

"Unsavory enough to harass some environmentalist when no one is looking. Most of the kids' parents make their living off the forest one way or another, and this political war has filtered down to the children."

"Mike wouldn't do anything stupid."

Emma hunched down to set the timer, nearly falling off the steps as her high heels wobbled. "Mikey is probably their ringleader. Their latest prank has all the earmark of his handiwork."

Ben pulled her away from the edge of the steps. He took the timer and hunched down to secure it to the post. "What prank?"

Emma sat down beside him on the top step, and set the clock and tested the string, making sure Mikey wouldn't see it but would still trip it. "Somebody built a fort of logs around an environmentalist's truck two nights ago."

Ben grinned, his teeth white and his eyes glistening in the moonlight. "That wasn't so bad. It's kind of brilliant."

"Very brilliant. As for being bad, there was no way to dismantle the logs without caving them in on the truck. Which is precisely what happened."

"Any number of kids around here must have access to a truck full of logs and a pulp loader. What makes you think it was Mike?"

"Because only Mikey would realize he could commit a crime without actually doing anything wrong. After all, they didn't touch any property, they simply built a log cabin. It wasn't their fault the truck was damaged. The environmentalists did that themselves when they tried to free the truck. What crime could the kids possibly be charged with?"

Ben sat down on the porch. "Hell, you're right." He wrapped his arm over her shoulders. "Mike's a genius."

"Doesn't he scare you sometimes?"

"He scares the hell out of me," he said.

Emma rested her chin in her fists. "Me, too."

"You've survived well enough."

"Only because Mikey's been charitable to me."

"I love your legs."

"Huh?"

"And your hair. You've fixed it just right to show off your lovely neck and your cute little ears. You look very delicious tonight, Miss Sands."

Emma shot out from under his arm and was halfway to the truck before he caught up with her.

"Was it something I said?"

"Thank you."

"For?"

"The compliment."

"Hmm. I don't suppose you've had many, have you? Here's another one: thank you for doing such a fine job of raising Mike. A father couldn't hope for a better son."

Emma stopped and stared. Had she just heard right? Was Ben *thanking* her for raising Michael?

"Say 'you're welcome,' Em."

"But you hate me."

He shook his head. "No, I don't." He shoved his hands in his pant pockets and rocked back on his heels. "Not anymore."

Emma took a step back, his words making her heart beat a little faster.

"I hated Kelly by the time I was done reading that

letter. Then I learned that *you* had raised Mike, so I turned my anger on you. But I can't hate you. You love him, Em. And that's something I understand."

He took two steps closer and put his hands on her shoulders. Emma feared he could feel her shaking, but she didn't pull away.

"That's what you think you've done, isn't it, Em? You think you've sold your soul by keeping Mike from me, that you've committed a sin neither I nor God can forgive."

He reached up and gently brushed a tear from her cheek, and Emma realized she was crying. Still, she couldn't move.

"I forgive you, Emma Sands, because I probably would have done the same." He lifted her chin. "Will you please stop worrying that I'm trying to take Mike away from you? Will you believe that I'm willing to share him?"

"I could have done something ten years ago, Ben. I could have done something *fifteen* years ago. Even then, I was old enough to know it's wrong not to tell a man he's fathered a child. I would never forgive anyone who did something like that to me."

Tears were running down her cheeks.

"Aw, hell, Em," Ben growled. He wrapped her up in his arms and rocked her back and forth—in the dark shadows of the pines, in the silence of the cold autumn night. "*That's* our problem. You can't believe I can understand why you kept Michael to yourself all these years."

"You shouldn't."

"But I do. Because I can *feel* your love for him."

Emma looked up. "But I can't even say if I would do things differently, given another chance. I honestly don't know if I would have the strength."

"You had the strength to mail the letter a month ago. Why then?"

Emma pulled away and walked to Ben's truck. "I didn't send you that letter. Mikey must have. He may only be fifteen, but come January, he's stepping into the giant world of college. He needs someone other than me to guide him, a father to show him the way. He needs you."

"And you, too."

"Not really. All chicks leave the nest eventually. Michael's flight may be earlier than most, but I'm already becoming his history. And he wants you to be his future."

"He's never intended to leave you behind. Haven't you figured that out?"

"I know I will always be his aunt. But he needs more."

Ben opened the passenger door and lifted her into the seat. He kept his hands at her waist as he stared into her eyes. "He can have us both."

"I have my own life to think about. I intend to leave this nest right after Mikey."

"*You* can have both, too, Em."

She shook her head and turned to face the front. A whisper of a sigh reached her just before he softly closed the door. Emma stared at his back as he looked out over the lake, his shoulders casting a broad, strong silhouette that could have been carved from black marble.

Chapter Ten

"Give me your *coat,* and I'll hang it up and get us some paper cups. Want something from the concession stand?"

Emma fingered the top button on her coat. The dance was being held in the fire station. They had moved out the trucks and decorated the building— tables had been placed along the walls, the lights were turned down, and a band was set up against the side wall. Emma had chosen a table way back in the corner, where it was hopefully dark enough for people not to recognize either of them.

"I'll keep it on a little while. I'm chilled."

Her escort lifted one brow. "What are you hiding under there, Emma?" He looked down at her bright red shoes and sheer-hosed legs. "I'm getting curious."

She opened the cooler they had brought and waved

him away. "Go get some cups and some ice. I'm not hungry yet."

After Ben walked off, she unbuttoned her coat, threw it over a chair, then arranged Greta's shawl, making sure she was covered from her neck to her waist.

What had possessed her to wear this dress?

She had two other dresses that were far more modest, but the devil-fairy had returned this afternoon.

"I want to talk to you."

Emma looked up to find Wayne Poulin looming over her, and he didn't look like he was planning to ask her to dance. "Hi, Wayne. What's up?"

He placed his hands on the table and leaned over, attempting to look intimidating. But she had never been afraid of Wayne Poulin, and she wasn't about to start now.

"I want you to keep that kid away from me."

That surprised her. "I doubt Mikey wants to be anywhere near you, Wayne. So I don't see the problem."

"He was in my room today. When I got home from work tonight, that kid was just leaving Greta's. And when I got up to my room, I realized someone had been in it. Snooping."

"I was in your room." Emma stood up, forcing him to straighten to look her level in the face. "I brought up your laundry for Greta and dusted a bit."

His eyes narrowed to slits. "You did more than dust."

Emma shrugged. "I probably moved a few things while cleaning. Sorry."

"What were you looking for?" Wayne crossed his arms over his chest. His gaze traveled up and down her, and his eyes gleamed. "You're looking a lot like your sister this evening, Emma Jean. Why's that? You got a hot date tonight?"

"The lady has a possessive date tonight, Poulin. So I suggest you move along."

Wayne Poulin swung around with a start. Emma saw his eyes widen when he recognized the speaker, and he had to tilt his head up as he took a step back.

"Sinclair!"

Ben set an ice bucket and a plastic cup on the table. He towered over Wayne by a good foot, and seeing them together face-to-face, Emma realized what she had known all along.

Benjamin Sinclair was not only tall, he was solid: the type of man who would never run from a problem. When he had left Medicine Gore sixteen years ago, he hadn't abandoned a pregnant girl—he had merely walked away from a disastrous love affair. Nothing could have dragged Ben from his child then, and a whole town full of animosity wouldn't be able to now.

Wayne had said Ben's name loud enough for the nearby tables to hear. People were turning. Conversations had ceased. And whispers arose all around them.

With a feeling of doom, Emma watched the men face each other. Wayne stood defensively, his hands balled into fists, his shoulders rigid, and his eyes cold. Ben appeared relaxed, but Emma knew he was ready for any attack, verbal or physical.

"Wayne was just thanking me for bringing up his laundry," she said into the silence. "I was helping Greta."

"Who's Greta?" Ben asked. He was looking at her, but Emma knew his attention was still firmly on Wayne.

"She owns the boardinghouse in town. She practically raised Kelly and me."

"Greta Lavoie," he said, nodding. "I remember now. Kelly took me over to her house for cake several times."

Emma glared at Ben. He winked back and reached into the cooler. He pulled out a bottle of whiskey and cracked the seal, poured some in a cup of ice, then put the cover back on. Then he pulled out a bottle of beer for himself and looked back at Wayne. "I'd invite you to sit with us, Poulin, but I no longer share my dates."

Wayne stalked away.

Emma quietly whistled between her teeth. "Are you *looking* for trouble tonight, or just trying to drive me crazy?"

Ben looked up from opening his beer, his gaze going to her shawl, then down to the red dress below it. His eyes stopped at the hem. Emma watched them widen before they rose to her face.

"Did you forget to put on the pants that go with that blouse?" he asked softly.

She tightened the shawl over her chest.

Ben walked around the table and held the back of her chair. "Sit," he quietly ordered. "And remind me to hold down the back of that dress when we dance."

"It's not that short."

He pulled out the chair beside her and sat down, effectively boxing her in against the wall, setting himself up as guardian of his domain.

Emma snorted just before she took a sip of her drink. He turned and looked at her, and caught her staring at him.

"What was that for?"

"You really are territorial. And either really brave or really dumb. Ben, if you want these people to accept you, you're going to have to walk the greatest distance. You're the villain here—not Wayne or Durham or anyone from sixteen years ago."

"I didn't do anything wrong. I was a kid on summer break, and I was working for something I believed in. Kelly just . . . she just happened."

Aware they were being openly stared at, Emma reached up and touched his sleeve. "I'm not the one you have to convince."

"Yes, you are. You and Mike. Everyone else can go to hell."

She brushed at his shoulder. "Oh, Ben. You're doing

a better job of fooling yourself than me. It's just as important to you that the people here believe you. If not
for yourself, then for Mikey."

He looked at her hand on his shoulder. "What are
you doing?"

Emma pulled away and smiled at him. "Nothing. I
just thought I saw a piece of moss clinging to you."

His frown deepened. "I think we should dance."

There were all of three couples on the dance floor
when Ben pulled her to her feet. As soon as they
reached the dance floor, his hand went to her back,
under the drape of her shawl. It stilled when five cal-
loused fingers and a wide scorching palm met bare skin.
He stopped moving his feet to the rhythm of the music.
"Don't you dare take that shawl off tonight, or *you'll* be
the cause of any war that breaks out."

Emma started dancing, but she had to shove Ben to
get him moving again. "If you think the back's bad, you
should see the front," she whispered, only to have his
arms tighten around her with enough force to make
her squeak.

"Oh, cut it out," she said with a laugh. "I'm sure
you've escorted plenty of women who've worn a lot
less."

His hand dropped low on her back, pulling her
closer. Emma gasped when her belly came into contact
with his arousal.

"Don't act so shocked," he whispered, moving them

gracefully through the waltz. "This happens every time I get close to you."

"Everyone's staring at us," she hissed.

"Then I suggest you cuddle closer if you don't want them knowing how you affect me."

"All hell could break loose any minute, and you're turned on?"

He leaned back to stare down at her. "That was your plan, wasn't it? To distract me—and probably your friends—from the real issue?"

Emma glared up at him. "I don't know *why* I bought this damn dress. I must have had a brain cramp this morning."

"And another one this evening, when you put it on? And then fixed up your hair? And slipped into those heels?" He slashed her a feral grin. "At least you had the sense to wear the shawl."

Emma leaned her forehead into his shoulder and sighed. "Yes, I still possess some semblance of sanity."

The song ended and Ben spun her around and nudged her toward their table. "I need a beer."

"Sinclair."

Emma turned at the guttural sound. She tried to step around Ben to see who had called his name, but his arm came out and stopped her. Holding her firmly, Ben stood and waited as the four men approached.

The band didn't start up another song. The musicians, along with everyone else, silently stared as Durham Bragg, John LeBlanc, Wayne Poulin, and Galen Simms stopped two yards in front of Ben and Emma.

Durham looked over at her. "Move away from him, Emma."

Ben gently pushed her away, his eyes never leaving his adversaries.

Emma stepped to the side and stopped, crossing her arms under her chest. "This is neither the time nor the place for this, Durham," she told him.

"I knew I recognized you, Sinclair." He shook his head. "You wouldn't have walked away two weeks ago if I had known who you were then."

"You spiked the trees," John LeBlanc accused from beside Durham. "You've come back, bringing even more trouble with you this time."

"I'm here for my son," Ben said, his voice laced with steel.

Wayne stepped closer. "You're welcome to take the little bastard and leave."

Other than balling his hands into fists, Ben didn't react.

"He's wanting to ruin another Sands first," Galen Simms added, and the four men took a collective step forward.

Emma quickly moved between them and Ben.

"You don't have your shotgun this time, missy," Durham hissed.

Ben's powerful hands grabbed her shoulders and all

but lifted her out of the way. Emma turned and looked up into the hard gray eyes of a man not pleased with her action. She slipped free of his grip and moved back in front of the men, out of Ben's reach.

But he didn't grab for her again, and Emma realized that Durham and John and Wayne and Galen were staring at her, their expressions turned from anger to shock. She looked back and understood why. Ben was holding her shawl in his hands.

Well, she certainly had everyone's attention now.

"For the record, gentlemen," she said, raising her voice to include the rest of the townspeople. "Benjamin Sinclair did not blow up the dam and kill my father. He didn't even know about any plans to do so." She lifted her arms and let them fall back against her sides. "Do any of you honestly believe I would let him in my home if I thought he was responsible for my father's death?"

"You're so blinded by your love for Michael, you probably would," Durham said.

Emma pointed her finger at him. "Mikey knows Ben didn't kill his grandfather. And I know it. Sheriff Ramsey did everything in his power to find the ones responsible. Even the FBI investigated, and *they* couldn't come up with a suspect. Every living, breathing male within fifty miles of Medicine Gore was questioned. Every tree hugger who had set foot in Maine that month was questioned. Including Benjamin Sinclair."

"How do you know that?" Wayne asked.

"I read all their reports. It was *my* father who died, and they kept Kelly and me informed."

The men looked past her, as if expecting Ben to confirm her story. Durham was looking thoughtful, as was John LeBlanc. Galen wasn't budging from his angry expression, and Wayne Poulin looked even more hostile than before.

But then, he had more reason to hate Ben.

"Every one of you has spent the last sixteen years focused on Benjamin Sinclair, blaming him for my father's death. If you had turned all the energy you've spent hating Ben into finding the men who actually did it, we could have had a conviction years ago."

"How can you be so sure?" Durham asked.

"She's sleeping with the bastard," Galen said, pointing at her.

"I am not!" She glared at all the men, daring them to utter another word.

"That's enough," Ben growled. Emma flinched when her shawl dropped over her shoulders, then she was suddenly imprisoned between iron-hard arms and an unmovable granite chest. "What you think, Simms, doesn't mean jack shit," Ben continued. "But she is right about one thing. Whoever blew up that dam has gotten away with it, and I intend to find him. You can help me or you can stay the hell out of my way—I really don't give a damn. But understand that your hostility is directed at *me*. Not Emma, and not Michael."

Stark, absolute silence followed.

"What makes you think you can find him after six-teen years, when the FBI couldn't?" John LeBlanc finally asked.

"I'm more motivated," Ben said.

"Whoever blew up that dam is long gone," Wayne said, his eyes narrowing. "Better you just take your son and leave."

"I have no intention of leaving."

Ben's anger was palpable, vibrating through Emma's entire body. She walked out of his arms and back to their table, where she opened the cooler and started repacking.

"We're not leaving," Ben said, coming up beside her.

She reached for her coat. "You're welcome to stay, but I'm going home."

A nasty word rumbled across the table as Ben picked up her coat and held it up for her.

"We are not going home," he told her through grit-ted teeth. He picked up the cooler, put his hand at her back, and ushered her past the stunned, staring faces of people who were supposed to be her friends. Her head held high, Emma mentally steeled herself for another scorching lecture.

But she understood male posturing. As she did with Mikey, she would simply smile and nod at Ben, swear she would act more wisely, then go on doing whatever she had to in order to keep the peace.

Ben placed the cooler inside the Suburban, slammed the door shut, then turned. Emma took a cautious step back. He looked madder than Mikey ever got, and far more intimidating than her father ever had.

"Don't ever step between me and danger again, Emma. There is a fine line between bravery and recklessness, and you crossed it tonight. Poulin and Simms were ready to explode, and neither man cared that you were in the middle." His hands tightened on her shoulders. "Contrary to what you think, you're not ten feet tall and bulletproof. You could have gotten hurt."

"So could a lot of innocent people. I stopped a brawl from breaking out."

"Stepping between angry men is never smart. It was sheer luck tonight that they backed down."

She frowned. "There wasn't an ounce of luck involved. I know these people. Durham wouldn't have let anything happen to me."

"I can fight my own battles."

"You weren't doing a very good job of it when I first found you."

He hauled her up against his chest, his arms wrapping around her like a vise, and Emma felt his chest expand as he blew out a sigh.

"You're going to be the death of me, Emma. I've finally been given a gift from God, but I will be too insane to enjoy it." He tugged her head back, lifting her

face to look at him, pulling at her hair until it fell
down her back. "I may lose a few of the battles, but I
will win this war, Emma Jean. And there can't be two
generals on the field."

"I wasn't trying to protect you; I just didn't want any
trouble. And I figured they would listen to me," she
quickly added when he took a deep breath to scold her
again.

He sighed instead. "The point I'm trying to drive
into that stubborn little head of yours is that you could
have gotten hurt tonight."

She shot him a sudden smile. "Is your ego strong
enough to go back inside and let me take off my shawl
for the rest of the dance?"

Sounding more like a mountain lion than a man, he
growled deep in his chest as his mouth descended on
hers. He was not gentle and she didn't expect him to
be. Anger and fear and the threat of violence often
turned into passion for men, especially when the object
of their frustration was within reach. And she reveled
in it.

It appeared he might really like her.

And damn if she wasn't liking him back.

Emma wrapped her arms around his neck, yielding
against him as she coaxed a different response. Slowly,
almost reluctantly, his arms loosened until she could
breathe again, and his grip relaxed into a caress.

He sighed into her mouth as he slid his hand down

to cup her bottom. And again she felt the evidence of his desire.

There was a fire slowly kindling in her as she let him lift her closer still, allowing her to wage her own assault. She explored the texture of his mouth, his hair beneath her hands, his heat that radiated clear through her coat. Even his smell enveloped her. He tasted of beer and delicious male essence, and Emma soon became drunk on him.

He broke away, sucking in a shaky breath. Every muscle she was clinging to felt like granite. Her head was spinning and everything had gone black except for the flashes of light swirling in her head.

"Open your eyes, Em."

That helped. Until she looked up at his face. She got dizzy again when her gaze locked on his, and she had to dig her fingers into his jacket to steady herself.

"If I take you home now, I'm going to lock us both in your bedroom. Then I'm going to strip off that dress and make love to you for two days straight."

How classic. Give a man a kiss, and he starts talking about bed. "Do I have another option?"

"We can walk across the street to the diner, and I'll buy you a meal first."

To fortify her for their lovemaking? How thoughtful.

But she wasn't ready to give her passion, to experience sexual bliss with the man she had loved since adolescence. What good would come of taking him into her bed and body when he intended to walk out of her life in two months with her nephew?

"I'm about to take you on the hood of this truck, if you don't decide soon."

Emma could feel the tension humming through him. And he thought she had been in danger at the dance?

"Dinner."

He looked momentarily confused, then his face darkened. Suddenly he released her, grabbed her hand, and started pulling her across the street.

Emma stifled a snort. Undentable ego, hah! She smiled, hoping the diner was warm and toasty, because she intended to take off her shawl to eat.

Chapter Eleven

The little witch had taken off her shawl in the diner. Ben shook his head as he escorted his date back to his truck. She had stuffed herself with potatoes and coleslaw and a hamburger that would have choked a horse. Then she'd followed everything with a monstrous dessert that had far more icing than cake.

He hadn't been able to swallow a thing.

Her coat was now buttoned up to her chin, thank God. Hopefully he would find the strength to take her home and leave her at her door.

That bright red dress was only slightly higher in the front than the back. And she was wearing a long string of pearls that nicely teased the top curve of her breasts.

Stunning breasts—full and soft—and she clearly wasn't wearing a bra.

"A cold front's moved in," she said, her breath fogging in the chilly air.

Cold front? He was hotter than a teenager in a whorehouse with a hundred-dollar bill.

"The dance is still going strong. You want to go back in?" he asked, stopping beside his truck.

"No. I think we should call it a night."

Something in her voice sounded odd—almost like fear. Emma Sands, the shotgun-carrying, night-flying spitfire, was afraid. But not of him—not exactly.

Maybe she feared the emotional danger he presented. Maybe the fact that she erupted like a long-dormant volcano every time they kissed scared the hell out of her.

Ben opened her door to his truck. "I'll take you home, kiss you good night, and see you tomorrow."

Wide, questioning green eyes looked up at him, and a sigh of relief escaped her as she turned to climb into the truck. Ben softly closed the door and walked around and climbed in his side of the truck.

"The evening wasn't a total waste," she said as he buckled his belt.

"Not for you. Your belly's full enough to last you the winter."

She smiled at him. "Thank you for dinner, but I meant the dance wasn't a waste. You accomplished a lot tonight."

He gave his attention to pulling out of the crowded parking lot. "How's that?"

"You finally came into town, were recognized, and faced your accusers. Everyone is going home tonight with something to think about. And since they all know you're here, you won't have to stay hidden at Medicine Creek Camps any longer."

That made him frown. "I wasn't hiding."

She waved that away. "Now when you come into town, there won't be an ugly scene. You won't catch anyone by surprise and they won't be so hostile."

"So that's why you agreed to come tonight? You wanted to be there for my grand reunion with Medicine Gore, so you could run interference?"

She lifted her chin. "I just wanted to go to a dance. It's been years since I attended one."

Ben blew out a tired breath. Arguing with Emma was an exercise in futility. "And now you think everything's fine?"

"No, they'll still be suspicious. But they'll also be more open-minded."

"Because of your resounding endorsement?"

"Because I gave them cold, hard facts to think about." Ben saw her lift her chin again. "And yes, because they know me. They know I wouldn't be caught dead with you if I thought you were responsible for killing my father."

"And what about Kelly? Will they forgive me for abandoning her and Mike?"

"Probably not. Although they won't put all the

blame on you. Kelly was . . . well, she was known for being a bit . . . impulsive." She turned in her seat and touched his sleeve. "They're good people, Ben. They just need time for the truth to sink in."

He looked down at her hand. It was a feminine hand, despite the short nails and calluses he knew were there. It was a strong hand, capable of holding a gun, of coaxing a plane into unthinkable flight, and of inciting his lust to new heights with the gentlest of touches.

"God, Emma, you overwhelm me," he said, covering her hand with his.

She squeaked and pulled back as if he had burned her. Ben opened his mouth to reassure her that she was safe for tonight, but one of the red idiot lights on the dash suddenly blinked on.

"Damn." He immediately shut off the engine, then let the truck coast to the shoulder of the road.

"What's the matter?"

"The oil light just came on." He put the truck in park, turned to her, and caught her smiling at him. "What's so funny?"

"This is what you get for spending a fortune for a sissified truck."

"Sissified?"

She waved her hand around the interior. "This isn't a real truck; it's a station wagon disguised as one. It's got leather seats and more frills than a Victorian teahouse," she added as she dropped her visor and opened the mirror. A set of lights automatically turned on. Ben heard a soft whir, and Emma seemed to magically rise in her seat. "It's a yuppy vehicle."

"I bought it for us."

"Us?"

"I thought the three of us could take a trip down to the coast some weekend," he told her as she magically descended back into position. "I want Mike to meet my older brother, Sam. He lives in Keelstone Cove."

She sobered. "Oh. Mike would love that."

"Only we're not even going to make it home, much less to the coast," he said as he opened his door, releasing the hood and stepping out. He heard Emma's door open also. "Be careful near that ditch," he warned, remembering she was wearing heels.

There was a short scream, a rustling of bushes, and then muffled grumbling from the other side of the truck. It took him no more than a second to reach her, but Emma was already struggling to her feet. Her long hair had got caught on a bush and she muttered a word that made him grin.

"Don't you dare say a thing," she hissed. The interior lights of the truck were bright enough for Ben to see her glare at him while she tugged on her hair.

"Let me get that," he said, reaching down to free her. "Emma, a lady is supposed to wait in the car when there's trouble," he said, shaking his head at the mess she'd made of herself.

"Thank you, Emily Post," she snapped. She grabbed his pant leg—much too high for comfort—and tried to pull herself up out of the ditch.

Ben reached under her arms and hauled her to her feet, and didn't let go until he had her seated in the truck. One hand on the door, the other on the roof, he stood and watched as she pulled down the visor again and opened the lighted mirror she had just scoffed at. She ran her fingers through her hair, then brushed at a bit of dirt on her cheek. "What's wrong with the truck?"

"How in hell am I supposed to know? Have you looked under the hood of one of these things lately?"

She nodded. "My new truck has more technology under its hood than the space shuttle. So what do we do?"

Ben reached into his jacket and pulled out his cell phone. "We call for a tow."

She peered out at the surrounding black woods. "I don't think we're within range, Ben. Medicine Gore is on the fringe of service, and we're a good five miles past that."

"The fringe of civilization, you mean," he muttered, opening his phone and checking for a signal. The little red light flashed up at him with depressing regularity. He looked up and down the road, finding nothing but black emptiness in each direction. "Then you will sit tight and I'll go for a walk. Which direction is shortest?"

"We're closer to Medicine Gore than home, but I'm going with you."

"Afraid I'll get lost again, madam guide?"

"I don't think we should separate. Someone might be lurking in the shadows, waiting for you."

He sobered. "You think this was deliberate?"

"New trucks don't just lose oil all of a sudden."

He cursed. "But you can't possibly walk in those shoes, Emma. You'll break your neck."

"I never leave the house unprepared. I tossed my sneakers into the back before we left. I've ended up walking more than once from a broken truck."

"That's right. Didn't Mike ask if you had run your truck into a creek *again*, the day you found me?"

"It was either that or run into a moose," she said, trying to jump down.

Ben grabbed her before she could go tumbling into the ditch again and sat her back up on the seat. "I'll get your shoes for you." He walked to the back of the truck, straining to see into the darkness behind them. Emma was probably right. Someone had tampered with the truck while they had been in the diner.

Poulin, most likely.

Of all the men, he appeared to be the greatest threat. Poulin would have no problem stranding them both in the middle of the woods on a cold night, and Ben made a mental note to keep an eye on Wayne in the future.

He opened the tailgate door and found a small bag sitting there.

"Here. What else have you got in there?" he asked, handing her the bag.

"A flashlight, a compact survival kit, and a package of Elmer Fudge cookies."

"All the necessities," he said with a chuckle. "How far to home?"

"Only eight miles."

"Eight!"

She stopped rummaging around in the bag and looked at him. "That's by road. We could cut cross-country and be there in five."

He shook his head. "Not unless you packed some pants in that bag." He blew out a breath and watched it steam up into the night. "If we stick to the road, we may get a ride." He looked at his watch. "The dance should be breaking up soon."

"Galen lives out this way."

"He probably helped Poulin ruin my truck."

"What makes you think Wayne did it?"

"Any other likely suspects?"

"No." She finished tying her sneakers and tossed her red shoes in the backseat before she jumped down. She was much steadier on her feet this time, and Ben saw the Maine Guide in her return.

Too bad. He already missed the unschooled vixen she'd been tonight, with her hair done up to expose her neck and her blush of red lipstick that had disappeared with her meal.

But he still intended to steal that dress and hide it until their honeymoon.

They walked in companionable silence for the first few minutes, and Ben realized he was happy. No matter that his truck had been sabotaged, or that the entire town of Medicine Gore distrusted him, or even that he was sexually frustrated by the woman walking beside him. He liked it here.

He enjoyed the sense of wonder and grandeur of these woods. He liked the overflowing emptiness of the land. He was even getting used to the unpredictable weather.

"I can't imagine wanting to leave here to go study the ocean," he said into the silence. "Is that what you really want to do, Emma?"

"I don't honestly know," she answered. "Sometimes I just wish that I had the choice."

"You've always had the choice. You could have sold everything and taken Michael with you."

She looked over at him, but Ben couldn't make out her features in the low light of the waning moon. They weren't using the flashlight because Emma had said it was easier to walk once their eyes were adjusted to the dark.

"I was too scared. It was easier to stay with what I knew rather than venture into the unknown. Especially with Mikey. If I had been alone, well . . . I don't know."

"You love it here. You've succeeded in your own right," he told her.

"I do love it. And I'll probably never leave," she agreed.

He folded an arm over her shoulder and pulled her against him, making walking awkward, but she didn't protest. "Once we're married, I could even move my base of operations here. Never say never, Em. Maybe we could spend several months of the year here, and the rest at Rosebriar."

But he was talking to himself, because Emma had stopped three steps back.

"What did you say?" she asked, her voice cracking in disbelief.

What *had* he said? Several months here . . . move his operations after they . . . oh, Lord, he'd said the *m* word out loud.

"You said 'after we're *married.*'"

"Yes. I guess I did."

She started walking again—in the opposite direction.

Ben ran after her. "Emma. Wait. I know it's kind of a shock, but . . ."

Aw, hell. He'd said it, he meant it, and he had to tell her eventually. He grabbed her arm and turned her around to face him. "Emma. I want to marry you."

"Well, I don't want to marry you. I don't ever want to get married."

"Why not?"

"Because I don't ever intend to fall in love."

"Why the hell not?"

She pulled herself free and started walking again. "Because every person I've ever loved has left, one way or another. Even Mikey will be leaving."

Ben caught her sleeve again, and spun her around, and held her firmly by both arms. "I won't leave you, Em."

"You already did."

"What do you mean? When?"

"Oh, Ben. I had such a crush on you sixteen years ago. I didn't even care that you were seeing Kelly. I was sure you would come to your senses eventually and notice me." She looked down at his chest. "I was so sure you would come back, and that I would be grown up enough for you by then." She looked up at him and the anguish he saw stole his breath. "It wasn't until Kelly left that I realized you were never coming back. So I simply stopped loving you."

He was frozen in shock. Then he crushed her to his chest so fiercely, it was a wonder she didn't break.

"It's me. *I'm* the one Mike was talking about. You're in love with *me*!"

He hugged her again, laughing at himself. "It's me!"

He was the one Emma had gathered her hope chest for.

But he was also the man who had broken her heart so badly she had abandoned her dream. Ben wanted to howl at the moon. He had been competing with himself all this time—and now he had to compete with her demons.

"I was fifteen that summer, Ben. It was puppy love, and I've outgrown it," she said into his chest.

He held her away. She was a gorgeous mess, her hair a tangle of knots and her eyes shining with tears.

She was beautiful.

This could work. It fit his plan even better. If Emma loved him she would be contented as his wife. They could have a good marriage; she would be happy, Michael would be ecstatic, and Ben could get his life back on track.

"Marry me, Emma. Marry me right now, and I promise to never, *ever* leave you again."

"You're not listening to me. I don't love you anymore."

Dammit, he might as well be talking to the trees. He turned them back toward Medicine Creek Camps and started walking again.

"If you loved me once, you can love me again. And, Emma?"

"What?" she asked, staring straight ahead.

He waited until she looked at him.

"I have more patience than you do."

They walked in silence for nearly two miles before the first headlights appeared on the road behind them. Emma pulled Ben into the ditch, then well into the woods.

"Hey," he protested. "We could get a ride."

"It's Galen."

"You can't possibly know that. He's still half a mile away."

"His truck has a whistle. Hear it?"

Ben didn't reply, and Emma looked over to see him rubbing his face with his hands. "I feel like I've fallen down a rabbit hole."

She patted his arm. "Try thinking of this as an adventure."

"All I wanted was a simple, old-fashioned date tonight."

Emma stifled a somewhat hysterical giggle as Galen's truck drove past, her senses reeling. Ben wanted to marry her! He was either nuts or he thought he had to marry her for Mikey's sake.

Which left her smack in the middle of two stubborn men and her own conflicting emotions. She could never marry Ben. She was barely surviving his courtship, if that was what he'd been doing all week. Her brain was screaming one thing, her body another, and her heart was trying very hard to stay neutral.

Her body might have won most of the battles, but the voice in her head was making itself known just as loudly. It was her heart, though, that was most in danger of surrendering. His declaration tonight that he would never leave her had been a powerful blow.

"Come on," she said. "There'll be other cars soon."

"I suppose I'm going to have to buy a new set of tires as well now," he grumbled, stumbling after her through the bushes. "Galen probably slit them on his way by."

He fell into step beside her as Emma set a brisk pace for home. At the rate they were going, it would be sunrise before they arrived. And she had to pick up a group of hunters at the seaplane base in Bangor at eight in the morning.

They were cutting it close.

"Everything just bounces off you, doesn't it?" he asked, his long strides easily matching hers. "No matter what gets thrown at you, you just deal with it and move on."

"I have other options?"

He was silent so long, Emma figured the subject had been dropped.

Then he said, "Like this night from hell. Most women I know would be a ball of tears by now."

"I'm sorry."

"Excuse me?"

"I'm sorry you have such bad taste in women."

She laughed and started running, but was saved from certain reprisal when bright lights suddenly crested the knoll ahead of them. "A logging truck," she said with another laugh when Ben's face became fully illuminated. Lord, she wished L.L.Bean could see their number one customer tonight. Her date was not weathering the evening well.

She looked down at herself. Neither was she.

"He's going the wrong way," Ben said.

"Right now, any way is the right one." She stood in the middle of the road and waved, then quickly stepped to the side.

The huge eighteen-wheeler, looking illegally overloaded, braked to a stop beside them, bringing a blinding cloud of dust with it.

"Little late for a stroll, ain't it, Emma Jean?" Stanley Bates asked from high over their heads.

"Our truck broke down and we need a ride, Stan. Can you take us to Medicine Creek Camps?"

He shook his head. "Sorry, chicky. There's no place to turn this rig between here and Medicine Gore. I'll haul you there, though, if you want. Hop in."

That was easier said than done for a woman wearing a dress that lacked inches in the length department. Emma had to slap Ben's hand away more than once and reposition it three times before she made it into the cab.

"You broke that new truck of yours already, Emma Jean?" Stanley asked, his words muffled by the spit of air brakes releasing.

"No. Ben's new truck broke," she shouted back over the rev of the engine laboring through the gears.

Stanley peered at the man whose lap she was sitting on. "Hey. I remember you. I gave you a ride out to Medicine Creek a couple of weeks ago. I see you found it okay. What's wrong with your truck?"

Emma answered. "The oil light came on."

Stanley looked over and suddenly seemed to notice all the leg she was showing from her thigh to her sneakers. She saw poor Stan's eyes widen just before his face turned a dull red.

"You . . . you been to the dance, Emma Jean?"

"Part of it."

"You wouldn't happen to be carrying any oil, would you?" Ben asked, yanking her coat down over her thigh.

"Ah . . . yeah. Sure. I got a couple of gallons," Stan said, ripping his gaze away to look at the road.

Emma nearly laughed out loud. Stanley Bates, like most of the men in town, hadn't seen her in a dress since Sable Jones's funeral. He looked as if he'd forgotten she actually had legs.

"I don't know if there's a puncture in the pan or if the cap was loosened," Ben continued. "But maybe we could stop and check."

"We can fix ya up, mister."

A heavy sigh hit the back of her head. "That's assuming I still have four round tires," Ben said.

Emma patted his arm. "If not, we can ride to Medicine Gore and file a complaint with Sheriff Ramsey. Then he can take fingerprints and issue a warrant for the arrest of the vandals."

He squeezed her.

Stanley Bates chuckled. "Like my daddy used to say, if they got tires or tits, they're gonna give you trouble."

Emma reached over and smacked Stanley's arm.

"Gosh, Emma Jean, I'm sorry. I didn't mean nothing by that. It just popped out."

"Aren't you running a little heavy tonight, Stanley? Your load looks pretty high to me," Emma said in response, giving him a good glare for insurance.

"Now, Emma, I said I was sorry."

"The guy was only stating a truth, Emma *Jean*," Ben added, pulling her back against him. "Don't threaten the man who's saving us from an all-night walk."

Within minutes they covered the distance it had taken them half an hour to walk. Stanley pulled the eighteen-wheeler to a noisy stop. After the dust settled, Ben climbed out, then gallantly—and somewhat lecherously—helped her down.

"I bet you're going to think twice about wearing this dress again, aren't you?" he whispered before he let her go.

"Oh, I don't know. I kind of like all the attention it gets me," she purred, bolting for the Suburban. She turned when she reached it, and saw Ben was just coming around Stanley's truck. He seemed to be adjusting his own clothes, tugging on the legs of his pants.

Stanley was already crawling under the Suburban, which in itself was an amazing feat. The man weighed a good three hundred pounds, and Emma feared he was going to get stuck.

"Your drain cap was loosened," he hollered from under the guts of the engine. "You're lucky you didn't lose it completely."

"And look," Ben added. "My tires aren't flat."

With much grunting, Stanley reemerged from beneath the truck. "Oil pressure's got nothing to do with tire pressure," he said, looking confused.

Ben appeared momentarily startled, then shook his head and chuckled. "I'll remember that," he told Stanley, who was already headed back to his truck for the oil.

"Open the hood. I'm guessing it will take five or six quarts," Stan hollered over his shoulder.

Ben unlocked his truck and popped the latch.

"You know, it's a good thing you had Emma with you, young fella. A man could get lost walking these roads at night," Stanley said as he poured oil into the filler pipe.

Ben walked around the truck with a flashlight, apparently checking for other damage.

"There ya go, Emma Jean. Your ride's full of oil and ready to go. Why don't you start her up," he instructed Ben, who was shining the light in the ditch beside the truck.

"Not yet. I found this in the ditch," Ben said, holding up a lug nut. He bent down to inspect the right rear tire. "The hub covering the lug nuts has some grease on it." He pulled out a pocketknife and pried it open.

The cover fell off and the flashlight showed that

only two nuts were left holding the tire on, and even they had been loosened.

Stanley whistled beside them. "Oh-ee. Someone don't like you." He looked more closely at Ben. "You one of them tree huggers?"

"No, I am not." He held the lug nut up in the light, looking at Emma. "We could have gotten hurt if we'd taken off without discovering this."

Headlights appeared on the horizon, coming from town. A short burst of siren sounded two seconds after the headlights landed on them.

"What in hell else can go wrong?" Ben said with thinning patience.

"That's Ramsey's Blazer," Emma said. "Why would he be out here?"

Ben sighed. "It must be Michael."

Chapter Twelve

Sure enough, Emma recognized the silhouette in the front seat of the sheriff's truck. His head hanging like that of a cooked goose, Michael Sands was a boy who knew he was in very big trouble.

"This is all your fault," she hissed at Ben as they rounded the back of the Suburban. "'Go out and get into boy trouble,' you told him. 'Hang out with your buddies,' you said. I swear, Ben, if Mikey ends up with a juvenile record—"

She was pulled up short. "This is one of those times when Mike needs a father, Emma. Please, let me handle this."

Damn, she hated when he threw her words back at her. She took a step back. He gave her a swift peck on the cheek and walked to the sheriff getting out of his truck.

Emma sidled over to within hearing distance, but then she caught sight of Mikey looking her up and down and grinning. She walked over to his window. "I'd wipe that smirk off my face if I were you." She opened his door, then noticed—

"Handcuffs!" She glared at Sheriff Ramsey. "You get them off him right now!" Running around the front of the truck, she shoved Ben out of the way. "You get those handcuffs off that child this minute, Ramsey, or I swear you'll never have clean sheets again." She pointed her finger at him. "If Greta finds out what you've done, you'll have burnt meals for the rest of your life. He's only a child!"

Ramsey snorted. "Michael is no more a child than I am. I was just teaching him a little lesson."

"On emotional scarring?"

"On what happens when you get caught in a criminal act," the sheriff returned, his face growing serious. "And what's going to happen if I ever catch him causing trouble again."

"It's okay, Nem," Mikey said from beside her. "Sheriff Ramsey is actually being lenient. I could be in jail now instead of being escorted home."

She turned to Mikey with a frown. "What did you do?"

Ramsey unfastened Michael's cuffs. "The boy was pulling another prank with his friends—adolescent stuff. I was trying to scare a little sense into him."

He pocketed the handcuffs, then brushed Emma's hair

over her shoulder in a fatherly fashion. "Nothing's going to happen to your boy, here." He looked over at Ben. "He's got a good head on his shoulders. He'll be okay."

"Can I go home now, sir?" Michael asked.

"I can't prove you were responsible for the earlier damage to the environmentalist's truck, Mike, but I caught you red-handed this time. You can go home, but if I ever see you in town after ten o'clock at night again, I'm going to haul your ass to jail. Do we understand each other?"

"Yes, sir."

Ramsey nodded. "Good. You're much better than your actions tonight, Michael." He looked from Emma to Ben, then back at Michael. "And you've got other things to be more interested in."

"He'll stay out of trouble, Sheriff." Ben guided Emma back to the Suburban. "Why don't you sit in the truck while Mike and I fix the wheel."

"You got car trouble?" Sheriff Ramsey asked.

Ben turned. "Just a loose wheel. We'll be fine. Thanks."

Mikey moved to flank her other side. Emma rubbed her forehead. She wasn't used to leaning on anyone, much less letting them coddle her. It kind of made her light-headed.

"Why didn't you tell Ramsey about the oil and the tire?" she asked.

"I'm not willing to stir up any trouble just yet, and

we can't prove anything. It could have been kids, thinking I was a tree hugger."

"What happened to the truck?" Mikey asked.

"It was sabotaged," Emma told him.

"Take this flashlight and see if you can find any more lug nuts in the ditch, would you, Mike?" Ben asked.

"If you folks don't need me anymore, I'll be on my way," Stanley said from the driver's side of his truck.

Ben pulled out his wallet. "Let me give you something for the oil, and for helping us."

Stanley waved the offer away. "I don't need nothing from you folks. Emma Jean's pulled my butt out of hot water more times than I can count."

"Well, thanks again for your help," Ben said. "It's appreciated."

"Thanks, Stanley," Emma called out from the Suburban's window, waving at him as he climbed into his rig.

Ben leaned his arm on the roof of the truck and stared at her, silent and thoughtful. She could practically see the wheels turning in his brain.

"I have to go away for a couple of days. I'm needed in New York. Why don't you and Mike come with me?"

Emma knew he was worried about their safety. "Unfortunately, I can't, I have a business to run." She looked at the clock on the dash. "In three hours I have to get in my plane, fly down to Bangor, and pick up some sports. The archery deer season starts Monday."

His frown deepened. "Hire it out. I want you two with me."

"Take Mikey. He would love to see New York."

"I want you to come, too."

"I can't." She reached out and touched his chest. "I'm not in any danger, Ben. You are. You don't have to worry about me."

"We'll discuss this after you get back tomorrow morning," he said, striding away.

Emma stared at the dark road ahead of them. Sheriff Ramsey had gone back to Medicine Gore, Stanley following him. The lonely stretch of road was covered in silence again, except for the soft murmurs of Mikey and his father working at the back of the truck.

Ben seemed truly worried. She'd heard it in his voice when he asked her to go to New York, and she had seen it in the taut lines of his face when she had refused. It was kind of nice to have someone worry about her.

Kind of . . . comforting.

She sat in the truck, soaking up the stillness of the night, and wondered if Ben even realized what was happening to him. He was gathering moss by the bucket load now. He had fallen in love with his son, he'd asked his son's aunt to marry him, and at the dance he had promised the town he would find the man responsible for blowing up the dam sixteen years ago.

Yup. He was definitely knee-deep in moss.

*   *   *

"I'd feel better if you were both coming with me."

"You're just worried about missing Mikey's cooking," Emma said patiently.

They were all seated around the kitchen table. Ben already had his bags in his truck, but he was making one last effort to get her and Mikey to go with him. Realizing she wouldn't budge from her position, Ben had conceded that Michael probably should stay with her. Emma had rolled her eyes at his reasoning, and voted that Mikey go see the bright lights of New York. Mikey had simply folded his arms over his chest and softly said he was staying.

So they were sitting at the table, having a good-bye snack.

"Don't feel so bad, Ben. You're not the first man who's had to deal with the two of us in our stubborn mode." She looked at Mikey and winked. "Judge Bracket didn't have any better luck."

Mikey chuckled as he set his cup of coffee on the table. "That man didn't know what to do with either one of us, did he?"

As she'd intended, the mention of a judge turned Ben's attention from his sulking. "Who's Judge Bracket?"

"He's the judge who awarded me custody of Mikey."

Ben gave her a curious look. "Did you have much trouble getting it? You couldn't have been twenty or twenty-one at the time, and you were single."

"I didn't apply for custody until Mikey was nearly eight and I was twenty-three. After Kelly left, nothing much was said about his living with me. Everyone in town, including me, thought she would be coming back soon."

"I was already going to school before Mom left," Mikey added. "So Nem didn't have to deal with enrolling me."

"So Mike was living with you for three years without the state knowing it?"

Emma reached across the table and touched his hand. "You have to understand, Ben. People around here usually saw Mikey with *me*, not Kelly. When a year went by and she didn't return, no one was willing to call the authorities. They didn't want to see Mikey taken away from me."

"So when did Judge Bracket become involved?" he asked.

"When Michael broke his leg and had to be taken to Bangor to have it set. The Greenville hospital thought he needed special attention, because it was a bad break. I signed the guardian papers, but I made the mistake of mentioning I was his aunt to someone in Bangor."

"All hell broke loose then," Mikey added, grinning in memory.

"Mikey called them the 'kid police.'"

"I was eight," Mike defended. "They wanted to take

me away from you and put me in a foster home until custody could be legally awarded."

"Jesus." Ben looked appalled. "They wanted to uproot a child from his home after he'd had the trauma of an operation?"

"Don't worry, Dad. Nem didn't let them."

"Darn right I didn't. I stole him out of the hospital once he was safe to travel, and flew him to Medicine Gore. I hid him at Greta and Sable's."

"But they must have come after you," Ben said, still looking horrified.

"When they arrived at my door, I gave them hell for losing my nephew." She laughed out loud. "You should have seen their faces when they couldn't find Mikey, and I kept raging at them that they had lost the kid."

Ben didn't laugh with her. "What about Judge Bracket?"

"I hired a lawyer and petitioned the state for custody. The courtroom was a zoo that day."

"I hobbled in on my crutches with Nem on one side of me, our lawyer on the other, and the whole town of Medicine Gore behind us," Mikey explained, grinning from ear to ear. "About ten social workers and state lawyers descended on me like vultures, asking me questions and calling for Nem's arrest."

Emma expected the coffee mug Ben was gripping to shatter.

"Judge Bracket just kept pounding his gavel and shouting for order," Mikey said.

"Were you arrested?" Ben asked, looking at her.

"On what charge? No one could prove I did anything wrong."

"That's not the best part," Mikey interjected. "Judge Bracket tried for over two hours to make sense of the whole mess. He wanted to know where my mother was, and we told him we didn't know. So then he wanted to know where my father was. Again, we told him we didn't know."

"Then Mikey told Bracket that if he couldn't stay with me, he would run away and disappear, just like his parents. By the time he was done with his little speech to the judge, there wasn't a dry eye in the courtroom."

Ben sat up straighter. "But the state would have looked for me before they awarded you custody."

Emma shook her head. "On the birth certificate, Kelly put that the father was unknown."

"*You* knew who the father was."

"Yes," she admitted. She turned her teacup in her hands as she looked him square in the face. "But I wasn't about to tell them. I would have lost Mikey."

Ben looked at his son, his face softening as he blew out a frustrated breath. "I see. And you weren't quite ready to find me yet, either."

"I was scared," the boy admitted. "Nem was all I had. I didn't want to go live with a stranger."

Ben looked back at Emma. "Most of the town knew about me; you said Mike's parentage wasn't a secret. No one said anything?"

"You weren't exactly well thought of. They didn't want to give a little boy over to a man they thought was a murderer."

Which reminded her—*somebody* had wanted to get Ben back here recently. "Hang on a second," she said, getting up from the table. "I have some stationery I want you to look at." She ran into her bedroom.

"Here it is," she said as she returned to the kitchen, setting the stationery she had stolen from Wayne on the table.

"What is it?" Ben asked, picking up the paper.

"Was the letter you received written on this stationery."

"It's nothing like the stationery I received. This is more like typing paper. My letter was written on ivory linen card stock. Where did you get this?" he asked, setting it back on the table.

Emma picked up her tea. "I stole that from Wayne's desk yesterday. I thought he might be bitter enough to write you, hoping to stir up trouble."

"You broke into his *house?*"

"He boards at Greta's, and she asked me to take his laundry up to his room. So while I was there, I . . . just . . ." She threw up her hands. "I thought Wayne might have sent the letter!"

Ben's face was unreadable. "I don't like this," he finally said.

"I didn't get caught. And it's only a piece of paper."

"No. I don't like that we don't know who sent me
the note. Nor do I like the fact that someone out there
has suddenly decided to meddle in our lives."

Emma looked over at Mikey. "Any ideas?"

"No. Everyone's known for years who my father is,
so I don't know why anyone would suddenly decide to
contact him now."

Emma shrugged. "It's probably just some busybody in
town." She stood and gathered the teacups. "We'll find
out who sent it eventually. Where is the letter anyway?
It might help if we saw it."

"It's in New York. I left it with a detective agency,
but I'll bring it back when I return. Emma, what are
these numbers on Poulin's stationery?"

She turned from the sink and found Ben studying
the paper. "Oh. Those are some coordinates I found
hidden under his desk blotter. I can't say why I copied
them, other than that they made me curious."

Ben's face darkened. "You snooped through his
whole room?"

"I was looking for the letters he claimed Kelly had
written him."

"This is northwest of here, Nem," Mikey said, studying the paper he had taken from Ben. "What did he
have these written on? A map?"

"No," she said, moving to look over his shoulder. "They were on a scrap of paper that was old and yellowed. Like I said, I just wondered why he had kept them."

Ben grabbed her by the shoulders and kissed her full on the mouth. Then he hauled Mikey up from his chair and gave him a hug that would have felled a lesser man. "I'll be back Tuesday morning. I expect to find you both here, with no broken bones or near misses. Be good and I'll bring you back something from New York." Those dictates given, he opened the door and left. Emma and Mikey looked at each other, then started laughing.

"Did you see that, Nem? There really *was* moss sticking to his jacket." Mikey ambled out behind his father. "I doubt even a good scrubbing could get it off."

Chapter Thirteen

"*Okay. Here are the* choices," Emma said as she entered the shed. "We can stack firewood, winterize the boats, and wash the plane and my truck, or we can go check out Wayne's coordinates."

Mikey looked up from the generator he was servicing. "I vote for the last one."

"Good. You go dig up the topographies for that area and find the handheld GPS. I'll pack us a lunch."

"We flying or driving?"

"Flying," Emma answered over her shoulder as she left. "You need another lesson in tight water landing. You came in much too hot at Smokey Bog."

Emma had two packs loaded and in the plane by the time Mikey arrived with his own day-trip gear. He had a roll of maps, the GPS, his shotgun, and Homer, their newest homing pigeon. Shaking her head, Emma took

Homer's cage and set it on top of the packs in the backseat of the plane so the bird could see out the window.
She climbed into the passenger seat and handed Mikey
his headphones as he settled in beside her.

"That's cheating, Nem. He can watch the terrain
and learn his way back."

"But think of the thrill for him. He can tell his buddies he actually flew over a hundred miles an hour."

"You spoil those birds."

"No worse than I spoil you," she shot back, pulling
out the checklist and handing it to him. "Like doing
the preflight inspection for you. All systems are go.
Let's take this bird into the sky."

"If Dad finds out about this, there'll be trouble," he
warned, checking the instruments and starting the
plane.

"Then we'll make sure he doesn't find out. Give me
the maps and get us airborne, Boy Wonder. We'll be
back before Ben calls."

"You think he'll call?"

Emma just snorted and opened the maps.

With the confidence of someone who knew he had
a guardian angel sitting on his shoulder, Mikey taxied
out to the middle of the bay. "Smile and wave to Crazy
Larry, Nem," he told her through the headsets.

"I don't see him."

"He's in his picture window, looking at us through
binoculars."

Emma picked up her own field glasses and looked toward the shore. Sure enough, there was Larry, eagle-eyeing them like the nosy pain in the neck he was. She felt like shooting him an unladylike gesture, but decided not to aggravate the situation. She smiled and waved instead, and watched as his jaw went slack and he instinctively waved back.

The old coot had rained holy terror down on them when Mikey had splintered his docks. The FAA had arrived and threatened to take her license away. And they would have, if not for Michael blatantly lying that he'd taken the plane without her knowledge. Even Sheriff Ramsey had been called to the scene. But having flown with Emma and Mikey when the boy had been at the controls, and knowing her influence with Greta, Ramsey had somehow ended up losing the paperwork.

Living in a small town sure did have advantages.

"Where do you want to land?" he asked, once they were airborne and heading northwest.

Emma punched Wayne's coordinates into the loran on the dash. "Let's fly to the spot and look around first, then find a pond nearby," she said, studying the map.

"What do you think we'll find?"

"I haven't a clue, Mikey. This could be a wild-goose chase, for all I know. It may simply be a spot Wayne needs to cruise for future cutting for the mill."

"You said the paper looked old."

"It did. That's what made me curious, I guess." She looked at him, but only saw her reflection in his mirrored glasses when he looked back at her. "You want to return and stack wood instead?"

He grinned. "No. It still beats working. And I'm up for a lesson from my favorite aunt any day of the week."

"Your *only* aunt. And the best darn instructor you'll ever hope to have. Why haven't you taken Ben up for a ride yet?"

"I offered. He said he's still recovering from his last plane ride."

"What do you honestly think of him? Does he measure up to your expectations?"

Mikey scanned the horizon and checked their progress down below. "Actually he does—and then some. I like him. He's intelligent and interesting and he's got a sense of humor. But I think he's a little . . . well, overwhelmed by . . . everything."

"That's one way of putting it. I don't think he knows what to do with either of us."

"But he is trying," he told her with all the sincerity of a loyal son. "But you know what I find the neatest?"

"What?"

"There's a lot more to him than he lets on. He supposedly got lost getting here, but I don't believe it. I think he was stalling because he was nervous about meeting me. But then there's this other side of him. It's not something anyone can see; it's more like a feeling I have. I don't think he's someone you want to cross paths with when he's truly mad. You might think he's a rolling stone, Nem, but I think he's solid granite. And if there's a fight to be fought, I'd want to be beside him, not opposite him."

Emma had to agree. There was much more to Benjamin Sinclair than he let on. There was a hard side. Maybe even a lethal side.

There definitely was a controlled side.

She remembered the morning they had awoken in the forest, and the gun he had pulled at the threat of danger. The same gun he hadn't drawn while four men beat him senseless, because he hadn't wanted things to escalate to the point of no return.

That required a strength most men lacked.

The day Galen Simms had attacked her, she'd gotten a glimpse of Ben coming near the edge of violence. But even then, it had been a controlled deadliness.

"You may be right, Mikey. I would bet Medicine Creek Camps that we've only seen the civilized surface of Ben. And like you, I don't ever want to be opposite him when that veneer comes off."

"Then you had better marry the man, Nem. For both our sakes."

"He told you!"

He grinned over at her. "I'm his greatest ally."

"Well, Mr. Ally, we're here," Emma snapped, refusing to discuss the subject. "Bank left and let's see what's down there."

Nothing was down there. Nothing but old-growth forest for miles and miles. They circled three times before Emma decided they'd have to put down and walk to the spot. She pointed out a marginal-sized pond and Mikey expertly circled the area, deciding how he wanted to land. Like the proficient natural bush pilot he was, he picked a spot and set the Cessna down with plenty of room to spare.

"Grab the GPS and Homer," she said as she reached behind them for the packs. "I would say we've got about a mile to go."

It turned out to be more like two, since they had to sidetrack around a deep gully. Using her handheld global positioning device, Emma was able to lock in the position and walk until the system said they were standing on the spot.

"There's nothing here," Mikey said. "Just trees."

Emma frowned. He was right; there was nothing but forest for hundreds of acres in all directions.

"I know I copied the coordinates down right. I double-checked." She laughed. "I dislike that man so much, I conjured up a mystery that doesn't exist."

"It still beats stacking wood."

"Not really. At least we would've had something to show for our efforts."

"Let's spread out and widen the circle," he suggested,

setting Homer down and dropping his backpack beside the bird. "Maybe Wayne found the site of an old logging camp from the last century. Or a rusting Lombard. There's supposed to be several of those old steam engines rotting away out here."

"Maybe this was an old meeting spot for him and Kelly." Emma dropped her pack beside Mikey's.

The boy shook his head. "Naw, it's too far out. They would have found a closer place."

Emma stared at him. "I was kidding, Mikey. And how can you talk about your mother as if she . . . she . . . well, as if she were just another woman?"

He put his hands on his hips and stared back, looking defiant and angry and lost all at the same time. "She stopped being my mother the day she left." His face sharp with anger and his chin held high, he continued. "For that matter, she never was much of a mother before she left. All my childhood memories are of you. Kelly was just a woman who lived with us."

"That's not true, Mikey. Your mother loved you the best she could." She wrapped her arms around his waist and hugged him. "She was just so lost inside, Michael. When Dad died, and she found herself pregnant, she never fully recovered. Being weak is not a crime, Mikey. It's human. And you have to love her no matter her shortcomings."

She sighed when she felt his unsteady arms wrap around her. "She was advised to put you up for adoption, but she didn't. As much as she was capable of, Kelly loved you. She just didn't know what to do with you once you arrived."

"You didn't seem to have any problem dealing with me."

She pushed away with a scowl. "Ha. I had more problems with you than I can count. I've spent the last fifteen years trying to keep one step ahead of you."

Michael let his arms fall to his sides as he looked around. "Does this place give you the creeps, Nem?" he asked softly.

Emma felt a sudden chill go down her spine at his words. She rubbed her arms and looked around. "Yes," she whispered. "Now that you mention it."

"I feel as though we're being watched," he said, stepping closer.

Emma attempted to shrug off the feeling. "It's probably just a bobcat. You know how they like to sneak around. I've been stalked by them several times while out hiking."

"That woodpile's looking pretty good, all of a sudden. How about we head back?"

Emma mentally shook herself. This was the forest they knew and loved, not the setting of a Stephen King novel. She walked over to Homer and took him out of his cage. "Not until we give this little guy a head start for home."

Mikey pulled a message canister from his pocket. "What do we want the note to say?"

"'The last one home is a rotten egg'?"

Mikey smiled as he wrote. "How about 'The last one home has to cook dinner'?"

Emma wrinkled her nose. "Or *be* dinner? Homer can't cook."

Michael stuffed the message in the canister and carefully secured it to Homer. "But he could pick up a few crickets on the way."

Emma rolled her eyes and released the bird. "Watch him, Mikey. You could take flying lessons from that little guy," she said as they watched the bird rise into the sky. He circled once, then twice, and landed on a branch fifty yards away.

"Well, that's a brilliant homing pigeon," Mikey said. "He's just sitting there, watching us."

"He's young. He doesn't know he's suppose to hurry along yet."

Mikey snorted. "He wants to ride back in the plane. Do you suppose the flight here messed up his internal compass?"

"Maybe he's just enjoying his freedom," Emma suggested, raising her hand to shade her eyes as she squinted up at the tree. "Or maybe he's enjoying the view."

"Or maybe we *will* have him for dinner," Mikey said.

Emma handed him his pack. "Come on, Daniel Boone. Let's look around and then get airborne ourselves. Those clouds look like another storm is headed in."

Mikey followed her line of vision as he hefted his pack onto his back. "There's supposed to be a cold front moving down tonight."

"It's early this year."

"We're ready for it. There's only two boats left to be put up. And snow will make good tracking for the hunters."

"Speaking of hunters, where's Pitiful gone off to? I haven't seen him all week," Emma asked, hefting her pack onto her back. "I hope he's okay."

"No one in their right mind would shoot that moose, Nem. He's no trophy with that missing antler, and no one would dare eat his meat. They'd be afraid of catching mad moose disease or something."

Emma fished out the GPS and turned it on, then studied the screen as the satellites lined up and gave her a reading. "I don't get it. Why would Wayne have kept these coordinates? His desk had no clutter, no scraps of paper anywhere else. Everything was organized and efficient. It doesn't make sense."

"Maybe this is where he buried all the bodies," Mikey suggested, raising his hands and pretending to choke someone. "He's probably a serial killer. He's certainly weird enough."

Emma shut off the GPS and slid it back in her pocket. "He is a little . . . different," she conceded. "But just because you don't like the man is no reason to brand him a psycho."

"This coming from the woman who ransacked his room looking for nonexistent letters, and who is now trying to find out what he's got hidden out here in the middle of nowhere."

"Maybe Wayne's running drugs, and he's using this as a drop site."

Michael slowly nodded. "That makes sense. He would have the opportunity to run drugs, since he can roam these woods without suspicion."

"It's a far-fetched idea," Emma said.

"But a brilliant one, Nem."

"Then where's all the drug money? Wayne's not exactly living the high life."

"He's socking it away. One day he'll just disappear, only to turn up with a new life in a faraway place."

Michael was clearly warming to the idea.

"Okay, Sherlock. Let's work out a scenario. How do the drugs get to this spot?"

"An air drop. Which Wayne picks up and brings into town."

Damn if that didn't make sense. "That would mean there has to be a road nearby."

Michael pulled out the topographical map from his pack and opened it, turning so the lowering sun would light it through the trees. "Here's one." He looked off to the east. "It comes in from the Golden Road, but according to the map, it's old. It may not be passable by truck."

"So we find it and see if its been traveled," Emma

suggested, picking up Homer's empty cage and heading east.

Mikey folded his map, leaving the area they needed exposed as he fell into step beside her. "And if it has? What then?"

Emma picked her way through the underbrush. "We could maybe have a talk with Ramsey. Tell him about our suspicions."

Michael snorted as he held a branch for her to pass. "He'll laugh us out of his office. We have nothing for proof but some illegally gained coordinates marking nothing."

Emma stopped and glared at him. "We're going to tell Ramsey our suspicions, and then we are dropping the whole thing. You are *not* going to look for proof, understand? You are *not* going to stick your nose into anything remotely dangerous."

"I wonder what Dad would think we should do?" he asked, knowing darn well that Ben would love to bring down a world of trouble on Wayne Poulin.

"If you tell Ben, then you're going to have to tell him we stuck our nose in this in the first place. How do you think he'll take *that* news?"

"He'll lecture a bit, but then he'll realize that maybe we can't pass up the opportunity."

"Michael Sands, I'm going to lock you in your room for a year," Emma said, pushing past him through the underbrush.

She'd opened a can of worms with this little excursion, and now she didn't know how to put the lid back on the damn thing. God help them all if Ben decided to get involved.

They found the road a quarter of a mile to the east. As the map indicated, it was an abandoned old logging road leading up a mountain that hadn't been harvested in over forty years. The bushes had grown in, but not enough to make passing impossible. Emma and Mikey stood in the middle of the old track, looking in both directions.

"It's passable here, but any number of old bridges or culverts could be washed out farther down," Emma said.

Mikey started walking toward the Golden Road, looking down as he went. "There's been traffic up here since last spring." He moved the bushes and checked their branches. "There's broken twigs here, but they're weathered."

"Any number of people like to see where these old roads lead," Emma said, trailing behind him and studying the gravel. "That doesn't mean it was Wayne."

They walked on in silence, looking for any signs of recent use. "Maybe this is no longer a drop site," Emma said after a time. "Maybe it never was."

Mikey suddenly stopped and hunched down, touching the ground in front of him. "This track is fresh," he said, looking around. He stood up and walked back a few steps. "And look. A truck turned here." He grabbed a bush and fingered a broken branch. "This is new."

Emma walked up and looked at the tracks in the road. They *were* fresh. She looked in both directions and then up the forested mountain. For the second time that day, a chill brushed down her spine.

"Someone was here today," she said, continuing on until she came to a mud puddle with a tire track through it, the ground still wet from the splash of the truck passing. "Not long ago." She turned to her nephew. "We're going back to the plane, Mikey. I don't like this."

"Aw, Nem. It's just getting interesting."

"No, it's getting creepy. What are the chances that two different parties ended up in this particular spot at the same time?"

"We couldn't have been followed. We flew here."

"But Wayne knew I had been in his desk. He might be checking to see if I discovered the coordinates and came here."

"He knew? How?"

Emma felt her face redden. "I must have rearranged something in his desk. Or maybe he counts his stationery."

Mikey did his own scan of the area, suddenly looking worried. "If Wayne's been using these woods to run drugs, then he knows them well. He'd know where we'd land our plane. Maybe we should head back and make sure it hasn't been discovered."

"We're going to check that plane out with a magnifying glass," Emma said as she started up the road, searching for a game trail that turned off to the northwest. "And then we're flying home and dropping this whole thing. It's not worth our getting involved."

She was talking to the trees. Mikey was still standing in the road, staring at her.

"Not worth getting involved? Nem, we can't just do nothing. The guy could be running drugs."

"It's not our problem. We'll tell Ramsey, and let him decide what to do."

"But where's your sense of citizenship?"

"It's hiding behind my sense of responsibility," she countered, walking back to him. "Your safety and my safety come first. Drug dealers are dangerous and without conscience, and we are not going to put ourselves in the middle of this."

He simply started walking up through the forest until they came to the mountain, then turned south and skirted it.

Emma walked quietly behind him. Well, she'd done it now. Michael Sands could be one stubborn, ugly dog when he got a bone between his teeth.

She knew he would go to Ben as soon as the man got back, and tell him their suspicions and persuade him to do something about it. And she would have absolutely no control over what they decided.

Michael Sands had apparently had enough of female guidance.

Chapter Fourteen

It took them half an hour to reach the plane, and it felt like the longest trek Emma had ever made. Silence can be such a wearing thing, especially when the longer it continues, the wider the void becomes. Right now there was a distance growing between her and Mikey nearly as wide as Medicine Lake.

"It looks to be riding low on one side," Mikey said as they approached the plane, speaking for the first time since they'd left the road.

Sure enough, one of the floats was sitting on the bottom of the pond, making the Cessna look like a wounded bird with its wings spread out for balance.

Dammit, someone was out here with them.

And whoever it was didn't want them leaving by air.

"We're going over every inch of it," she said, remembering Ben's tampered-with oil pan and lug nuts.

Scrambling onto the still-floating pontoon, Emma opened the engine cowling and peered inside with a small flashlight. Running her light along the wiring and hoses, it wasn't long before she found trouble.

"He wasn't a very imaginative saboteur," she told her nephew as she fingered a severed hose. "He simply cut the fuel line in half."

"Then he doesn't know you very well. You always shut off the fuel," Mikey answered, unlocking the door to the plane and throwing their packs inside. Then he climbed up onto the wing. Emma heard him sigh. "He snapped off the radio antenna."

Emma walked to the back compartment of the plane and rummaged around in her toolbox. Mikey had more confidence in her preparedness than she did. She doubted she had any fuel line, or anything else she could substitute. She always kept her plane in perfect flying condition, and the fuel line was not something one expected to break.

"What's the damage to the float?" she asked as she searched for anything resembling a hose.

"It looks like he took an ax to it just below the waterline. Any luck with the hose?"

"No, Mikey. I don't have one."

"Are you sure?"

She popped her head out and bent to look under the fuselage so she could frown at him. "The plane had its annual inspection just last month. Why would I need to carry around a bunch of spare parts?"

"Maybe because you have this thing about always being prepared? So what are we going to do?"

Emma looked around at the beaver flowage and the endless forest. "We walk."

Mikey looked around also. "Right into an ambush?"

The sun chose that very moment to hide behind a cloud, adding its own warning.

"Then we fly out," she said with more confidence than she was feeling.

"How?"

"We conjure up some Yankee ingenuity and make this lady flyable. Here," she said, handing him the pieces of hose she had removed from the engine. "Find a way to splice this while I check for other damage."

Mikey took the hose, they ducked into the back compartment and began to search for something useful. Emma looked at the engine again.

Ten minutes went by before she felt a tug on her shirt. "Here. This is the best I can do," Mikey told her as he handed up the repaired fuel line.

Emma looked at it, then at her nephew. "Duct tape? What have you got stiffening it so it won't collapse?"

"I pulled some conduit out of the tail section. It was tight, but I was able to slide the severed ends of the hose over it and tape them together." He hesitated, giving her an uncertain look. "It should hold long enough to get home. But even if it works, we still can't fly with that hole in the float," he added, glancing at the sunken pontoon.

Emma smiled at him, nodding in approval and reassurance. The poor boy had been asked to do something that put both their lives on the line, and he didn't like it. She worked the repaired hose back into place.

"We've restricted the flow somewhat, but if it can get us airborne, then you've worked a miracle, Mikey. Now let's see about floating this plane. Grab that bicycle pump and truck tire tube from in back, would you?"

"But the float has a hole the size of a basketball, Nem. Duct tape won't hold, and a rubber patch will never be strong enough to withstand the pressure."

"We're not going to patch it. We're going to stick that tube in the float and pump it up," she told him, smiling as his eyes widened in disbelief.

"What makes you think that will work?"

"Remember Jack Frost? The guy who was here last summer?"

He suddenly laughed. "Do I. He flew floatplanes in the Gulf of Mexico, didn't he, servicing the oil rigs?"

"Yup. And Jack told me that most of the pilots down there always stick a deflated truck tube in each of their floats. If they get a bad leak or damage one of them, they can pump up the tube to displace enough of the water to take off and land."

Her nephew looked more skeptical than impressed. "There's got to be a lot of drag."

"It'll work." Emma jumped down in the water, wincing at the cold. "I got us into this mess, and I'm going to get us out. By air."

Michael hunkered down on the float above her and unscrewed one of the portals. "If anyone can do it, you can. And I'm sorry."

She continued stuffing the giant tube through the portal. "For what?"

He took over the chore, not looking at her as he spoke. "For shutting you out this afternoon. For getting carried away by this whole idea of chasing down some drug runners. For being mad at you." He finally looked up. "For forgetting that you love me, and that you were only worried about my welfare."

"Heck, I remember what it's like to be young and full of dreams and curiosity and adventure."

"But you never got to fulfill any of your dreams, did you? You got me and Kelly to look after, a huge mortgage to pay, and a boatload of sports to babysit."

She squeezed his leg. "I got something a whole lot better. I got you. As the song says, I thank God for unanswered prayers. I wouldn't trade my life with you for any of my childish dreams. I love you, and I love the life we've had."

"It's not over, Nem. It's just changing. For both of us."

"That's right. And if you don't want to discover what's under your father's civilized veneer, we'd better get ourselves out of here and home before he calls."

He quickly finished stuffing the tube in the float and pulled the stem up through the opening.

They took turns pumping, a long, tedious undertaking since the bicycle pump had to lift most of the weight of the plane. While Mikey pumped, Emma used the duct tape to cover the jagged edges the ax had made in the pontoon. It took nearly half an hour before they were satisfied the float was riding high enough to taxi on.

With a sigh of relief, Emma looked at her watch and then at the sky. "We'll just make it home before dusk, thank God. I sure as heck don't want to be landing this crippled bird in the dark. If we flip her, we'll be fighting blindly."

Wiping her hands on her jeans, Emma looked at her nephew, who was scanning the woods and looking more worried than a mouse at a cat show. "It will be okay, Mikey. The fuel line will hold, and so will the pontoon. Turn us around and climb in."

He did as he was told, pushing them out into deep water, then climbing in the plane and putting on his headset. Emma turned over the prop. The Cessna sputtered alive and immediately began pulling them through the glassy water of the pond.

Emma took her time taxiing, listening to the engine and watching her gauges. She gave it some throttle and felt the plane pull harshly to the right, the pontoon on that side plowing the water. Damn, she wished this pond was bigger—she'd like to have more room to ease the weight of the plane onto the left pontoon and into the air, not force it up at full power.

But she didn't have that option.

She turned into the slight breeze and shoved the throttle forward. The plane immediately responded, thrusting them back in their seats as it attempted to rise onto the surface of the pond.

It wasn't a very comfortable—or graceful—journey skyward. Emma had to fight the controls all the way, praying the repaired hose would allow enough fuel through it to give them the power they needed. Water sprayed against the prop and the engine and Mikey's window. The Cessna shuddered and shook, and finally came up on the step of the floats.

Mikey let out a whoop as they lifted into the air, at the exact same time the window beside Emma shattered into a million spider veins. She instinctively ducked and banked the plane to the right.

"The trees!" Mikey shouted.

Emma eased back to the left just as the window behind her shattered and a bullet lodged into the ceiling. She pulled back on the yoke until the stall alarm sounded, then she forced the plane into another tight bank to the right, aiming at the narrow valley at the head of the pond.

"Dammit, Nem! We won't make it!"

She pulled back on the yoke and the big, beautiful

Stationair did the impossible as it clipped the tops of the trees in its struggle to fly.

There was another sound at the rear of the plane, which Emma guessed was another bullet hitting the tail.

"Someone's shooting at us!" Mikey hollered, turning to look at the back of the plane. He twisted around and looked up at the ceiling, then at the window beside her. "We were shot at!"

"Take the yoke. Now," Emma ordered, lifting her right hand to her left shoulder.

He grabbed the yoke with shaking hands, his expression stark with fear.

"Keep climbing, Mikey. And head for Greenville."

He looked over at her, and through the haze of tears nearly blocking her vision, Emma saw his eyes widen in horror.

"You've been shot!"

"I don't think bad, but it burns like the devil. Take us to Greenville and set us down as close as you can to the shore."

"Jeez, Nem. Are you bleeding bad?"

She carefully turned in her seat to open one of their packs. Her shaking hand was slick with blood as she worked the zipper and pulled out a shirt. She balled it up in her fist and put it over her left arm, gritting her teeth to stifle a groan.

"Well?" Mikey asked, trying to divide his attention

between flying and looking at her wound. "Can you stop the bleeding?"

"I'm trying, Mikey. Give it a second."

He patted her knee. "I'm sorry, Nem. I just don't like seeing you hurt."

"You never did." She let go of the shirt long enough to wipe the tears from her eyes. "Remember when I fell on the dock and hit my head?"

"I remember you bled like a stuck pig. Like you're bleeding now. Maybe you're a hemophiliac. You could bleed to death before we get to Greenville."

"Don't go inventing trouble," she said as she fashioned the shirt into a bandage, using her teeth to tighten it.

"Is . . . is the bullet still in your arm?"

"I don't know."

He groaned, as if he were in more pain than she was. "Damn, I wish we had filled the woodshed today."

"Well, we didn't. And we may still have to pay our dues for being curious. There's Greenville. I'll take the yoke. I want you to open your door and look down at the pontoon, Mikey. See if it's still intact. We hit a few of those trees pretty hard."

His face went completely white, and Emma watched him uncurl his hands from the yoke as she took control with her right hand. He opened the door, having to force it against the wind, and looked down. When he closed it and looked at her, his face was even whiter than before.

"The tube's deflated and hanging half out. As soon as we land, that float's going to drag us over."

Emma gritted her teeth. "We have two choices. The water or the trees. Which one do you want to land us on?"

"Me!"

"There comes a time when every pilot has to make the decision to sacrifice his plane to save himself," she told him, looking him straight in the eye. She tried moving her left arm and found it nearly impossible. "Personally, I'd choose the trees. I don't know if I can swim out of an upside-down plane right now."

"You're asking me to crash the plane?"

"An *emergency landing*, Mikey. There's a difference."

"I know. I know." He stared down at the lake below them. "We've practiced the procedure often enough."

"And now you get to try it for real."

He turned to her. "I could kill us both."

"Not if you focus on the principals I taught you. Full flaps, slow speed, and just fly it into the softest trees you can find," she said, her voice steady and low. "It's all a matter of deciding to do it, and doing it right. You've got the skill, Mikey."

"But *you've* actually done it before, Nem. Couldn't you take over long enough to get us down?"

"This is the ultimate chance for you, Michael."

"This is no time for a lesson!"

"Pick your spot, Mikey. The sun's setting. And I'm bleeding."

He gritted his teeth as he leaned forward to look out the window. "I don't know why I'm worried. If we make it down okay, Dad's going to kill us anyway when he gets back." He banked the plane down to the right. "There, Nem. How about those trees?"

"Maybe we should buzz the seaplane base and flash our lights, to let them know we're in trouble."

He all but dove for the base in the cove.

Emma watched out Mikey's window. She couldn't see out of her own; it was too shattered, with one neat little hole at shoulder height. They dove low over the seaplane base, and Emma saw several men look up at them.

"They saw us. Bring it down now, Mikey."

"You're sure the water wouldn't be better? There's help right there, Nem. They can get to us quickly."

She shook her head, closing her eyes as a wave of pain shot down her arm. "The water's unpredictable."

"Here goes!"

He lined them up for an approach to a planting of young fir growth, as though he were lining up to a runway. Then he pulled down full flaps, causing the plane to feel as if he had put on the brakes. Their packs shifted in the backseat, and Emma's arm throbbed as it banged against the door, making her bite back a moan.

"Just fly it down, Mikey." She kept her voice calm and coaxing. "Bring back the throttle. That's it. Easy, now. This is just like a glassy water landing. Let the plane fly into the trees. Flair, Mikey. Nearly stall it. That's right, you've got it."

At first it felt as if they were landing on a huge ball of cotton when the pontoons lightly brushed over the treetops. As they slowed even further and settled deeper, the soft cushion of fir got denser. And harder. Tops snapped below them in a sudden rush, just before the plane itself started shuddering.

"Flair out, Mikey. Flair!"

The plane squealed in protest. The stall alarm blared. The pontoons caught on the thicker trunks, violently jerking the Cessna as metal gave way to wood, the noise of ripping aluminum and snapping trees deafening. A branch finished shattering the window beside her and the thrust of her body against her harness was nearly unbearable.

It lasted only seconds.

And in the end, they ended up upside down anyway.

Michael was out of his seat belt first, hitting his head as he fell to the ceiling. He righted himself and carefully unbuckled Emma's belt, catching her in his arms and easing her down. Then he kicked open his door and pulled her out with all the care of a father handling his infant for the first time.

Emma was laughing and praising him and bawling like a baby the whole time. He pulled her a safe distance away from the plane, propping her up against one of the lifesaving fir trees to examine her, all but counting her fingers and toes. He pulled off his shirt and held it up to her shoulder.

"You're one big mess, Nemmy." He looked back at the plane and then at her, grinning like a drunken fool. "But we did it! We walked away from my first official crash."

"Not many people have crashed so gracefully, Mikey. You did good, big man. You earned your wings today."

His euphoria suddenly vanished. "We've still got to face Dad."

Emma smiled. "Which means you get to earn your *son* badge next—because you're the one who gets to tell him," she said, just before everything went black.

Chapter Fifteen

*B*en *stood outside the* small, rural hospital's room, not ready to face what he would find inside. Not until his anger cooled. Not until his hands stopped shaking. And definitely not until he trusted himself not to strangle the woman who seemed determined to give him a heart attack.

He was afraid that if he walked in there right now, he would lash out at Emma with the full force of the wrath he was feeling. Then again, he could just as easily crawl into bed with her, wrap her in his arms, and weep with relief.

So he stood silently outside the door, blatantly eavesdropping on the conversation taking place between his son and the woman he intended to marry as soon as he could find a preacher.

"You look worse than I feel," Emma said, her voice a mere croak.

Ben moved just enough to see Mike standing beside the bed, his posture subdued, his face bruised, the flowers he'd brought forgotten in his hand.

"I . . . uh . . . Dad's here," the boy whispered as he moved closer. "And you know that civilized veneer we talked about?"

"Y-yes."

"Well, it's gone, Nem."

Ben very nearly smiled when he saw Emma's eyes widen in horror. Then she looked more closely at her nephew. "He didn't lay a finger on you, did he?" she asked, her voice stronger—and outraged.

"I almost wish he had. He's angry enough to kill someone, but I don't think we're the target he's looking for."

Ben saw Emma heave a giant sigh. She looked damn good for someone who had been shot and then managed to survive a plane crash. Her left arm was bandaged against her ribs and there was another bandage on her forehead, but otherwise she looked fit enough to face him.

He pushed the door open and quietly walked in.

"Give your aunt her flowers, Mike," he told his son as he approached. He laid a gentle hand on the boy's shoulder. "You're strangling them to death."

Deep jade eyes the size of dinner plates stared up at him from the bed. Ben moved closer, and carefully touched his lips to her cheek. "Hello, Emma. Been keeping out of trouble while I was gone?" he asked softly.

She shook her head, then suddenly started nodding it up and down, her eyes still huge and unblinking. It looked to Ben as if she'd stopped breathing.

"So you've earned the present I brought you from New York?"

Hesitant, and clearly suspicious, she nodded again. Ben kissed her again, this time on the lips, then walked over and opened the window. He nodded to the man outside, and gave a low whistle through his teeth.

A large German shepherd lithely bounded through the window into the room.

A surprised squeak came from the bed.

"Meet Beaker, Em." He touched the dog's head and turned to Emma, bringing Beaker with him. "He's six years old and he wants to move in with a family. He's tired of city life, and is looking forward to retiring to Maine."

The recipient of this gift was eyeing the shepherd with ill-concealed horror. Beaker was eyeing her in return, his nose pushed through the rails of the bed and his tongue lolling off to the side.

"Retiring from what?" she asked in a barely audible voice.

"Beaker's been a personal security dog for the last three years."

"What happened to whoever he was guarding? Did he eat them?"

Ben pushed Beaker's head out of the way and dropped the rail on the bed. He sat down by Emma's hip and patted the bed beside her. Beaker immediately accepted the invitation and lifted his front paws onto the bed and sniffed her.

She squeaked again and tried to scoot over to the other side. "I don't think you're supposed to bring a dog into the hospital, Ben. It's unsanitary or something."

"Beaker and I won't tell if you don't." Ben frowned. "You're not afraid of dogs, are you, Emma?"

"N-no. Not small, harmless dogs with teeth the size of toothpicks."

He looked over at Mike, who had taken two steps back. The boy's face looked as pale as Emma's.

Well, hell. The Sandses were afraid of dogs.

Ben cupped Emma's hip just as Beaker leaned forward and gave her a wet lap on the hand. She whimpered at the gentle greeting.

"Beaker won't hurt you, Em. Actually he's partial to women." He looked at Mikey. "He likes boys, too," he added as he pushed the dog down.

"We . . . we can't have a dog at Medicine Creek Camps, Ben," she said, her voice growing stronger in direct relation to Beaker's distance. "They chase deer."

"Beaker won't. He's been trained to stay close to people."

Her gaze was on her new pet, who was now eyeing Mike with interest. The boy was all but plastered to the wall, and it looked like he'd stopped breathing, too.

"Good God, people. He's not going to eat you," Ben said with waning patience. "He's a fine dog and will be a good addition to the household."

"He's nearly as big as Pitiful." Emma pushed a button and lifted the head of her bed.

She immediately stopped when Beaker turned at the noise.

"Then the two of them should get along great." Ben stood up, his hands on his hips and his expression showing that his patience was gone. "Beaker needs you as well as the peace and quiet of your woods. You're going to have to coddle him. Take him with you wherever you go. He loves riding in the truck."

He started out of the room. "So make peace with the animal, Emma. You're all that's standing between him and a nervous breakdown."

"Wait!"

He stopped and looked back at her.

"Where are you going?"

"To clean up the mess you started yesterday."

He stopped just outside the door, and waited to see how the three inside were going to deal with one another.

"Walk over to this side of the bed," he heard Emma whisper. "Slowly, Mikey. Don't spook him."

Ben leaned forward to peek in the room. Mike was

making a Herculean effort to unglue himself from the wall. The boy slowly inched his way around Beaker, never taking his eyes off the dog.

"Nice dog," Emma said softly, staring at Beaker. She had her water pitcher in her hand, looking ready to hurl it at the poor, unsuspecting dog should he attack her nephew.

Ben shook his head. They were petrified of a gentle dog?

Well, Beaker was gentle with his *charges*. The highly trained guard dog could rip an assailant into pieces if he wanted to. He was intelligent, perceptive, and vigilant, having been trained at one of the best facilities in the country.

Ben only hoped the poor animal had plenty of patience.

"He doesn't look that mean, Nem," he heard Mike say, now that the boy had the safety of the bed between them. "He's kind of handsome. And look at his eyes. They're sort of sad-looking."

"They look crafty to me. Who knows what he's really thinking?"

"Dad wouldn't have brought you a dangerous pet, Nem. Beaker was trained to protect the people he lives with, not eat them."

Ben saw Emma eyeing Beaker with suspicion. "I don't like dogs—especially when they're bigger than me. One bite and I could lose an arm or a leg."

"Aw, Jeez, look at him. We're hurting his feelings. We should talk to him."

"Why don't you walk over and pet him, then?"

Mike vigorously shook his head. "Nope. You heard Dad. Beaker's your dog. *You* should make the first move."

Emma glared up at her nephew and then at the doorway. Ben moved back into the shadows and waited.

"I can't believe he has the nerve to bring a dog in here!"

"I don't think anyone would have stopped him if he'd brought him in the front door. They scrambled into action when he asked to see your doctor. I actually tried to hide behind the vending machine."

"He just dumped this animal with us and left! He didn't even ask how I was feeling," Emma said, sounding utterly dejected.

Ben hadn't trusted himself to mention her condition, much less how she'd gotten here. But he'd read her chart three times. She had a flesh wound in her upper left arm that had required ten stitches, but the bullet hadn't done any major damage. She had a nasty bump on her forehead, her right ankle was wrapped because of a sprain, and she had bumps and bruises that she'd certainly feel tomorrow morning.

The doctor had said Ben could take her home this evening.

As for Beaker, he was more than ready to begin his

new job as her personal guardian. *Ben* was the one on the edge of a nervous breakdown.

"That's what scares me, Nem. He hasn't said a word about the crash or your arm, or even asked how it happened. He just showed up here and asked to speak to whoever was in charge. Then he hugged me for two solid minutes, and told me to come in here while he spoke with the doctor."

"I . . . I think maybe I should stay with Greta a few days," Emma said. "You could, too, if you want."

"In the same house as Wayne?"

So that bastard Poulin was somehow involved in this, was he? With renewed anger, and now with a direction to aim it, Ben left the hospital.

Emma had been expecting a lecture, and would have preferred it to that peck on the cheek and a *gift* that had teeth the size of elephant tusks.

She'd nearly killed his son, and now she'd opened a can of worms that had left her with a wound that ached like the devil, a nephew who was bruised and battered, and a tangle of metal that had once been her plane.

And a dog.

Emma ignored the beast that fell into step beside them as Ben carried her up to the house. Mikey was trailing behind, still looking a little lost as he carried the flowers he'd brought to the hospital.

Emma looked over Ben's shoulder at the cove, where her Cessna usually sat. She'd loved that plane. She had scrimped and saved and extended herself to buy it five years ago. It was the workhorse of her business. Now it was gone, and she was laid up for at least a month. She'd have to call all the sports she had booked for this month and cancel their reservations.

Deer hunting season was her most lucrative time of year. Now she was going to have to return all the deposits and eat the loss, and leave a lot of people disappointed.

"Do you want me to take you to your bedroom, or do you feel like sitting up for a while?" Ben asked as they entered the kitchen.

Which was already occupied.

Her curiosity outweighing her fatigue, Emma said she'd sit at the table. "Mikey. Could you make me a cup of tea?" she asked as she eyed the two men standing by the counter.

Not appearing surprised to find men in his house, and with the energy of someone glad to have something to do, Mikey put the kettle on to boil.

Emma studied the two men with open curiosity.

Ben cleared his throat. "Emma. I would like you to meet Atwood," he said, gesturing to one of the men. "He's my secretary in New York."

The man smiled. "Nice to meet you, Miss Sands."

Emma stifled a snort as she shook his hand. Secretary, her ass. Atwood looked like he ate babies for breakfast. There was no way those beefy hands dallied on a keyboard all day—nor could she see him answering phones and serving coffee to clients. His hard, piercing blue eyes never stopped moving, as if he expected someone to come crawling out of one of the cupboards with a machine gun.

The other man, who was dressed like Paul Bunyan, looked like he hunted down the babies for Atwood's breakfast.

"This is my brother-in-law, Skyler," Atwood said, now standing back by the counter. "Mr. Sinclair was nice enough to let him join me for this trip. He's on hiatus."

From some battlefield, Emma decided.

Ben had returned from New York with a security dog, two bodyguards, and who knew how many other foot soldiers lurking in the shadows. She'd bet Medicine Creek Camps that for every man standing in her kitchen there were at least three more wandering around town right now.

When pushed, Benjamin Sinclair was apparently going to push back with enough force to start World War III.

Mikey must have spilled his guts last night when he'd called his father to tell him what had happened, and Ben had immediately assembled an army.

"Have either of you been to Maine before?" she

asked, already knowing the answer. The closest either of these men had come to this wilderness was shopping at L.L.Bean or Cabela's.

"No, ma'am. We're used to slightly warmer country," Skyler said, giving her a smile that was more feral than friendly.

Emma sighed and rubbed her forehead. "Well, you might as well make yourself at home in cabin five. It's suddenly vacant." She looked at Mikey as he set her tea on the table—along with a bowl so full of Elmer Fudge cookies, they were falling out. "We've got to call all my bookings for the rest of this month and cancel them, Mikey. Tomorrow you can help me send back their deposits."

"Oh, Lord, Nem. I hadn't thought about that. You can't guide and we don't have a plane anymore."

"That's only a temporary problem. The Cessna was insured. I'll start hunting for a new one tomorrow."

"You're going to be busy tomorrow," Ben said, sitting across from her and grabbing a handful of cookies.

"Doing what?"

"Recuperating." He popped an Elmer Fudge into his mouth.

She was going to have to teach him how to properly eat the cookies, she decided, ignoring his unsubtle suggestion that she sit back and do nothing. She attempted to pull the two halves of her own cookie apart but her left hand failed her, and the cookie went sailing through the air. Beaker caught it before it could hit the floor.

"That's good, Em," Ben said, smiling at her, knowing damn well she hadn't intended to feed the beast. "Keep giving him treats. That will help you two bond."

She glared at the dog, who was looking at her with huge, expectant brown eyes. Her heart melted—a little bit.

He was such a quiet dog. And unobtrusive. He merely padded along with them like a silent shadow. He seemed polite, too. On the ride home from the hospital, Beaker had sat in quiet joy in the back, looking out the window at the forest zooming by.

"Chocolate's not good for dogs," she said, taking another cookie and managing to get this one open. She scraped off the chocolate center with her teeth and then carefully extended the vanilla cookie to the dog.

Just as carefully, Beaker took it from her, his soft muzzle brushing her fingers. He inched closer, leaning against her leg, and set his chin on her knee.

A dog. A huge, quiet, burned-out dog that was trained to kill.

And he was hers.

"Where's he going to sleep?" she asked.

"With you," Ben answered.

"What if I roll over in the night and squish him? He might get mad."

"We can make him a bed on the floor."

Emma looked back at the dog. "That's not very comfortable. You said he needed peace and quiet and plenty of rest because his nerves are frazzled."

Atwood suddenly began coughing.

"Get Mr. Atwood some tea, Mikey. And Mr. Skyler, too. Gentlemen, come sit down and have some cookies."

The men looked at Ben, as if seeking his approval.

"We don't stand on ceremony here," Emma said with the authority of a hostess in her own home. "Just grab a mug from the cupboard and Mikey will pour you some tea. Have you had supper?"

"Yes, ma'am," Skyler answered, doing as he was told.

"Please drop the 'Mr.,'" his brother-in-law added, joining them at the table. "It's just Atwood and Skyler."

"I will, if you stop calling me 'ma'am,'" she told them, smiling at the table full of testosterone. Her kitchen looked like a convention of warlords.

"Are you feeling up to telling us what happened yesterday?" Ben asked, once they were all seated and sipping tea.

So the cease-fire was over, and the interrogation was about to begin. Emma shrugged, and immediately regretted it as pain shot down her arm and across her back. "You know about the coordinates I found in Wayne's room."

"Yes."

"Well, Mikey and I decided to go see what they were."

"What did you find?" Ben asked, leaning forward.

"Nothing."

He stared at her.

"There wasn't anything there, Dad," Mikey added, sitting beside her—and away from Beaker.

"Are you sure you had the right spot?"

"Yes," Emma answered. "We checked and double-checked. And I know I wrote them down right."

"We think it was probably a drop site for running drugs," Mikey said.

"You mentioned something about drugs last night, but I couldn't make it all out." Ben cleared his throat, again frowning at Emma before he looked back at his son. "You were bombarding me with all sorts of news."

"There was just forest for miles and miles," Emma said, drawing Ben's attention again. "So we started guessing why Wayne would have kept those coordinates in his desk, and the only thing that made sense was a drug drop."

"We found a road nearby," Mikey said.

"And we found recent tire tracks," Emma added. "That's when we decided to come home."

"And your plane had been vandalized?" Ben asked, his eyes darkening.

Emma nodded. "Someone had cut the fuel line and taken an ax to one of the floats."

"I don't get it," Atwood suddenly interjected. "You may have been able to repair the fuel line, but you never could have gotten airborne with a punctured float. How did you do it?"

Mikey answered, "Nem had a tire tube in the plane. We put it in the float and pumped it up, displacing enough of the water to float the Cessna well enough to take off."

"And land?" Ben asked.

"And land," Emma confirmed. "But someone started shooting at us just as we got airborne. We clipped a few trees, and the tube got damaged. So we had to crash the plane."

All three men looked as if she and Mikey were missing some rooms upstairs. Ben had gone completely white.

"You crashed the plane on purpose?" Skyler asked softly.

"Mikey did," she told the three horrified men. "It's common practice when the alternative is certain death."

Ben stood up, pushing his chair back with enough force to tip it over. Skyler and Atwood winced at the sound. Beaker lifted his head off her lap.

"Oh, for the love of God," Emma said with exhausted impatience. "I'm a bush pilot, Ben. It's what I do for a living. Yesterday wasn't the first time I've lost a plane, and it probably won't be my last."

"Yes, it damn well will be," he gritted out, leaning his hands on the table and glaring at her.

Beaker growled low in his throat, and Emma instantly warmed to the dog.

Without even thinking, she patted his head to let him know she approved of his courage. Even if she had fangs the size of Beaker's, Emma wasn't sure she would have the nerve to growl at Ben.

Clearly startled, Ben looked at Atwood. "He can't growl at me," he told his "secretary."

Atwood smiled. "He just did."

Ben sat back down, glaring at Emma's new protector. He cleared his throat again, and seemed to be trying to remember what they'd been talking about.

"Did you happen to see who was shooting at you?" Skyler asked.

"We were kind of busy trying not to litter the mountainside," Emma answered, idly petting her new guardian.

"What about you, Mike? Did you see anything?" Atwood asked.

"I had my eyes closed."

"How about a guess, then." Ben looked at Emma. "Who do you *think* was shooting at you?"

She shrugged her good shoulder. "If I had to guess, I would say it was Wayne Poulin."

"Why?"

"Because he knew I had been snooping in his room. And if those coordinates are important to him, he was probably checking to see if I had been out there."

All three men silently mulled over her theory. Emma stood up and grabbed the cane Mikey had hooked on the back of her chair and Beaker stood as well.

"I'm going to take a nap," she said as she started hobbling out of the kitchen.

"I'll carry you," Ben said, moving to intercept her.

Beaker moved between them, the hair on his back raised, and growled.

Ben stopped and his face reddened. "Goddammit! Beaker!"

The dog advanced a step, his growl rising in volume.

"Maybe you should try feeding him cookies, boss," Atwood suggested, sounding like he was strangling on a laugh.

"I'm going to feed him to the crows," Ben said through gritted teeth. "Beaker. Sit!"

The dog ignored him.

Emma laid her hand on Beaker's head. "It's okay. Let's go have a nap, and leave these men to contemplate the future." Then she looked at Mikey. "Why don't you call Stanley Bates and see if he'd be willing to haul our Cessna home."

Mikey nodded, staring at the dog as if it had two heads and a forked tail.

Satisfied the remaining males could get on with their foolish little war without her, Emma led Beaker into her bedroom and softly closed the door. The dog stood looking up at her, his tongue lolling out of the side of his mouth and his eyes a soft liquid brown.

"If I let you up on the bed with me, do you promise not to hog it?" Emma gingerly sat down and patted a place beside her. "You promise not to eat me if I wake you up from a sound sleep?"

Beaker eagerly accepted her invitation, jumping up and plopping himself down right in the middle.

Emma carefully settled on what space was left, making sure she didn't jar her throbbing shoulder.

Beaker immediately snuggled against her.

There was an advantage to having a big dog, Emma decided. Beaker radiated a pleasant heat down her entire back, supporting her at the same time.

Maybe, just maybe, she'd keep him.

Chapter Sixteen

Five days. Five long, boring days of being treated like an invalid by five males, one of which had four legs and a cold nose.

She was totally sick of it. Her ankle was healed, her shoulder couldn't move but it was out of the sling, and her beautiful house looked like a dust bowl. It was time to clean it out, and Emma started with her watchdogs—including the four-legged one.

"Are you headed into town again this morning?" she asked Ben over her cup of tea, sitting across the table from the man who could, with just a look, send her pulse into overdrive.

She'd been getting a lot of those looks lately— whenever he was home. Ben had been leaving the house every morning for the last five days, returning only for supper. He called her every noon to check on how she was feeling, but Emma knew he was really checking to make sure she was behaving herself.

"Yes," he said, his piercing gray eyes sending another ripple of awareness down her spine as she tried to remember her question. "And what are your plans for the day?"

"I thought I would do some dusting."

"You're not well enough to do housework," he said with all the concern of a man who didn't see dust or cobwebs or accumulating laundry.

"I think I can manage a dustrag. And the first thing I'm cleaning out is all you men. Mikey's going to school, and Skyler is taking him. I want him to pick him up this afternoon also. Atwood can go to cabin six and do 'secretary' stuff. And you're taking Beaker with you into town. That poor beast is more bored than I am," she finished, raising her chin.

He merely smiled. "Are we driving you nuts, Emma?"

"I can't turn around without tripping over testosterone." She set her cup on the table with a thunk. "It's bad enough I have to stay cooped up all day; I don't need an army of guards watching my every move."

His frown returned. "You're liable to get an idea into your head and take off or something."

"A person can only take so much coddling, Ben."

He stared at her, his face chiseled stone. Emma felt another ripple run down her spine. Ben hadn't said one word about her nearly getting his son killed six days ago. And not once had he commented on the tangle of metal, now sitting behind the garage. He didn't speak of Wayne Poulin or the coordinates, of drug running or the shots fired at them. Nor did he mention the bullet wound in her shoulder.

Ben looked down at Beaker, who had sidled over and set his chin on her knee. "I suppose you could use a break," he said, his face softening. "You're too independent for all this attention, and Beaker and I could use a little time together."

Immensely pleased with her little victory, Emma patted Beaker on the head as she took a piece of toast from her plate and fed her new friend.

Ben pushed his chair back and walked over to the counter, where he grabbed the bowl of Elmer Fudge cookies. He returned to the table and proceeded to pick out a cookie, break it apart, and use a table knife to scrape the chocolate center into his plate.

Beaker immediately raised his head to watch.

Ben performed his little operation on two dozen cookies, making a huge pile of vanilla wafers. Then he swept them up and stuffed them in his pocket.

"Bribery, Ben?" Emma asked with a laugh.

"Self-defense," he answered as he stood up. "Come on, Beaker. Let's go for a ride." The dog stood, his tail wagging as he stared at Ben's pocket.

Ben walked to the door and opened it. "Come on, Beaker. Outside."

Her faithful guardian obediently trotted to the door, but stopped and looked back at her with uncertainty. Emma nodded. "Go on, boy. Go for a ride."

The dog bounded outside.

Ben let the screen door slap closed as he walked back to the table, and grabbed her chin in his hand. "Now that he's out of the way . . ." he whispered, just as his mouth captured hers.

Emma's toes instantly curled, and she had to grab the table for support. Holy hell, he was dangerous to her heart. But she wouldn't allow her fears to rob her of this enjoyment anymore. She wrapped her good arm around his neck and kissed him back.

That was all the invitation he needed. He carefully pulled her to her feet and into his arms, wrapping her in his warmth and strength and sweet-smelling maleness. Her head reeled with unleashed passion. The very floor beneath them rumbled. Dishes rattled. A pot on the counter crashed to the floor.

Emma pulled back and looked up at him. "How do you keep doing that?" she whispered in awe.

His frown made her laugh out loud.

"Jeez, Nem! That was a powerful one," Mikey said as he ran into the kitchen, sliding to a sudden stop when he saw his aunt in the arms of his father.

Emma realized she was clinging to Ben and stepped back.

The kitchen door banged open, and Atwood and

Skyler came running into the kitchen, Beaker fast on their heels. The two men's eyes were nearly bugging out of their heads; Beaker was whining and looking for a place to hide.

Emma laughed out loud.

"What was that?" Atwood asked. "Maine doesn't have earthquakes, does it?"

She shook her head. "Not usually. But we do get little rumbles every once and a while. Just enough to rattle the dishes."

"That was more than a rattle," Skyler interjected.

"It's the earth rebounding from being crushed by heavy glaciers thousands of years ago," Mikey told them. "Or it might be the hot springs," he said, looking at Emma. "They could be rumbling back to life."

Emma preferred the image of Benjamin Sinclair's arms upraised, commanding nature to his will. She forcibly shook it away. "Well, gentlemen. Since you're all here now, Ben has something he wants to tell you."

Ben looked at her, the spark of passion still in his eyes. "Maybe you should tell them, Emma, since you're so full of . . . surprises this morning."

Fighting down the heat suddenly threatening to color her face, Emma looked at the three expectant men, and at Beaker, who was sitting and staring up at her.

"Ah . . ." She looked at Mikey first. "Ben and I were thinking it's time for you to go back to school."

The boy immediately shook his head. "I want to stay home a few more days."

"I think you're over the trauma of crashing our plane, young man. You've milked it long enough."

"But—"

"Go to school, Mike. Skyler, you'll take him and pick him up," Ben added, looking at Skyler, who nodded in return.

"Atwood," Ben continued, "why don't you see about filling that woodshed out back."

Atwood quickly nodded, seeming relieved not to have to spend another day lurking close to the house.

Ben turned to her. "And you won't lift anything heavier than a dustrag?" he asked, looking skeptical.

She placed her right hand over her heart. "I promise not to get into any trouble," was all she said in agreement.

He kissed her firmly on the lips. "I'll be home early," he said, and walked out the door, calling Beaker to follow.

Emma went to the sink, and with a slightly trembling hand and pink face, she picked up the fallen pot. "Have a nice day, gentlemen," she said without looking up as they silently filed out the door. Each of them stopped only long enough to dip into the bowl of cookies on their way out before letting the screen door slam behind them.

Emma eyed the empty bowl. They were going through

the Elmer Fudge cookies like kibble. She didn't know where they had come from, but there was a whole case in the pantry. And there always seemed to be a large bowl of them on the counter. She had decided it was magic, because one minute she'd notice the bowl was empty, and the next minute it would be full.

Her little addiction seemed to be contagious.

It was three o'clock before Emma heard the kitchen door slam again over the voice of Mary Chapin Carpenter coming from her earphones. She looked up from the paperwork scattered over the table to see Ben and Beaker walk in, both looking like they owned the place.

Beaker trotted up and immediately pushed at her arm for attention. Emma pulled off her headset and shut off her radio, then reached down to greet her pet.

"Something smells good," Ben said, shedding his jacket. "What's in the oven?"

"I got sick of Mikey's cooking." Emma patted her dog. "He's got this thing about spices. That's turkey you're smelling."

Ben looked concerned. "How did you get it in the oven with only one arm?"

"I called in reinforcements. Greta put the turkey in the oven," she explained, looking back down at her paperwork. "You can either wash the potatoes or help me figure out how I'm going to come up with the funds for a new plane."

"You said it was insured," he said, scanning the paperwork from over her shoulder. "So what's the problem?"

"They're not paying out until the FAA has finished its investigation. I . . . um . . . I don't have an instructor's license, and Mikey isn't old enough to solo yet. And word's out that he was at the controls at the time of the crash. The investigation could take months." She tapped her pencil on her financial worksheet. "And I don't have months. In the winter I change the pontoons to skis and fly ice fishermen into remote ponds and biologists in for animal counts. I need to replace my plane."

"I'll give you the money," he said, rolling up his sleeves and going to the sink, apparently confident the problem was solved.

"No."

He stopped in midstep and turned. "No?"

Emma picked her words carefully. "I appreciate the offer, Ben, but I don't want your money. Don't take it personally. It's just that I . . . I wouldn't be comfortable," she finished, looking down at her papers.

He walked back to the table and stood over her, and silently waited. He was going to take it *very* personally, she realized. He'd made a generous, innocent offer, and she'd rebuffed him, no matter how diplomatically. Several long seconds passed before she found the nerve to look up.

"I can just write you a check."

"I know you can, but I want to do this myself. Paying for a new plane isn't the problem; it's waiting for the insurance to pay that's got me stumped. I just thought that with your business background, you might have an idea how I can temporarily shuffle my money around."

He suddenly turned and headed back to the sink, once more rolling up his sleeves. "You need an accountant for that."

Emma blew out a breath with enough force to ripple her papers. He wasn't angry; he was hurt.

She began gathering up her papers into an unorganized pile. Hell. She felt like throwing the papers into her woodstove, then crawling in behind them. She hadn't meant to hurt Ben.

The last paper to go on her pile was one Emma didn't recognize. It was legal length and folded in fourths, and she knew it hadn't been there ten minutes ago. She opened it up to read it, but didn't get past the first line.

The silence that suddenly fell over the room was so absolute, Emma could hear the blood rushing through her veins. The pounding of her heart was deafening. The room around her receded into the recesses of her consciousness as she opened her mouth and closed it again.

She finally found her voice, which didn't seem to be

hers at all. "This is an application for a marriage license."

"Yes," came a solid, faraway voice from right beside her.

"It's all filled out."

"Only one line's still blank," Ben said.

Emma stared at the document. Every piece of information about her was there, from her birth date and birthplace to her parents' names and her Social Security number. Everything was filled in for Benjamin Sinclair as well.

"Michael. Your middle name is Michael," was all she could say, fixated by that one small fact.

"Kelly knew my middle name."

Emma finally looked at him. "This is a *marriage* license application," she repeated.

"Yes."

"And all I have to do is sign it, and we can get married."

"You would also have to show up for the ceremony."

"Are you . . . is this a proposal?"

"I believe I already proposed. This is the next step."

Emma rubbed her forehead. "I don't remember a proposal, exactly. I do remember you mentioning your plans for *after* we got married. You said something about running your business from Maine."

He pulled her hand away from her forehead, holding it in his as he went down on one knee. "Sign it, Emma."

"I . . . I have to think about this," she whispered, tugging on her hand.

"You *have* thought about it."

"I've had plenty of other things on my mind lately."

"You're going to sign it eventually, so why not take this load off your shoulders now? Sign the paper and I'll take care of the rest."

"Just like you plan to take care of me?"

He shook his head. "I have no intention of taking over your life, Emma. You'll be just as independent after we're married as you are now. You just won't be alone anymore."

He was telling her to trust him.

Which she already did.

He was telling her they could spend the rest of their lives together.

Which she wanted to do very badly.

He was saying he respected her independence.

Which she needed to keep in order to survive.

But he wasn't telling her that he loved her.

Emma's eyes locked with his, and that was how Greta found them.

"Land sakes, that boy can fill a hamper with clothes!" her friend complained as she walked in from the great room. She came to a halt in midstride and stared. Her eyes widened when she spotted Beaker sitting next to the stove, eyeing her back.

Greta returned her gaze to the table. "It's nice to see

you again, Benjamin Sinclair." She set her basket down and wiped her hands on her slacks before she reached out in greeting. "You might not remember me. I'm Greta LaVoie, a friend of Michael and Emma."

Ben stood and accepted Greta's hand, taking it between his as he smiled down at her warmly. "Miss LaVoie. I certainly remember you bake the best cakes this side of the Canadian border."

Greta, who wasn't charmed by the best of men, blushed like a peach. "So you finally came," she said, clasping Ben's hands within hers. "I'm so glad. Michael's been wanting to meet you for a very long time."

"I'm deeply glad to have discovered him," he answered before pulling away.

"And now you'll protect him and Emma from whoever's trying to kill them?"

"What makes you think someone wants to kill them?"

Greta frowned up at him in disbelief. "They were shot at. Their plane crashed. They know too much."

"Half the county knows as much as they do by now."

Greta nodded. "You just keep that boy out of this logging war. And who's this?" she asked, going over to the German shepherd.

"That's Beaker. Emma's new pet," Ben told her.

Greta looked at Emma. "But you're scared to death of any dog larger than a squirrel." She looked at Ben. "Emma Jean was chased halfway across town by a Doberman when she was seven. I had to walk that child to the store for six months after that. She had terrible nightmares for years."

"She likes Beaker."

Greta began petting the dog, who welcomed the attention.

Emma looked down at the table, picked up the application for her marriage license, and quickly signed on the one remaining blank line. Then she folded it back into fourths and pushed it to the center of the table.

A large hand swooped down and grabbed it, and Emma watched it disappear into Ben's shirt pocket. She lifted her gaze to find piercing gray eyes staring back at her with triumphant satisfaction.

By God, she'd done it now.

Chapter Seventeen

It was well into the small hours of the night—the time when the mind is drugged with sleep, when dreams and reality mesh. Emma came awake slowly, her senses rousing one by one. The now familiar warmth snuggled against her side comforted her, as did the peaceful shadows of her room and the feel of her own pillow under her head. Only her nose was at odds with her surroundings, nudging her further awake.

She was smelling springtime. Flowers. Specifically, roses.

A sound was her second clue all was not right within her realm of security. From the floor came the soft noise of Beaker contentedly gnawing on a piece of rawhide.

Which meant the warmth beside her was not her dog.

Adrenaline fired her awake into frozen awareness.

The heavy warmth beside her rose to loom like a dark specter as the blankets tightened, entrapping her.

"Sshhh. Don't panic. It's me."

"Ben?"

"You're a sound sleeper. I've been lying beside you for nearly an hour."

Emma tried to throw off the last cobwebs of sleep. She was suddenly living her long-held dream of sharing a bed with Benjamin Sinclair. All of her fantasies bubbled to the surface—the warmth of his body, the welcome weight pushing against her, the feel of his breath on her face. His smell invaded her senses, making it impossible to tell reality from longing. She closed her eyes, savoring the feel of his weight.

"Wake up, Emma," he whispered.

"I don't want to."

"I want you awake when I make love to you, Em."

She opened her eyes and found his face mere inches from hers, his eyes aglow with reflected moonlight, his mouth a white gleam of humor.

"Okay," she sighed.

"Oh no. I want to hear the words first."

"Words?"

He blew an impatient sigh, wafting her hair. "The words to back up that paper you signed today, that give me permission to be in this bed." He softly kissed the end of the nose. "I need to hear them soon, before I go insane."

"I do trust you, Ben. With my life, my home, and my nephew. I trust you."

The moonlight illuminated his frown. She knew what he wanted to hear; she just wasn't sure she could say it out loud.

"And?" he growled, every muscle in his body tightening.

"And I think you're the most handsome man I've ever met. You're more beautiful than a sunset, and more solid than the mountains. You're more man than I ever hoped to be with."

Suddenly his hands were in her hair, capturing her head while he lifted her face and kissed her full on the mouth.

No vision from her imagination could ever consume her so completely. No other man could waken her feminine yearnings as fiercely. Emma parted her lips, matching his passion with her own. She tasted him, pulling his essence into herself as she struggled to free her hands to gather him closer.

He broke the kiss, drawing in a shuddering breath that matched hers, and stared down at her with eyes the color of polished lake ice.

"I swear, Ben—if the ground starts shaking again, I'm going to scream."

He laid his forehead on hers. "I'm about to forget all about my noble intentions, your sore shoulder, and the words I'm still waiting to hear."

"I can give you what you want without saying it out loud, Ben."

"No," he said, lifting his head. "We'll seal our bond tonight, Emma, but not until you surrender yourself. You can be strong and stubborn and fearless with the rest of the world, but with me, right now, you need to let down your guard. No pretenses. No digressions. I want you warm and soft and vulnerable, and that begins with you saying the words out loud."

He was done with the chase, and he wasn't about to settle for a compromise. He wanted total, complete, irrevocable surrender.

"I love you," she whispered. "I always have and I always will. I've been waiting fifteen years for you to come for me."

She waited, then said, "I'm not the only one baring her soul here, Sinclair."

"Don't you know that I love you!" His mouth captured hers again, making her burn all the way to the center of her being.

As a declaration of love, it was about as romantic and subtle as a bull moose bugling its intentions. Ben tore the blankets from the bed and fell on her with all the finesse of a man well beyond his patience. Completely naked, he scorched her skin right through her flimsy nightgown.

Smelling roses again, Emma opened her eyes to see petals floating through the air, set off by the blankets thrown to the floor. She was completely surrounded by rose petals, and by the man who had strewn them over the bed while she slept.

With an eagerness that matched his, Emma wrapped her arms around Ben's neck and met his passion, raining kisses over the hard planes of his face, feeling the scratch of his beard tickle her with joy.

"I love you," she whispered into his ear just before she lightly bit it.

He laughed out loud, the sound warming her. He found the neck of her nightgown and ripped it down to her waist as he pulled it from her shoulders. Another cloud of petals filled the air, dancing in the moonlight as lightly as her heart.

He suddenly stopped above her, then leaned down and softly kissed the bandage on her left shoulder. "My God, I could have lost you." He gathered her against him fiercely. "I nearly lost you."

"Sshhh. I'm okay, and I'm here," she whispered, hugging him just as fiercely. "Love me, Ben, and see if you can make my dishes rattle again."

He lifted his head and returned her smile. "Oh, I intend to. I may even crack a few of them," he finished, cupping her left breast.

Emma sucked in a surprised breath as he moved his thumb across her nipple, and she arched her back in eager acceptance. She used her own hands to explore his chest, which was wide and hard and hot, and dug her fingers into his shoulders when he took her nipple into his mouth.

She moaned, kissing his hair and running her fingers through it. She felt his hands at her waist, pulling her panties down, along with what was left of her night-gown. Within seconds she was as naked as he was.

"You've got the body of an angel," he whispered as he moved back over her, bringing her into intimate contact with the proof of his desire. "You're *my* angel."

Impatient, she wrapped her legs around his hips and placed the heart of her womanhood at the tip of his shaft.

"Wait," he gritted, trembling with restraint.

Ignoring him, Emma lifted her hips, sheathing her-self over his manhood as she exerted pressure with her legs on the back of his. He finished the task with a groan, burying himself deep within her.

She squeaked at the discomfort of the invasion, bracing her hands on his shoulders as if to hold back a mountain. He instantly stilled.

"You're damn tight, Emma."

"You're damn big, Ben."

He smiled at her as he slowly started to move, caus-ing a sensation so exquisite Emma was afraid she might have left nail marks in his chest.

Not that he seemed to notice. His head was thrown back and his eyes were closed, and she could see he was caught in a maelstrom of pleasure. Tentatively she began to move her own hips.

"Be still," he gritted through clenched teeth, looking down with eyes darkened with desperation. "Or this is going to be over before it begins."

She reached up and wiped the sweat on his forehead. "And I thought you were a powerful god," she said, lightly tugging his hair. "You're merely mortal after all."

He shut her up by capturing her mouth with his, and began moving more earnestly as he reached down and found the very center of her nature.

Emma ignited like a volcano, molten white heat consuming her as she cried out in convulsing pleasure. The moon and all the stars flooded the darkness that had surrounded her heart all these years. She became one with the man of her dreams as she felt him shudder deep inside her, his own cry softly echoing through the room.

She tried to calm her racing heart as she held Ben close. Small convulsions continued to rack her body, pleasant little ripples of waning ecstasy. Breathing, which she desperately needed to do right now, was nearly impossible.

She shifted in an attempt to wiggle free.

"Are you hurt, Emma? Did I injure your shoulder?" he asked, concern rousting him as nothing else could.

She smiled up at him, and pulled him down to her side as she continued to cuddle him close. "No. I just needed some air."

He returned her smile with a cocky one. "I take your breath away?" He brushed the hair back from her face. "Not bad for a mere mortal."

As if his teasing had awoken the gods of the underworld, the soft rumble of trembling earth approached, growing more ominous in volume until even the bed began to shake. The windows rattled in their sashes. The lamp on her nightstand clinked with growing violence.

Beaker whined.

Emma gasped. "Dammit, Benjamin. Cut that out!" she hissed.

He jumped out of bed and nearly fell. "Me? It's your damn hot springs!"

She sat up, hugging the blankets to her chest as she looked at him.

"This is getting eerie." He caught her staring, and grabbed a pillow and held it at his waist, covering up all the best parts. "What's happening in your woods?"

Emma sighed. "You're not superstitious, are you?"

The bed dipped and she found herself flat on her back, Ben looming over her again. "It's not funny." He kissed her to stop her laughter. When he was finished with that chore, he kissed her again. Emma guessed the second time was just to prove he could without the windows rattling again.

"I have to go," he whispered into her mouth.

"Why?"

"It's nearly dawn. And when Mike catches us in bed, I want us to be married."

Emma sighed again. "Yeah."

"So when will that be, Em?"

"Well . . . when do you want to get married?"

"Tomorrow."

She burst out laughing again. "How about next spring?"

"How about later this week?"

"A Christmas wedding, then."

"Thanksgiving."

"But that's only two weeks away!"

"Two damn long weeks, if you ask me. What's the problem, Emma?"

"I want a nice wedding. It's the only one I'm going to have."

Ben heaved a mighty sigh. "You can have as nice a wedding as you can put together in two weeks. That's as long as I'm waiting."

"Or?"

He smiled but he didn't look amused. "Or I will shanghai you on one of my cargo ships and have the captain marry us at sea."

"That's . . . you can't . . . oh, okay. Thanksgiving, then," she conceded, sealing her bargain with a quick kiss. "In my church. With Greta as my maid of honor."

"I don't care if Pitiful stands up with you as long as

it's legal." Ben stood up and began hunting for his clothes.

Emma unabashedly watched, her knees tucked under her chin, admiring the play of muscles that made his movements efficient and graceful.

"Thank you for the roses. I've never received flowers before," she said as she picked up several petals and held them to her nose.

"You're welcome." He kissed her and walked out of the room.

As soon as the door closed, she scooped up a hand-ful of petals and inhaled their scent with gusto. She fell back on the pillow, letting the petals cascade over her face as she closed her eyes and inhaled again.

Damn if they didn't smell like moss!

Though he considered himself firmly grounded in real-ity, there were times Ben could actually *sense* some-thing lurking, preparing to pounce. It was never anything tangible or even definable, just a feeling of impending disaster.

He believed in the mysteries of this world, and he also believed there were things beyond human under-standing better not dwelled on. But mostly Ben be-lieved his gut when it was telling him something was wrong. And for the last week, it had been telling him something was very wrong in Medicine Gore.

There was evil walking these woods, threatening

Emma and Mike and the new life Ben had found with them. They thought Poulin's coordinates were a drug-drop site, but he felt they were part of something much more ugly. He'd first noticed it two days ago when he'd checked them out himself, and he felt it now, as he stood at the spot they marked.

"A dog would help," Atwood said from ten feet away, scuffing at the ground with his foot, disturbing years of rotting leaves. "One of those dogs used to search for bodies after disasters."

Ben turned to the quiet, intelligent detective. "It's been ten years."

Atwood shrugged as he continued to walk in circles, scanning the forest floor. "Dogs have remarkable noses."

"When we get back, call one in. But keep it quiet. I don't want Emma or Mike to know what we're doing until we've found something concrete."

"I'll put Sklyer on it."

Ben fought the chill that suddenly ran down his spine, hunkering deeper into his parka as he shoved his hands in his pockets. "Why don't you head into town and try to find out where Poulin has disappeared to," he suggested. "If it looks like he's really out of town, you may get your chance to check out his room."

Atwood looked up and grinned. "A little more sub-tly than your lady did?"

Ben lifted a brow. "I'm assuming you have more ex-perience at that sort of thing."

"I can get in and out without leaving any tracks," he drawled as he walked to Ben. "What about the old lady?"

"Emma said Greta was coming out to Medicine Creek this afternoon to start the wedding plans."

Atwood's face lit up. "Congratulations. You're really going to tie the knot?"

"Just as tight as I can."

He had no second thoughts about marrying Emma and legally adopting Mike. And if the small army he'd brought from New York couldn't put Wayne Poulin away, Ben was taking his new family to the other side of the earth until this was finally settled. One way or another, he wasn't letting the evil touch them.

"Go ahead on back," he told Atwood. "I'm going to hang around a while longer." He looked at the forest again. "The key to this puzzle is here. I can feel it."

"We rode out here together. How you planning on getting home?"

Ben shrugged. "I tossed a pack in the truck before we left. I'll walk back."

Atwood looked incredulous. "It's over twenty miles."

"It'll give me time to think. And according to the map, those old hot springs are between here and home. I think I'll stop and check them out."

Atwood turned wary. "That could be dangerous, what with all the tremors lately. There could be noxious gases escaping."

Ben started walking to where they'd parked the Suburban. "I'll be careful."

Atwood fell into step beside him. "You want me to do any checking on the dam that was blown up fifteen years ago while I'm in town?"

"Leave that to the others. We'll get together tonight and discuss what we've found." He stopped and looked back at the forest. "My gut says it's all connected. I don't know how yet, but I think Poulin had something to do with Charlie Sands's death and Kelly's disappearance."

At the truck, Ben pulled out his pack and the high-powered rifle he'd borrowed from Emma's gun cabinet that morning. Then he lifted out the small cage that held Homer.

"You're really getting into this woodsman stuff, aren't you?" Atwood said with a chuckle.

"When I mentioned to Mike I was coming out here, he asked me to bring Homer with me and let him go. He wants to find out if the bird can find his way back without the benefit of having flown here," Ben said.

The wilderness did intrigue him, though. More than that, he was beginning to find a contentment he hadn't known existed.

Atwood shrugged and climbed into the driver's seat.

Ben settled his pack on his back, and picked up his rifle and Homer. "While you're in town, find out when the plane will be in. Push it if you have to. I want it here by Thanksgiving."

Atwood grinned. "A wedding present?"

"Yup. That way she'll have to accept it."

"She's gonna be one grateful bride. The plane you ordered makes the stealth fighter jet look like a relic. It's got every electronic toy known to man."

"Every groom deserves a grateful bride, don't you think?" Ben said as he slapped Atwood on the shoulder. "I'm counting on it."

Atwood started the truck and drove off. Ben watched the Suburban slowly make its way down the overgrown road, waiting until it was out of sight before he headed back to the one spot in this vast, beautiful forest that seemed to be lacking a soul.

The fall morning was crystal clear, the sun bathing the land with warmth. Yet when he stepped into the realm of Wayne's coordinates, it was like stepping into a cold, lifeless circle of evil.

Chapter Eighteen

"*Beaker, I'm going to* step on you if you don't get out of my way," Emma warned for the fifth time.

For some mysterious reason, the dog had been glued to her side all morning. She had already given the clinging animal numerous cookies trying to calm him, but now she was feeling ill from eating all the chocolate centers.

With a sigh of defeat, she sat down on the couch and patted a place beside her. Beaker immediately jumped up and laid his head on her lap.

"What's bothering you?" she asked, scratching his ear.

He lifted only his canine brows and whined.

Emma gave him the attention he needed as she stared into the crackling fire in the hearth. Maybe the dog had caught the mood of the lodge's other inhabitants. It was like there was a pregnant cloud hanging over Medicine Creek Camps. Heck, even the woods had been rumbling.

The phone rang, and Emma got up to answer it. "Hello."

"Emmie? Is that you?"

Emma went utterly still.

"Are you there, Emmie? Hello?"

"K-Kelly," she whispered. "Kelly? Is that you?"

"Hello, sister."

Emma gripped the phone with both hands. "Where are you?"

"In Bangor. I need you to come see me, Emmie. Right now. Please? I have to talk to you."

"You're in *Bangor?*"

"At the mall. I'll be at the center court waiting for you. Hurry up."

"Wait. Kelly!"

A dial tone answered her urgent plea.

Emma stared at the phone until it started buzzing loudly. She finally set it down, though it took her three attempts to put it on the charger because her hands were shaking so much. And still she continued to stare, not seeing anything but Kelly's face in her mind's eye.

Kelly hadn't even asked about her son. Emma's gaze drifted to the picture on the mantel, of her and Kelly and five-year-old Michael on his first day of school. "What sort of mother doesn't even ask about her son?" she whispered into the stark silence.

Beaker whined and nudged her thigh. Emma looked down at the dog staring up at her with large brown eyes. "Maybe she's . . . do you think she could be scared, Beak? Ten years is an awful long time."

Emma knelt down to hug the dog, and let out a shuddering sigh. "Here I go again, making excuses for her. But just hearing her call me 'Emmie' . . . I—I guess I should pity her more than hate her." Emma buried her face in Beaker's neck. "She missed so much not being here to watch Michael grow up."

Emma considered stopping at the high school and picking up Mikey before heading to Bangor. He deserved to see his mother, and truth be told, she wasn't sure she was emotionally strong enough to face Kelly alone. "No, that wouldn't be fair to Mikey," she muttered into Beaker's neck, stifling a sob. "He *deserves* this reunion to be right here, in his home, where he'll have some sense of control."

Emma finally stood up, brushing away the tears streaming down her face, and took a deep breath. So Kelly wanted to talk, did she? Well, by God, she would talk to *all* of them, Ben included. She intended to drag her sister back here kicking and screaming if she had to. "Come on, Beak. We're going for a ride."

She blindly strode to her truck, and Beaker jumped up on the driver's seat ahead of her. He stood in her spot, whining, not letting her in the truck.

"I know you don't want me going anywhere, Beak, but I have to go get Kelly."

The dog whined, not budging an inch. Emma ended up pushing him over and scooting behind the wheel despite his protests. "If you don't want me leaving you here, you better hush up and sit down. It's a two-hour ride." Emma started the truck and backed it out of the yard, spitting gravel as she headed for the main road.

The dog scrambled to remain upright. "It's okay, Beak." She pushed him into a lying position. "That's a good boy. You like riding. Just relax and watch out the window."

Emma took a deep breath to calm her racing heart and slowed the pickup to a safer speed. She was contemplating various ways to approach Kelly when she rounded a curve and had to slam on the breaks to avoid running into Wayne Poulin.

Great. Just what she needed right now.

Unless Kelly had called him, too, and he'd been on his way out here to tell her?

His truck had obviously broken down. The hood was up and he hadn't even gotten it off to the side of the road. He was standing by the driver's door, his hands on his hips and his beady little eyes narrowed against the dust.

Emma shut off her truck and stared at him through the windshield. A growl rattled low in Beaker's chest.

She wasn't getting out of the truck. Wayne Poulin had a two-way radio, just like everyone else, and could call for a tow.

He walked up to her door and Emma rolled down the window just enough to speak to him.

"I need a ride into town," he said without greeting.

He certainly didn't sound as if Kelly had called him. "I'm in a hurry, Wayne. And I'm headed in the opposite direction. I'll send someone back—"

He reached in his jacket pocket and pulled out a gun, which he aimed at her face. Beaker's low rumble escalated to a vicious growl as he tried to crawl over Emma's lap and put himself between her and the danger.

Wayne moved his gun in Beaker's direction. "Settle him down, Emma, or I'll shoot him. I'm going to climb in the back, and you're going to move your truck into the trees to your right. Don't start it until I'm settled. Understand?"

Holding on to Beaker's collar and pushing him down in the seat beside her, Emma nodded. Wayne scaled the side of her truck and crouched behind her. Beaker nearly tore her hand off as he strained to face the threat.

"It's okay, Beak. Take it easy," she said, watching Wayne in her mirror.

He tapped on the glass with the barrel of his gun. "Start the truck and go slowly," he said. "Don't try anything, or I'll pull the trigger."

She believed him. She'd never trusted Wayne, and she certainly didn't doubt the man was mean enough to shoot her or her dog.

The question was, why?

Kidnapping her didn't make sense, so why was he pulling this stupid stunt?

Emma started the truck and put it in gear, letting it idle its way into the woods.

"That's far enough. Now shut it off," Wayne ordered.

She did as she was told and sat there, staring straight ahead, one hand on Beaker to keep him calm. She was afraid that as soon as she opened her door, all hell was going to break loose.

"Now get out."

Very firmly, Emma commanded Beaker to stay. The dog whined in protest, his hackles still raised, his eyes never leaving Wayne as he moved to her door. Emma opened the door and tried to scoot out and keep Beaker inside.

His gun poised, Wayne pulled her door all the way open.

Beaker lunged.

So did Emma.

The gun went off and she heard a yelp as all three of them fell to the ground. She dove for Wayne just as he was taking aim at her dog again.

"Run!" she screamed, kicking at Beaker as she tried to get the gun.

Wayne pulled the trigger again right next to her ear, deafening her to the point of pain. An outraged snarl erupted from Beaker as he darted for the safety of the bushes. Wayne fired again. There was no yelp, only the cracking of branches as the dog fled.

Emma lay on the ground on her back, holding her left shoulder. She didn't know which hurt more, her ear or her old wound.

"I've got three bullets left, Emma. Give my any more trouble and I'll use every one of them on you. Now get up," he said as he hauled her to her feet.

Emma stifled a cry of pain, afraid Beaker would come running back to help her. Wayne kept darting looks at the bushes as he dragged her over to his truck.

"Shut the hood," he ordered, holding her captive by her hair.

She did as he asked, and he hauled her around to the passenger side of the truck.

"Open it and get in."

She opened the door, but before she could get in he pushed her down on the seat, spinning her around while letting go of her hair to grab one of her arms.

"Put your hands in front of you." He darted one more look at the woods, then tucked his gun in his belt. He reached in on the floor of the truck and got a rope and tied her hands together.

"What's gotten into you, Wayne? Why are you doing this? I didn't find *anything* at those coordinates."

He finished tightening the knot, then glared at her. "I'm taking you out of the equation. Once everyone realizes you've run off like your sister, Sinclair will take his kid and go back to New York. Then I'll finally be home free."

Take her out of the . . . "Are you nuts? Nobody's going to believe I've run off! They know I'd never abandon Mikey."

He used her bound hands to haul her into a sitting position, shoved her feet inside, and pushed the lock on the door but didn't shut it yet. "They'll believe it once I start the rumor that Sinclair paid you a tidy sum to disappear so he could have the boy free and clear. And that if you didn't take the money, he'd ruin your business and take his son home anyway."

"You're crazy. No one would believe something like that."

He laughed insanely. "They've believed all the other rumors I've been spreading for the last ten years. They'll believe it, all right, because everyone knows bad blood always wins out." He stepped back with a twisted grin. "That dress you wore to the dance certainly showed everyone you're no better than your sister," he added, slamming the door shut.

Emma drew in a shuddering breath as she slowly lifted her hands to work her sore shoulder. Wayne took a hesitant step toward where Beaker had disappeared, his gun in his hand, the hammer cocked to fire. He waited, listening, and Emma prayed her dog was smart enough to stay hidden. Getting himself killed wouldn't help her; it would only empower Wayne even more.

He finally gave up and came back to the truck. Without saying a word, he got in, started the truck, and headed away from the main road, deeper into the forest.

Emma slouched down so she could see the road behind them in her side mirror. She hoped Wayne's first shot hadn't been deep enough that Beaker would bleed to death. She didn't see any sign of her dog, her truck . . . or anything else to say she'd even been there.

Chapter Nineteen

For forty minutes Emma rode in frightened, painful silence beside the man she'd known since childhood.

It was as if something in Wayne had snapped. She had never liked him, but now he appeared to have traveled beyond reality into darkness. He was sweating. His face was flushed and he gripped the steering wheel with white-knuckled tension.

It hadn't taken Emma long to realize where they were going. The bumpy, overgrown track was leading to the coordinates she wished she'd never found.

Wayne was staying off the Golden Road, a private gravel highway used by the paper mill to transport logs. There would be plenty of trucks on the Golden this morning, which was probably why Wayne was avoiding it.

So they were taking the long way, which involved a maze of unused tote roads that made the going slow and arduous, and painful to her throbbing shoulder. The entire right side of her body was bruised from banging against the door, since her tied hands made her unable to brace herself against the rougher spots in the road.

She kept peeking in her side mirror for any sign of Beaker. She didn't know much about dogs, but she didn't think they could travel nonstop for great distances, especially wounded. Yet Beaker seemed more remarkable than most. Maybe . . .

"Who called me pretending to be Kelly?" she finally asked into the silence.

If she'd been thinking with her head instead of her heart, she'd have realized it wasn't Kelly earlier.

"A friend from Greenville." Wayne looked over, his smile nasty. "Charlene thought she was setting you up for a surprise party." He reached over and roughly tugged on her hair. "Surprise, Emma."

She pulled away, banging her side against the door again. "What's this all about, Wayne? What did you mean, you're 'taking me out of the equation'?"

The rough road drew his attention and she didn't get an answer. She banged her head against the rifle in the gun rack behind her. A few strands of her hair caught on it, and she barely stifled a whimper when they hit another bump and it pulled the snarl out by the roots.

They finally reached the spot in the road where Emma and Mikey had found the tire tracks almost two weeks ago. Wayne suddenly let loose a curse. Emma followed his gaze and saw that the ground around the mud puddles was wet.

Which meant someone else had been there this morning.

Wayne looked past her to the mountain above, his eyes assessing. He opened his door, grabbed the rifle from behind her head, then hauled her out his door by her bound hands, driving her hip into the steering wheel and pulling on her wounded shoulder.

He relentlessly pulled her down the road, scanning the forest as he walked. Suddenly he stopped and hunched down by a puddle, trying to read the tracks. "They've left already," he said, standing and dragging her into the forest.

Taking advantage of the fact that Wayne was paying attention to his surroundings, Emma tripped him when he ducked under a branch, jerked free of his grip, then ran back through the path they'd made.

Emma heard snapping branches behind her as he scrambled to his feet in pursuit. Her bound hands made it nearly impossible to balance herself as she pushed through the snagging bushes and stumbled over roots. Wayne tackled her just as she made it to the road. He landed heavily on top of her, driving her into the ground, and Emma cried out in pain.

Wayne grabbed her hair, growling with frustration.

"Why are you *doing* this!" she cried.

He got to his feet and pulled her up by the hair again. Emma kicked him, and he smacked her side with the butt of his rifle, making her draw back against the pain.

Still without speaking, he took her deeper into the forest again, shoving her ahead of him, using his rifle to prod her in the back whenever she stumbled.

It seemed forever before he jerked her to a stop. Emma looked around and realized that they were standing at the exact same spot she and Mikey had found. Only now the earth was well trodden, the leaves and pine needles scuffed in places. Wayne also looked around, and realized his secret place had been invaded.

He shoved her hard, and Emma fell back with a scream.

"This is your fault," he growled. "I had the environmentalists stirred up enough to pass the no-clear-cutting legislation." He waved the gun barrel at the forest. "This would have remained untouched. Everything would have stayed safe." He pointed the gun back at her. "Your snooping ruined everything."

Emma scooted back out of his reach. What he was saying didn't make sense. Wayne would want the clear-cutting legislation to be defeated, not passed. His livelihood depended on cutting down trees. "You've been the one fueling this war all along? Why?"

He hunched down in front of her, sitting on his heels and balancing against his rifle. "This section was marked for clear-cutting next summer, which means there would have been men and large machinery all over these woods. I couldn't have that."

"Because it would have ruined your drug-running operation? You could just find another drop point."

He looked startled, then suddenly barked in laughter. "Drug running! Is that what you think?"

Confused, Emma nodded.

He laughed again. "You're dumber than your slut of a sister, you know that? I'm not running drugs."

Emma didn't like the sound of his laughter. Wayne wasn't just trying to cover his tracks; he truly was insane.

"Then what's this all about?"

He jumped to his feet, lifting his hat off, then re-settling it into place. He repeated the ritual several times, and began pacing in front of her, a sweating ball of nervous energy, his eyes pinpoints of madness. He pulled the handgun from his belt, still holding his rifle in his other fist.

"Kelly wouldn't stop probing, either, until she found out my secret." He stopped and pointed the handgun at her. "When I tried to explain it had been an accident, she still didn't believe me. She went ballistic and said she was going to tell Ramsey."

Emma felt the blood drain from her face. "What did you try to explain to her?"

He stopped pacing and stared at her with a surprised expression on his face. "That I killed Charlie."

Emma stiffened in shock. "Wha . . . ?" Her mind reeled as images of her father's body suddenly surfaced; beaten and battered by the force of the water carrying him down the valley below the dam. And more images: of Kelly's melancholy and the months of pregnancy that followed, of Wayne's public decree that the environmentalists were responsible, and that Benjamin Sinclair had led the terrorist act.

"*You* blew up the dam?" Emma stared back at him as her anger began to surface. "But why? Why did you kill my father? "

He started pacing again. "I blew the dam to make it look like Charlie got caught in the flood, but he was already dead. He blamed me for getting Kelly pregnant." Wayne stopped pacing again, the handgun hanging in his hand. "When I told him his slut of a daughter had slept with Sinclair and that it was his kid, Charlie exploded. We fought. It was an accident, I tell you! So I blew up the dam to cover my tracks."

"And then you blamed Ben."

His eyes ignited with hatred. "The bastard should be rotting in jail."

"Kelly didn't run away, did she, Wayne?" Emma said, as things slowly began to fall into place.

"You'll find out soon enough, Emma Jean. Assuming

there really is an afterlife." He pulled back the hammer on the revolver and aimed it at her.

Emma picked up a handful of dirt and threw it at him just as a blur of brown fur suddenly raced in from the left, landing on Wayne with an ungodly snarl of outrage. Wayne screamed in surprise. Beaker grabbed his arm with deadly precision, and the two of them tumbled away.

Emma didn't wait to see who won. She jumped up and ran up the mountain, since he had the truck keys in his pocket. She had also noticed the two-way radio had no microphone; Wayne must have hidden it before he'd ambushed her.

Her only hope lay in the forest.

Emma flinched at the explosion of gunshot behind her but didn't look back. She couldn't let Beaker down by getting caught again. She heard no yelp of pain, only Wayne cursing and the breaking of twigs as Beaker ran away in the opposite direction.

Could a dog be that smart? Could he actually be trying to divide Wayne's attention?

Emma dashed up the mountain. Wayne couldn't effectively pursue her while staying on guard against Beaker, so her odds of surviving had improved immensely. But the going was difficult, and her bound hands made progress slow. Winded, Emma finally stopped behind a tree to work at the ropes with her teeth.

Wayne was a good woodsman, and the knots were

stubborn. She heard a noise coming up the mountain, and leaned over to see Wayne picking his way toward her. He spent just as much time looking behind himself, and Emma smiled. Beaker had escaped and Wayne was worried. She definitely had a chance.

She began moving again, this time in a more deliberate direction. There was a large, deep chasm between here and the beaver pond where they'd parked the plane almost two weeks ago. If she could get across it and then destroy her route, Wayne would have to walk two miles out of his way to get to her.

With every step she took, Emma knew she was putting more distance between herself and Wayne. She was in excellent shape despite her wounded shoulder; a lifetime of hiking had made her legs strong and her mind sharp.

Wayne was also at home in the woods, but even while he was hunting her, he was also being hunted by Beaker. And the man *was* demented; she'd seen it in his eyes when he'd pointed the gun at her and pulled back the hammer. Wayne Poulin had slipped over the edge of reality, which meant his perception would be skewed.

She made steady progress, and soon heard the roaring of water cascading over boulders in its rapid decent down the mountain. With an urgency born of desperation, she walked along the eastern edge of the gorge, looking for a fallen log she could use to get across.

The only one she found was wedged high up on a

precipice, which meant she had to get her hands free. Emma found a jagged rock and began rubbing the rope against it, all the while scanning the forest behind her, knowing she'd never hear Wayne approach over the roar of the falls.

Her hands were a bloody mess by the time the ropes finally gave way, and Emma scrambled up the giant boulders to the fallen tree.

It was a long way down the churning icy water, and the log looked skinny and unstable. Emma carefully stepped onto the log.

The sound of gunfire stopped Ben in midstride, and its direction had him running back. Those hadn't been hunting shots: they'd been too sharp to be from a shotgun and too muffled to come from a high-powered rifle. Which left only a handgun.

And people didn't usually hunt with handguns unless the target was human.

Ben came to a sliding stop when he finally spotted the prey in the distance, and his heart stopped. Emma was on a log spanning the gorge, trying to walk over the roaring brook.

He broke into a sweat. There was no way she could make it. The log was too unstable, too high, and too rotted. But he couldn't take his eyes off her to see what she was fleeing from; nor could he holler for her to go back, as she'd never hear him.

Then he heard the crack of another shot, this one sharp, telling him it came from a high-powered rifle. He saw the bullet slam into the log just beneath Emma's feet.

He also heard Emma's scream of surprise, and helplessly watched her fall.

He started running parallel to the gorge, moving with the current and watching for Emma to reemerge. Shedding his rifle and gear, Ben swiftly climbed down the boulders. He saw Emma coming toward him, fighting to stay atop the froth as she slammed into rocks and debris. He lay on a boulder on his belly and extended both arms, bracing himself for leverage.

He caught her by her shirtsleeve and pulled, then wrapped his hand around her arm. She nearly hauled him in, the current was so swift. He was afraid he was pulling her shoulder from its socket but refused to let go, even when she slammed up against the rock he was on.

He heard the air rush out of her lungs as she screamed in pain, and he reached down with his other hand and grabbed her belt. Adjusting his position for maximum purchase, he pulled her out of the icy water with one swift motion.

She came up swinging, clipping him on the side of his head with her free hand. The attack was so unexpected, Ben tumbled off the boulder, pulling Emma into his arms to save her from another battering. They landed against a large rock, Emma on top. She reared back to take another swipe at him, but stopped mid-swing, her eyes wide with surprise.

"Ben!" she yelped, grabbing his jacket. "What are you doing here!" Not letting him answer, she tugged at his jacket and scrambled to get up. "We've got to get out of here. Wayne's trying to kill me."

She started up out of the gorge, but stopped when she realized he wasn't following. "Come on—he's carrying a small arsenal!"

With barely controlled rage, Ben picked up his pack and rifle, grabbed her hand, and started walking along the gorge upstream. Emma ran to catch up.

"Oh, the log. Good thinking. We've got to toss it in the water so he can't follow," she panted.

The sweat was cooling on his forehead, reminding Ben that the temperature was in the low forties. Emma had to be freezing. When they reached the spot below the log, Ben settled her into a safe crevice. She finally seemed to be coming down from her adrenaline high. Her face was a mask of pain, and her shivering was so bad he could hear her teeth chattering over the noise of the waterfall.

He eased her down between two boulders and set the pack in front of her. Her eyes widened when he repositioned his rifle onto his shoulder by the sling, but that was all the reaction he got. Her strength was gone, sapped by the cold water. Bruises were already turning purple on her forehead, and a cut was oozing blood from her hair.

Ben still couldn't speak, his voice caught in his throat at the sight of her. Reining in his emotions, he leaped over the rocks toward the log bridge, keeping as low as possible. Once on top, he pulled his rifle up and scanned the forest on the other side of the gorge.

Poulin was probably downstream, looking for evidence that Emma hadn't survived her fall. He didn't know Ben was here, and that was a mighty big advantage. Wayne wasn't expecting his prey to shoot back.

Ben began to push the log down into the falls, but suddenly stopped to study it. With a little work he could booby-trap the bridge, and hope Poulin *did* try to use it to cross the gorge.

He used his knife to hack a wedge in the bottom of the rotting tree, which he propped up with a small stone. He tested the log for stability, satisfied Poulin would be too intent on finding Emma to notice his handiwork. Then he spent several minutes scanning the forest downstream again.

He caught a glimpse of something moving up the gorge and sighted in on Wayne, his finger on the trigger. But he wasn't able to get a clear shot. Wayne was jumping from rock to rock, darting in and out of sight. Ben decided not to wait any longer. Wayne was still on the other side of the gorge, and Ben didn't want to give away his presence.

He climbed down and returned to Emma. She was still sitting where he'd left her, her arms wrapped around herself, no longer shivering. As gently as he could, he pulled her wet sweater off and replaced it with his parka, then grabbed her face between his hands and made her look at him.

"Emma, listen to me. We've got to keep going. Can you walk?"

She nodded, cupping his hands with her own. Ben kissed her on the forehead. "Good girl. Any suggestions as to which way?"

"N-north. We're going to have to go north b-before we can head east."

Ben looked north, and realized it was all uphill.

"Is there anyplace we can hide, Emma? We've got to stop long enough to get you warm."

"Th-there's the headwaters of Medicine Creek. And some caves just above it, on the other side of this mountain."

Which meant they would still have to travel uphill. She didn't appear able to walk *down* the mountain, much less up it.

He wanted to hold her until she was warm. "Come on, honey. We've got to move," he said, gently lifting her up.

He positioned his pack on his back, slung the rifle over his shoulder, and wrapped one arm around her waist for support. They began the arduous journey, and Ben was damn proud of the effort she made to keep up.

It wasn't long, however, before her stumbling became impossible to deal with. He reached inside his parka and found her skin was dry but cold, unable to produce enough body heat to keep her core temperature up. Whatever energy she could muster was being used to keep her moving.

"How much farther?" he asked, stopping to let her catch her breath.

She looked around, trying to read the forest. "Another half mile, I think," she said, her breathing labored and her words barely audible.

Ben looked over their back trail before he reached down, placed his shoulder into her stomach, and lifted her over his back in a fireman's carry. "If we're going to make it, I'll have to carry you."

When he guessed he'd traveled far enough, he set Emma on her feet and held her steady. "Where?" he asked.

"There," she said, taking a stumbling step. "Maybe a hundred yards up there."

Great. More uphill. He guided her progress with a hand on her waist as she led him to a blind cliff with fallen rocks at its base.

"There's an opening to the left of those trees," she said weakly.

Ben scooped her up in his arms and picked his way through the jumble of weather-worn talus. He heard the trickle of water before he saw it. Steam emanated from a crack in the cliff as water gurgled directly out of the mountain and flowed toward the valley below. The first thing he noticed as he approached was the heat; the second thing was the smell of rotten eggs.

Sulphur? That meant the cave would be uninhabitable.

Ben set Emma in a concealed spot before he took off his pack and leaned his rifle against a rock next to her. Then he carefully tested the temperature of the water.

The spring wasn't hot, but warm enough to produce steam in this cold weather. He moved to the entrance of the cave and peered inside, sniffing the air, faintly smelling sulphur. He decided to move Emma just inside the mouth of the cave so there would be plenty of fresh air.

He made his way back down to where he'd left her, only to find her staring at his pack. "Ben? Your backpack is making funny noises."

Chapter Twenty

"*Oh, shit! The bird!*" Ben grabbed the canvas bag and unzipped it, peeling back the top flap. He pulled out the small dented cage and peered inside.

The pigeon peered back at him.

"Homer!" Emma cried, her voice weak but with welcome animation. She looked at Ben. "How come you have him?"

"Mike sent him with me this morning. I put him in my pack to protect him from the cold." He set the cage inside the entrance. "Let's get you out of those clothes," he said when he returned, and lifted her to her feet. "The entrance is just big enough to get through. I brought some dry clothes with me. We'll get you into them, then I want you to sit near the mouth of the cave."

"But it opens up into a small room," she said, hobbling over the rocks beside him, leaning against him when she nearly fell.

"There's been a lot of seismic activity. I don't know if it's stable or gaseous."

She stopped and glared at him weakly.

"What?" he asked.

"You put Homer in the cave."

"Damn right I did. He's our canary. If he croaks, we're outta there."

She gasped, and Ben carried her the rest of the way. As soon as they were completely inside the cave, which indeed opened up into a small chamber, he felt the warmth. It was no sweat lodge, but it was just what Emma needed. As he undressed her, she sat like a child.

He was starting to get really scared. This wasn't at all like Emma. She was a proactive person, not passive. And she still wasn't shivering.

Ben dumped the contents of the pack onto the cave floor and rummaged through its contents until he found a sweatshirt. He pulled it over her head, silently thanking Mike for helping him pack that morning.

Ben had been appalled at the things the boy had insisted he take: a complete change of clothes, a first-aid kit, a flashlight, a pot, rifle shells, four different maps, and the GPS. The pack also contained a survival kit that held matches, fishing line, safety pins, aluminum foil, a candle, a mirror, and duct tape.

Ben found the socks and put them on her feet, then

worked the jogging pants over her legs. They were his and would probably come all the way up to her arm-pits. As he worked them on, he noticed one of her knees was swollen and both legs were marked with bruises. Her skin was icy cold to the touch.

He was sweating.

He shook his parka and laid it on the floor, eased Emma down onto it, then crawled behind her and wrapped her up in his arms, cocooning her in his heat.

Ten minutes passed before she stopped shivering, and Ben took his first easy breath since he'd found her. She was going to be okay. He continued to hold her until the shivering ebbed to tiny spasms, eventually stopping completely. She finally stirred with a moan.

"Thank you," she whispered, turning to face him. She reached up and cupped his cheek. "You saved my life."

"Are you lucid enough to explain what you're doing here? I left you in front of a roaring fire with a book."

She lowered her gaze and began picking at a button on his shirt. "Kelly called me," she whispered.

He stiffened, then lifted her face up. "Kelly's dead, Emma."

"I know now," she whispered. "Wayne tricked me. I think he killed her. How . . . how do you know Kelly's dead?"

Ben cupped her head, pulling her face into his chest. He couldn't look at her anguish any longer. "Atwood and I decided Wayne's coordinates were her grave."

She popped her head back up to look at him. "When?"

"A few days ago, after we came out here and looked around ourselves. The investigators I have working in New York couldn't find a trace of her; it's as if Kelly disappeared off the face of the earth ten years ago. And when I came out here, it was as if . . . that's when everything added up."

He ran his fingers through her hair, wishing he could soothe her sadness. "Your sister would have contacted you if she were still alive. She never would have abandoned you and Mike. People mature. They regret decisions. They wonder. Kelly couldn't have stayed away. That meant she must be dead."

Emma buried her face in his chest with a sob. "I've spent the last ten years of my life hating my sister, and all this time she's been dead!" She looked at him, grabbing his shirt in a desperate grip. "She never abandoned us. She never abandoned Mikey. But . . . she did leave a note. She said she was leaving, and that she would call us."

"There's a good chance Kelly *was* leaving. I think she was scared of Wayne, and she felt the safest thing to do for Mike was to leave. I also think she did plan to contact you when she was safe. Only she never made it out of Medicine Gore—Poulin got to her first."

She hid in his shirt again. Ben wrapped her up in as fierce a hug as he dared, and rocked her back and forth.

"He killed my father." Emma looked up again, and Ben saw outrage through her tears. "Then he set it up to look like you were responsible!"

He sighed, not really surprised, as he brushed the tears from her face. "Yeah. And it worked well for him."

"Until Kelly found out."

"And you went snooping in his room."

"He's the one who got the environmentalists involved, too. He knows this area is slated for clear-cutting next summer, so while he *appears* to be on the side of the mills, he's been quietly stirring up trouble."

"The logging operation might have uncovered Kelly's remains. And Poulin knew he would be the prime suspect."

"We have to stop him before he gets away," she said, trying to sit up.

He held her down. "We've got to get ourselves out of here first. Poulin doesn't know I'm with you. He thinks he's hunting a battered, half-drowned woman, so he'll have wasted a lot of time looking for you downstream. Does he know about this cave?"

She settled back against him. "He must. He's cruised these woods for the mills. This is his backyard."

Ben sat up, bringing Emma with him. "Then I'm afraid we're going to have to keep moving. Do you think you're up to it?"

She stared at him with an expression of surprise. "What?"

She suddenly hurled herself into his arms and kissed his chin. "I *love* you, Ben."

"I'm pretty sure we established that fact last night," he said with a chuckle, feeling her body was once more producing its own heat.

She popped her head up, clipping him in the chin. "Was it just last night?"

Ben kissed her deeply, tasting her sweet aliveness. He urged her mouth open with his tongue and invaded it with the passion of a man very grateful to have his woman alive and well again.

She kissed him back, matching his desperation. Within seconds Ben felt sweat running down his forehead, and it had nothing to do with the warmth of the cave.

He broke off reluctantly, and gently held her away from him. "We've got to keep moving, Emma."

Her flushed face suddenly brightened. "Beaker's out there somewhere."

"What?"

"It's amazing—he followed Wayne's truck all the way out here! He saved me, attacking Wayne just as he was going to shoot me."

"Where's Beaker now?"

"Probably stalking Wayne."

Ben smiled. "Then it's three to one. Poulin doesn't stand a chance."

"He may be crazy, Ben, but he's also smart. Don't underestimate him."

"Don't worry, I won't." He started repacking his backpack. "What's our best way back home?"

When he didn't get an answer, Ben looked up to see Emma holding Homer's cage, a speculative look in her eye. "We can send a message. When Mikey gets home from school, he'll check out the coops. We can use Homer to call in the cavalry."

Ben reached into his pocket for the message canister and a pen. "What should we say?" he asked, pulling out the piece of paper inside.

"Just write, 'Trouble. Medicine Creek. Poulin.' And sign it Emma and Ben," she instructed as she took Homer out of his cage.

Ben saw her kiss the bird on his head.

"I'm glad the fumes didn't get you, little one," she whispered, holding the bird for him to attach the canister.

Then Ben walked to the entrance of the cave and released him.

The bird soared into the sky, circled once, and landed in a tree a hundred yards away.

Emma sighed. "He does that sometimes. He's just learning."

"Great." Ben turned and scanned the forest below, but he couldn't see very far. The trees were thick, growing right up the side of the mountain to the base of the cliff. He turned back to help Emma out of the small entrance. "Are you okay to travel?"

She was a god-awful mess. Her long hair was a tangle of knots, half-dried and still wet in places. Her face looked like a prizefighter's after a rough bout in the ring. His clothes hung from her slender frame, pooling into a folded mass of wrinkles at her ankles. He couldn't see her hands; the sleeves of his sweatshirt were so long that they dangled empty-cuffed.

"I can make it."

He frowned. "Maybe you should stay here. I could turn the tables on Poulin by doing a little hunting myself since I have the element of surprise."

"No offense, Ben, but your battlefield is usually a boardroom. This is Wayne's turf. And he's truly insane."

She started down the mountain.

There wasn't one blasted spot on her body that didn't ache, and there were a few places that outright pained her. But Emma kept walking, concentrating on putting one foot in front of the other, determined to lead Ben out of the woods.

This was a hell of a mess, and it was all her fault.

If she hadn't gone snooping in the first place she'd be home right now, making wedding plans. Instead, she was running for her life with Ben, away from the man who'd murdered her father and sister.

"Slow down, Emma," Ben said. "You're going to burn out."

They had twenty-six miles to go before they were

safe, but she stopped and waited for him to catch up. She knew he was slowed down from watching their back trail.

"We're not going to make it before dark," she said when he reached her. "We'll have to find a safe place to bed down."

"Any suggestions?" he asked, brushing the hair off her forehead.

"I'll tell you if you share some of that food in your pack," she teased.

The poor man looked so stricken, Emma was immediately sorry for asking. "Lord, Emma, you must be starving," he said as he shrugged off the pack.

She took the pack and looked inside, and found a container of Elmer Fudge cookies. "No more than you," she said, opening the lid and grabbing one. She popped the entire cookie in her mouth, and immediately thought of Beaker. Was he still stalking Wayne?

"What's the plan?" Ben asked around his own mouthful of cookie.

"Medicine Creek starts up on the mountain, and gathers water from various streams as it flows down to Medicine Lake. So we just follow the creek, and come out at Medicine Bay and my camps."

"How far?"

Emma reached into the pack for some water before she replied. "We're still about twenty-six miles from home, but beavers dammed the stream about four miles from here and created a nice little pond. There's trout in it the size of baby whales."

Ben ate another cookie, his eyes darting up the trail they'd just walked down.

"I keep a canoe stashed there," Emma said, regaining his attention. "And the stream is navigable below the pond . . . for a while."

He lifted a brow, silently asking her to explain.

"About eight miles before home, there's a monster set of falls and then some pretty mean white water. Do you have any white water experience?"

His frown returned.

"That's assuming the canoe holds up," she added before she popped another cookie in her mouth.

Ben looked at the rifle leaning against a tree, then back up their trail, and then at her again. "I'm not sure you're in any condition for that kind of trip. Your limping has gotten worse the last couple of miles. Maybe I should turn the game on Poulin. Then we can take our time getting out of here."

"No, you're *not* hunting Wayne. I'm not kidding, Ben. The man is too good." She shoved the package of cookies in the backpack, then held the pack for him to put on. She grabbed the rifle and started off downstream.

"Emma, wait."

"We're walking out of here, Ben. And that's final." She wondered how seaworthy the old canoe really was.

* * *

"I owe you an apology," Emma said two hours later, collapsing onto a rock by the pond's edge as Ben sat beside her and shrugged out of his pack. "I really thought you were a 'take charge' kind of guy, that in a crisis things would have to be your way or no way." She leaned against him as she continued. "But you're going along with my plan, even though I know you're dying to go after Wayne."

He wrapped an arm over her shoulders and cuddled her against him, resting his chin on her head. "I like to think I'm man enough to listen to an expert. In fact, I'm betting our lives that you're more knowledgeable than Poulin."

She stared up at this man of her young dreams, and her heart started to race. He was hers. He belonged to her, just as much as she belonged to him. "It's going to be okay, isn't it?" she asked, gazing into his eyes. "Our getting married, I mean. It's really going to work."

He turned her more fully to face him. "You're just deciding this now?"

Emma ran a finger over his stern jaw. "I know you said I'd still be independent, but you can't blame me for having doubts. You do get a little bossy on occasion." She leaned up and kissed his chin. "But you're being so . . . democratic today."

His expression darkened. "Don't paint me pretty, Emma. If I had a choice, I'd have chained you to that couch this morning to keep you safe. I'm just dealing with the circumstances as I get them. Next time I might not be so cooperative."

She stroked his clenched jaw and turned to look at the pond. "I'm ready for some supper. Did your son put any fishing tackle in that fancy pack of yours?"

Silence answered her, and Emma knew he wasn't pleased at how their conversation had ended. She smiled toward the beaver pond. Benjamin Sinclair was practically blanketed in moss.

They sat in quiet companionship, soaking up the peacefulness of the pond as they rested. Emma's joints soon began to stiffen, however, protesting today's punishment. She tried to relax them without letting Ben know just how badly she hurt, straightening her swollen right knee as she fought the urge to rub it.

"How are we going to cook the fish we catch?" he asked. "We can't risk a fire."

"You can build a small fire in the dense forest," she told him. "Use dry wood so it won't smoke, and wait until it's dark enough so the smoke can't be seen. The breeze will scatter the smell enough that Wayne wouldn't be able to find the direction it's coming from."

She stirred from the comfort of his lap. "I'm going to check out the canoe."

He helped her stand, but didn't let go of her. "I think I should check our back trail first." He looked over at the forty-foot bluff rising up from the opposite shore of the pond. "If I climb up there, I might be able to see if Wayne's behind us."

Emma reached down and got the rifle. "Don't . . . oh, just be careful," she muttered, handing it to him.

She couldn't tell him not to shoot Wayne; that was Ben's decision. Given the facts, and the position they were in, she wasn't sure what she would do herself.

He kissed her, ending it much too soon, then pulled a handgun out of the back of his belt. "I assume you're familiar with pistols?"

Emma took the gun and nodded.

"And I assume you're not afraid to defend yourself?"

She nodded again.

"Don't overcook the trout," he said as he walked into the woods.

Emma watched until he was out of sight before she walked over to a huge tree that had fallen into the pond. She pushed the dead brush and cattails aside to uncover an ancient green canoe, used what strength she had left to turn it over, and quickly stepped back in case any critter had made her boat into a home. Nothing scurried away, and Emma began examining it for holes.

It was in decent shape, despite the years it had spent exposed to the elements. She pulled out the oars from underneath the seat and tested their strength, and decided they would work. Now to catch some dinner.

Emma found the kit she insisted must be in every pack leaving the house. She pulled out the fishing line and bobber, then turned over a rock and searched for grubs. She found several juicy ones and baited the hook, walked out on the fallen log, and tossed the grub into the water as far as she could. The bobber followed and settled nicely onto the surface of the pond, and she waited for a hungry fish to come swimming along. She split her time between munching on Elmer Fudge cookies and watching the bluff on the opposite shore. There was no sign of Ben yet, so she turned her attention to the handgun he'd given her. It was a neat little cannon, of a caliber that could blow a hole in an elephant.

It was also the weapon of a man who meant business.

Emma knew then, as she held Ben's pistol in her hand, that he would take advantage of any opportunity Wayne Poulin presented.

Tears fell onto the gun in her lap, large drops that bore witness to ten long years of pain. So many lies and misconceptions, so many moments of despair, when she had silently railed at her sister for abandoning her and Mikey. So much energy wasted on hate.

And now, so much regret.

Mikey would be devastated. Emma knew that he, too, had spent many nights lying in bed hating his mother. What kind of guilt would he place on himself?

And what must Ben be thinking? Did he blame himself for any of this? For her father's death or Kelly's? Could he have changed the course of history if he'd stayed?

She wiped her face with the back of her hand, but it did no good. The dam broke on her heart, and giant sobs racked her as she buried her face in her knees.

Chapter Twenty-one

"*Look who I found,*" Ben said as he walked into the makeshift camp Emma had put together.

"Beaker!"

"Easy, he's in pretty bad shape," he warned, setting the dog beside her.

"Oh, you poor baby," she crooned as she began inspecting him.

Ben sat down beside Beaker. "He's got a wound on his chest, but it seems to have stopped bleeding. And he was limping when I found him."

"Look at the pads on his feet," she said, rubbing him under the chin and kissing his head. "Oh, Ben. He followed Wayne's truck all the way from my road. He's a hero."

"Damn right he is," Ben agreed, suspecting it hadn't

been training that had pushed the dog to such limits. Beaker was in love with Emma.

Weren't they all?

Her face, though lit with joy at seeing her dog, was red and puffy, with dirty streaks running down her cheeks. If he didn't know better, he'd swear Emma had been crying.

"Is that supper?" he asked, pointing at the foil of expertly cleaned trout.

"Yes. They're all ready to be cooked. Would you mind taking them deeper into the woods and building a fire?"

She must be tired if she was asking for help—or her knee was hurting her badly. Ben reached for the fish. "Just point me in the right direction."

"It looks dense enough over there. Just set the fire low, and place the fish on top as soon as it catches. Twenty minutes ought to do the trick."

Ben was gone less than half an hour, and when he returned Beaker and Emma were sound asleep, cuddled together on his parka.

So he ate all three trout himself.

And they were delicious.

He didn't feel the least bit guilty, because he had decided to have Emma home by breakfast tomorrow morning. He left the two of them asleep while he dragged the canoe down over the beaver dam, loaded their supplies inside, then walked back to the pond to wake them up.

"Come on, Em. We've got to go," he whispered, gently shaking her awake.

"It's dark," she muttered, sitting up.

"Your eyes will adjust. Come on. The canoe's loaded and in the stream."

She stared up at him in confusion.

Ben sighed. "I've never known anyone to sleep as soundly as you do."

"Beaker would warn me if Wayne showed up," she said, trying to rise.

She gasped when her knee failed to support her. Ben grabbed her under the arms and lifted her to her feet, reached down for his handgun and tucked it into his belt, then tucked the parka around her.

"My knee stiffened up."

"I'll help you. It's not far. Come on, Beaker."

"Are you sure you're ready to run the river at night, Ben?" she asked, hobbling beside him.

"I think it's the safest way," he said, guiding her over the beaver dam. "If we wait until morning, we'll be sitting ducks. Poulin can't shoot what he can't see."

She looked up at him, and Ben could see a brilliant smile slashing across her face. "Why, Mr. Sinclair. I do believe you have the makings of a woodsman."

"Are there any surprises I should know about between here and the falls?"

She shook her head. "No. It's mostly flat water. The current will pick up as the stream gathers more tributaries, but we'll still have to do a lot of paddling."

Ben helped Emma into the front of the canoe and put Beaker in the middle. The dog whined and tried to jump out.

"Beaker, stay," Ben commanded, shoving off before the dog could dump them.

Emma picked up a paddle and pulled them into the stream, which was narrow just below the beaver dam, but quickly opened up into a winding dead water. Ben put his shoulders into each stroke, intent on getting to the falls by daybreak.

It was still solid night when they arrived.

Ben heard the roar of the falls at the same time he felt the canoe pick up speed. Beaker sat up. Emma pointed her paddle to the southeastern shore, and Ben guided the canoe to the bank.

"It's going to be a treacherous portage this time of night," she said, scrambling awkwardly onto the shore. Beaker wasn't any more graceful as he jumped and missed, falling back into the water with a yelp. Ben grabbed him by the skin of his neck and hauled him onto dry land. The dog immediately shook, soaking everything within ten feet.

Emma gave a pleasant if tired laugh. "You think Beaker is wishing he was back in the city?"

"No offense, but I wouldn't mind being back there myself." Ben looked at the narrowing creek, which disappeared into the blackness a hundred yards downstream.

Damn he was tired. His arms burned so badly, he wished they would just fall off. His back ached. His eyes felt like they were lined with sand, and he had blisters on both palms.

And they still faced eight miles of white water.

"Can you walk, Emma?" he asked, moving closer to be heard over the roar of the falls.

"I will. I just have to work the stiffness out."

"Do you want me to take a look at that knee? Maybe wrap it with something?"

He thought she smiled, but she could be wincing. The dim moonlight made it impossible to tell.

"Thanks, but I'd rather not know how bad it is until I can do something about it."

He reached out and cupped her cheek. "You're amazing, Emma Sands," he told her, kissing her dirty nose.

She covered his hand with her own. "I'm very glad you're here, Ben. I might not have made it without you."

He kissed her full on the lips, and she responded with passion, warmth, and a little desperation.

"You're sweeter than an Elmer Fudge," she whispered, then wrapped her arms around his waist and squeezed. "You're freezing! Here, take the parka for a while," she said as she worked her arms out of it.

Ben stopped her. "Not yet. I'll be a ball of sweat by the time I get this canoe down the falls. Keep it on," he gently ordered, zipping it back up.

Beaker suddenly came to stand next to them, his hackles raised and a low growl rumbling from his chest. Ben stilled, his handgun in his fist, his eyes trying to pierce the dense undergrowth as he followed Beaker's stare.

"Wayne," Emma said on an indrawn breath, scrambling to her feet. "He could have found our trail and realized I was heading home. We didn't exactly cover our tracks. He'd try to cut me off by traveling straight through the woods." She stared up at Ben in horror. "And he'll know I'm not alone anymore."

"Is there a reason *we* didn't cut straight through the woods?"

"I never would have made it with my bad knee. The terrain's too rugged."

"Beaker could be growling at an animal."

"You going to wait around and find out?" she asked. "We have to portage now! Once we get into the white water, Wayne won't be able to catch us on foot."

He handed her the rifle and pack, and tucked his handgun back in his belt. Ignoring his burning muscles, he hefted the heavy canoe out of the water and began dragging it over a ledge to the left of the falls.

Beaker silently disappeared into the darkness.

The sharp crack of a rifle suddenly split the night, and the tree beside Emma splintered with the impact of a bullet. Ben dove for her, throwing her to the ground and covering her head with his arms.

"It came from the other side of the stream," she said,

turning her face toward his. "I saw the muzzle flash."

"He's shooting blind. He just saw movement. He still might not know I'm here," Ben said, easing off her. "I'm going to keep dragging the canoe down through the trees. The noise of the falls should cover the sound." He handed her the rifle. "Try to cover me." He grabbed her chin and looked directly into her eyes. "If you get a clear shot, can you take it?"

Her eyes huge with worry as she tried to pierce the darkness, she nodded.

"Good girl. Don't try anything foolish," he warned. "I'm counting on you to be right here when I get back. Understand?"

"I promise not to move from this spot. Get the canoe down to the water."

"I'll be back in ten minutes."

"Where's Beaker?"

"Hunting." He started dragging the canoe again.

His last look back showed Emma lying on her stomach, her rifle aimed toward the other side of the falls.

He didn't doubt she'd pull the trigger, but he hoped like hell it didn't come to that. For all of her strengths, Emma was a gentle soul with a tender heart. He hated to leave her in the position of having to take another person's life, no matter how unredeemable that life was.

Ben was halfway down the ledge when the next rifle shot pierced the darkness and ricocheted on the rocks across the falls.

Yup. Emma had pulled the trigger.

Their game was up. Poulin knew she was armed, which meant their element of surprise was gone.

Ben finally reached the bottom of the falls, only to find a frothing, turbulent pool completely surrounded by sheer ledge. If they got in the canoe here, Poulin could pick them off as easily as shooting fish in a barrel.

Hell. It was time for another plan.

Ben looked up and saw the first whisper of dawn lighting the sky. He left the canoe on the ledge by the pool and pulled his handgun out of his belt. He'd tried to do things her way, but now it was time to join Beaker.

First, though, he needed to let Emma in on his plan so she didn't accidentally shoot him. But just as he started up the trail, a deep rumbling came echoing down the mountain. The ground started to tremble, and Ben had to grab a tree for balance. Rocks poured down from the ledge as deadly missiles, some of them as large as basketballs. The tree he was holding shook as if attempting to shrug him off as the valley awakened with violent energy.

Emma tucked herself against the trunk of a giant pine tree to ride out the earthquake. Medicine Creek boiled with fury as huge boulders lost their footing and tumbled into the water. The ledge of the falls split with explosive booms that sounded like gunfire, reverberating through the granite beneath her in undulating waves.

Her first thought when the ground quieted was of Ben. He was below the falls, in the path of a deadly landslide of falling rock and small trees that still fell with lethal frequency. Her second thought was that the roar of the falls had subsided to a more gentle sound, like that of a gushing faucet that had suddenly been turned off.

Medicine Creek had been dammed up by the falling debris.

Emma moved away from the swiftly rising water and scanned the opposite shore, able to see it clearly now that dawn blanketed the forest with dim light. Wayne was still over there someplace, waiting for her to move. She quietly started in the direction Ben had gone, sliding down the path, praying she wouldn't find him buried beneath rubble.

She lost her grip on a tree root and fell into his lap.

He caught her with a grunt. "Following orders as usual?"

"We've got about two minutes before the rising creek decides *this* is the easiest way down the valley," she told him, grabbing his hand. "The falls were dammed by the earthquake."

He reversed her grip on his and began pulling her back up the path.

"The canoe's destroyed. And it's too light out now to use it anyway," he said, helping her over a steep spot.

"Then let's head due east, away from the stream."

He shook his head, still climbing. "No. If that pigeon of yours made it home yesterday, help will be arriving soon. They'll be looking for us along Medicine Creek."

Emma forced Ben to stop by grabbing a tree trunk and hanging on.

"What?" he asked.

"Wayne will see them coming! He'll kill Mikey if he gets the chance."

"He won't get the chance," Ben said, pulling her behind him again. "I intend to kill him first."

Emma followed in silence. Water was already creating a new channel around the dammed falls. She hoped the creek was overflowing on the opposite shore as well, forcing Wayne out of his hiding place.

When they reached the overflowing stream, Ben headed toward the falls. There was enough light now to see the giant boulders and broken ledge blocking it, forming a bridge they could use. He stopped before crossing and turned to her, his face harder than the granite she was standing on.

Michael had been right. When Ben finally shed his veneer, he was scary.

"I need you to stay here," he said harshly, leaving no room for discussion.

Emma didn't argue.

"Cover me as I cross. Then keep an eye out for Atwood and Skyler. Fire two quick shots if you see them coming up the stream."

"What about Beaker?" she asked softly.

He looked across the natural bridge. "He's out there, watching and waiting."

"You'll be careful?"

He gently kissed her. "I love you, Emma. And I'll be back. We have an important date in two weeks, and I intend to be there to see what you think of my wedding gift."

He kissed her again, then pulled out his handgun and walked away.

Emma lifted her rifle to her shoulder and steadied it on the boulder she was leaning against, watching the opposite shore for any sign of Wayne.

Chapter Twenty-two

The earth continued to rumble with occasional shivers, rattling small rocks and rippling the ever deepening water. Medicine Creek finally found its new route around the dam, and its newly created falls cascaded down the path Ben had used to portage the canoe. Small trees were uprooted and earth and mud gave way with devastating effects. Her retreat was cut off. She was trapped except for the route Ben had taken across the old falls.

Emma wished she were here under different circumstances as this wonder of nature played itself out. She was witnessing no more than a gentle blip in the life of the earth, but to her it was mystical.

Michael would be fascinated.

She thought of her nephew, knowing he was valiantly coming to her rescue. She didn't doubt Homer had found the lodge eventually, and that Mikey had found the message they'd sent. And she knew nothing would stop him from trying to save the two people he loved. She knew she didn't have to worry about him barging into an ambush, as Mikey was smart enough to be cautious.

Sometimes he seemed as mystical as the land he'd grown up in. He knew things: when the rain was coming, when the seasons were changing, and when weather was brewing. He was able to read the signs like a soothsayer, and had surprised Emma more than once with an urgency to batten down the camps and secure the plane. When no more than a rainstorm was forecast, Mikey would make her prepare for a gale, and he was rarely wrong.

He would know Wayne was near, and would come with stealth and purpose.

Which scared her. As much as she didn't want Wayne's blood on Ben's hands, she certainly didn't want Michael involved. He was too young and innocent to become embroiled in the mess.

The forest behind her suddenly erupted in a flurry of breaking branches and heavy breathing. Emma swiftly turned, only to lower the rifle barrel when Pitiful came charging toward the stream. The animal's eyes were huge saucers of brown with white rings of panic surrounding them. His nostrils were flared and his sides were heaving as he broke through the trees, his single antler pulling down branches.

Unable to understand what was happening in his woods, the panicked bull splashed into the receding waters of Medicine Creek, letting out a bellow that sounded like a desperate child calling for help. He stood in the middle of the stream, shivering with fright and panting.

"Pssst," Emma hissed, trying to draw his attention. "Pitiful."

The young bull cocked his head in her direction, let out a loud bugle of joy when he spotted her, and came charging through the water toward the dam. Emma stepped behind her rock for protection.

Wayne Poulin grabbed her around her throat in a hold that nearly cut off her air.

"Drop the rifle," he said, pulling them both out of reach of the confused moose. "Who's here with you?"

She didn't answer, and he tightened his hold on her throat.

"It's . . . it's John," she gasped, tugging on his arm so she could breathe.

"John Lakes? The old hermit?"

"He found me yesterday and was helping me home."

"Where is he now?"

"Our canoe got damaged, so he left me his rifle and went for help."

"Call off that moose or I'll shoot it," he warned.

Pitiful was trying to climb up the steep bank of the stream, becoming more frantic with each unsuccessful attempt.

"I can't control him, Wayne. He's just a scared, dumb animal."

Wayne aimed his handgun at Pitiful. Emma bit his arm. He screamed and used his gun to strike her in the head, but she ducked, taking the blow in her shoulder. She elbowed him in the ribs as hard as she could, kicking him in the shin at the same time. But her right knee gave out, and they both fell to the ground.

With a curse of outrage, Wayne secured his grip on her, hauled them both to their feet, and started dragging her over the bridge the earthquake had made.

Bellowing, Pitiful turned in the water to follow.

Halfway across the old falls, Emma heard a deadly snarl just before Wayne screamed in pain. His arm around her slackened as he turned to face the new threat.

Emma broke free, but her feet got entangled in Wayne's, and they both fell onto the edge of the boulders. She saw that Beaker had a death grip on Wayne's arm holding the gun . . . just as she tumbled over the edge of the dam.

It took Ben several precious seconds to realize he was actually seeing a battle among a man, a woman, a moose, and a dog. All of which was taking place on top of a forty-foot-high bridge of granite that was too narrow to hold more than one of them.

He watched helplessly as Emma fell. He started out onto the bridge, but stopped when he saw she'd only fallen about ten feet, landing on a ledge wide enough to hold her safely. She was dazed but alive, which freed Ben up to deal with Poulin.

Beaker was making a mess of the man. The shepherd had been waiting for this moment, but Wayne still held his gun, and was slowly forcing it down in the dog's direction.

Ben raised his handgun and aimed it at Wayne, waiting for a clear shot.

In the end, Emma's pet moose struck the fateful blow. The panicked bull finally found a foothold and pulled himself out of the water, his head lowered for purchase, and his single lethal antler rammed into Wayne Poulin's ribs.

Poulin was thrown into the air with enough force to send him sailing out over the falls. He hit several outcroppings on the way down, finally landing in the pool at the bottom. Ben ran to the edge and looked down to see Poulin's broken body floating facedown in the water.

Then he looked over at Emma.

Her head leaned back against the granite ledge, and her eyes were closed. She didn't open them when she spoke. "Ben?"

"I'm here."

"Get me down."

She still hadn't opened her eyes. She wasn't looking down, and she wasn't trying to look up at him.

"Are you afraid of heights, Emma?" he asked, under-
standing finally dawning when he saw her death grip
on the ledge.

"Yes!"

Ben was incredulous. "You're a pilot, for chrissakes.
You spend most of your time in the air."

"I'm not wearing any wings at the moment, Sinclair.
Get me down—now!"

"I've got to go find my pack, Emma. There's a rope
in it."

"Wait!" She finally opened her eyes and tried to
look up, then gasped and shut them again.

"What?"

"Is . . . is Beaker okay?"

"He's fine, Em. He's standing right beside me."

"And Pitiful?"

"I assume so. He ran off."

"I heard Wayne fall, Ben. It was a sickening sound."
Her voice shook with distress. "Is he dead?"

"He's dead."

"I—I wish I wasn't glad."

"Emma, will you be okay while I go find our pack?"

"It's probably all the way to Medicine Lake by now.
Climb down and get me."

She still refused to open her eyes, so she couldn't see
that it was a ten-foot drop to the shelf she was on. It
was probably just as well. She also couldn't see it was
another thirty feet to the bottom.

Two quick gunshots cracked just below them, and Ben saw Atwood, Skyler, and Mike making their way to the foot of the pool where Poulin was floating.

"What was that?" Emma called up to him.

"Mike's here with reinforcements. I bet the boy's got some rope."

He heard her sigh.

"Nem!" Mike called from below. "Are you okay?"

"Get me down, Mikey!" she hollered, her eyes still closed and her head still leaning against the cliff.

Mike looked up at his father and waved. Ben gave a sigh of relief, sat down on the bridge above Emma, and put his arm around the softly whining Beaker. The dog didn't like seeing her distress any more than Ben did.

"Just a few more minutes," he assured the dog. "We'll get her up here safe and sound." He petted him. "You did good, fella. I think there are a lot of cookies in your future."

Still shaken from her ascent from the granite shelf, Emma found herself arguing with four determined males. The fifth, four-legged male hadn't stopped licking her since she'd made it to the top.

"I am not flying out of here in a helicopter," she told the men again.

"It's already on its way," Atwood said with a frustrated sigh.

Mikey should have been on her side, but the boy just

kept shaking his head as he looked at her, the worry evident in his expression. "It's the quickest way out, Nem. You can't walk, and there's no place for a plane to land."

Emma grabbed Beaker's nose in an attempt to get him to stop licking her. "I'm not getting in a helicopter, and that's that."

"Why the hell not?" Ben asked.

"Because helicopters are unnatural machines."

Skyler snorted. "They're remarkably nimble," he said, apparently taking offense. "And perfect for situations like this one."

"How are they unnatural?" Ben asked, looking genuinely interested.

"They don't have wings. And all their spinning parts are trying to get away from each other. Do you see anything in nature that flies without wings?"

Her answer seemed to shock them. Except Mikey. He was well aware of her feelings toward helicopters. And although he might agree with her in theory, he obviously wanted her out of these woods badly enough to put her in a helicopter.

She wanted out, too. But in one piece.

She looked at Mikey. "I can make it to where the white water flattens out. There's enough room there for a floatplane to land."

"But there's not a pilot in Greenville who'd be willing to try it," he answered, shaking his head. "You're the only one who would dare."

Emma looked toward the sound of a helicopter approaching from the south. "That thing is older than I am," she said as the aging Huey beat the air in heavy, pulsating thumps.

Ben got within an inch of her nose. "You're getting in that helicopter and going to the hospital," he said with the determination of a man who had been pushed past his limit.

"Someone's got to lead Pitiful home," she said. "He's panicked from the earthquakes."

"I will, Nem," Mikey offered.

"That chopper can't hover forever, Emma," Ben interjected. "So what'll it be? Trussed up like a Thanksgiving turkey or sitting in the basket like a dignified woodswoman?"

"You're riding with me," she countered, glaring right back at him.

The smile he gave her was purely male. "Oh, you can bet on it. I'm going to see that you're examined from head to toe."

Emma closed her eyes. And she didn't open them for the hair-raising ride up the grappling winch, or the treetop ride over the countryside, or even for the gentle ride in the elevator of the hospital.

Because she fell sound asleep in the warm, safe, capable arms of the man she loved.

Chapter Twenty-three

*I*t *took the authorities* nearly a week to find, identify, and finally release Kelly's remains to Emma and Mikey. Her nephew had come to her two nights ago and asked if he could bring his mother home to Medicine Creek Camps for the wake, to let the townspeople pay their respects.

Emma had thought to have a quiet affair with only Ben and Greta present. But she soon realized how badly Mikey needed to perform this act for the woman for whom he'd had so many conflicting feelings for most of his life. So she had agreed, and they'd made a place for Kelly's closed coffin in the living room.

And the townspeople, themselves likely sorry for having judged her, had come.

On the day of the funeral, the procession to the graveyard where Charles and Miriam Sands were buried was a long one. Cars and pickups and even logging trucks lined the road beside the small cemetery. The ceremony was brief, the faces of Medicine Gore contrite. They were all guilty of condemning a woman who had tried her best to keep her son safe from the evil that had been living with them for sixteen years.

Flowers overflowed the gravesite, spilling onto Emma's mother and father's graves. The weather was glorious, warm and embracing.

Emma didn't cry. She had purged herself that afternoon on the mountain, high up in the land her family had called home. She had made her peace with her sister, silently thanking Kelly for Mikey, and laid her quietly to rest, knowing the boy was finally safe.

As for Mikey, it was as if he'd suddenly had a weight lifted off his shoulders. The burden of being abandoned by someone who was supposed to love him was gone. Though sad and remorseful, he walked taller and seemed more peaceful.

So Emma didn't cry for her sister as the minister finished his eulogy and the townspeople gave her their sympathy on their way out of the cemetery. Nor did she cry when Ben led her away.

She didn't shed a tear until she turned back looking for Mikey, and saw him all alone, his jacket on the ground and his sleeves rolled up, slowly shoveling the earth over his mother.

Then she doubled over in pain.

Ben turned her into him, burying her face in his chest. "Sshhh, Emma. It's okay."

"I can't stand for him to do that, Ben. He shouldn't be alone. He shouldn't be doing that!"

"He has to, Em," he told her, hugging her close. "It's the last act a son can do for a mother he loves."

"Help him."

"No, honey. He doesn't need me. He needs to be alone with Kelly. Come on," he said, turning them toward his truck. "Everyone is waiting at Greta's house."

The entire town was gathered on the lawn, the porch, and inside the huge kitchen and parlor, as they had been when Sable died.

Emma had her emotions under control by the time they arrived, and felt she held up well, even when the condolences turned to questions. She actually smiled when the questions turned to apologies to Ben.

John LeBlanc led the crusade. "Well, Sinclair. We're sorry for thinking you had anything to do with the dam being blown up sixteen years ago. It came as quite a shock to learn that it was Poulin."

"It was Poulin who first cried that Sinclair was responsible," Durham added, coming up and handing Emma a glass of punch. He looked at Ben. "I'm, ah, sorry for the little misunderstanding that day, Sinclair. No hard feelings?"

Ben didn't answer immediately. "I'll get back to you on that," he said, his arm around Emma's waist.

"Rumor has it you're planning on marrying our Emma Jean." John looked at Ben with assessing eyes. "That right?"

"Next week," Ben confirmed. "The day after Thanksgiving."

Durham looked at Emma. "You're staying here, aren't you? You aren't selling Medicine Creek Camps?"

Ben answered for her. "No, she's not. I'm going to move my office to Medicine Gore."

Both men widened their eyes and Durham choked on his punch. "But I thought you owned some huge shipping company. How you gonna run something like that from way out here?"

"With satellites, modems, faxes, and computers." He gave Emma's waist a gentle squeeze. "And if I can find myself a good pilot, I can commute to New York when I need to."

Durham and John looked floored. "What about all the people who work for you?" John asked.

Emma looked at Ben. This was the first she'd heard of his plan.

"Nothing in New York will change. But there's a fine workforce here, also."

"We're loggers," Durham said. "We don't know nothing about computers."

"It will be steady, year-round work," Ben said.

Durham and John both frowned, their bushy eyebrows drawing together. Emma laughed out loud. "Your wife might become a career woman, John. And during your off season, you'll be doing the cooking."

Both men turned and beat a hasty retreat, mumbling that they needed something stronger than punch.

"Do you have a place in your company for a spry old woman, Mr. Sinclair?" Greta asked as she took the men's place.

"I'm sure I can find something."

"Well, Emma Jean. I must say, when I sent Ben that letter, I certainly wasn't expecting the results I got," Greta said.

"*You* sent the letter!" Ben said.

Greta nodded, smiling like a well-fed cat. "Damn right I did. I figured it was time you came back and righted a few wrongs." She looked at him, her eyes narrowing. "I didn't realize that the greatest wrong was living under my own roof. Thank you for fixing things, young man."

Ben smiled, took the old woman's hand, and kissed it. "I'm glad to have been of service. And thank *you* for giving me my son and Emma."

Greta blushed to the roots of her gray hair as she turned to Emma and winked. "Your mother's wedding dress is in my attic. Charlie asked me to save it for you girls."

All three of them turned when the kitchen door

opened and Mikey finally walked in. Emma started toward him but stopped when he smiled at her.

He looked surprisingly . . . peaceful. His jacket was thrown over his shoulder, his tie was pulled free and hanging down his front, and there were streaks of dirt on his cheeks. But he looked serene.

"I'm starved, Aunt Greta," he said as he walked over to the punch bowl and downed two cups without stopping. "What's to eat?"

Greta hauled him over to the counter and began filling him a plateful that would choke a horse.

"He's going to be okay, isn't he?" Emma asked Ben.

"He's okay right now, Em. He's found himself." He smiled at her. "And thanks to your meddling friend, we all found each other."

"I'm so glad," she whispered, wrapping her arms around him and hugging the man of her dreams to her heart.

Epilogue

As weddings went, this had to be the nicest one Emma would ever see.

It didn't matter that she was limping as Mikey and Beaker walked her down the aisle, or that there was a stain on her mother's dress that she had decided to leave in, or that it was pouring cats and dogs outside. It didn't even matter that Pitiful had broken one of the windows of the tiny clapboard church, and knocked over a vase of flowers trying to see what the love of his life was up to.

She didn't even bat an eyelash when the ground rumbled with gentle shivers.

All that mattered was that Ben was waiting for her at the end of the aisle.

But it wasn't until the vows were said, the rings exchanged, and the kisses given, that Emma noticed the boutonnieres in Mikey's and Ben's jackets, and she burst into laughter.

Both men were wearing sprigs of moss.

Letter from Lake Watch

Dear Reader,

I didn't start out writing my stories for you, but rather for me. A switch, quite literally, flipped on in my brain just shy of my fortieth birthday, and unseen forces sent me scrambling to a computer when the imaginary people plaguing my dreams started insisting—quite loudly—that I get their stories down on paper. I wrote my first books in blissful ignorance, unschooled in such things as style, grammar, pacing, story arc, or plot. My only concern was to shut those people up.

Ironically, considering I was a voracious reader, it never dawned on me that anyone else would be interested in reading *my* stories. I just wrote them just so that I could read them, and then I shoved them in the closet and started writing another one. But I eventually realized my characters didn't really exist, because it takes someone *else* to read them to bring them to life.

A thought is merely a thought until it is shared, and

only then does it become a tangible thing. Until some-one other than me reads one of my stories, it is only a massive collection of words. That's what language is, after all: a means for one person to convey their thoughts to another.

How cool is that? It doesn't matter if you're in Europe, Africa, Australia, Asia, South or North America, or even on the moon when you read one of my books, as you read, you are giving my characters life. You are see-ing them through your own unique perspective based on *your* life experiences; judging them by *your* personal eth-ics, *your* hopes and dreams and emotional needs.

So for taking these people out of my head and put-ting them into yours, I thank you.

And I'm quite sure my characters also thank you.

If you connect with them—if you love them or hate them—then I've done a good job. If you laugh out loud, get flustered, teary-eyed, disgusted, or downright angry, then I have managed to give you a very real experience.

Only if you are indifferent do I feel that I've failed.

I don't like every person I meet. Do you? I don't agree with everything everyone says, nor do I like some of the situations I find myself in, either. And I certainly don't like how life turns out sometimes. So I don't ex-pect my readers to like everything in my books, and, quite honestly, I hope you don't.

When I pick up a book to read—be it from a favorite author, or one I haven't tried before—I am usually searching for an emotional fix, depending on my mood at the time. Personally, I have only one requirement: that I don't walk away from a story feeling bummed out, desolate, or without hope. I read romance novels because I *like* happy endings, and for that reason alone I write them.

And I may be going out on a limb here, but I'm guessing that *you* read romances because you also wish to walk away believing that no matter how dire things seem, there is always hope. This need for a happy ending is sort of a universal theme, isn't it? Hope is the ultimate human emotion. It is powerful enough to get us out of bed every morning even when that happy ending seems impossible, and it is as vast and timeless as the ocean.

It wasn't until my first book was published, *Charming the Highlander,* that I realized I no longer was writing just for myself, but for you, too. A good friend and very wise woman told me—when I first started dealing with editors, book reviewers, and bestseller lists—that *no one* can be in my studio with me, telling me how to tell my stories. I couldn't let anyone sit on my shoulder censoring me, directing my creativity or insisting I make a character or situation fit their personal sensibilities.

So I'm still writing foremost to please *myself*, and until that thought in my head is completed to my satisfaction, nobody reads my story—not my editor and certainly not you. And then the delicate dance begins, and we all come together to engage in a universal conversation of love and hope and happily ever after.

Within days of my first book getting published, I started getting e-mails to my website from women the world over, telling me how something—a scene or character or situation—touched their hearts. I was blown away, as it still hadn't really dawned on me that my stories might have any sort of impact on others.

Well . . . try as I might to keep my writing studio free of *earthly* voices, I can't stop you—my reader—from sitting on my shoulder. Only instead of censoring or directing me, I feel you cheering me on! So this is my shout-out to you: Thank you for your letters, for enjoying my stories, and for telling me that you do.

That's not to say that I don't have my critiques, but realizing I can't please everyone all of the time, I've decided to write stories for those of you who like reading them. If you like them, then feel free to tell me; if you don't, then also feel free to tell me. Remember, it's indifference that hurts. If I can't get some sort of rise out of you, then I haven't written a story that involves real people, much less the very real situations that greet each one of us every morning when we open our eyes.

So you just keep on reading, and I'll keep on writing.

Until later, from LakeWatch . . . keep reading,

Janet

Turn the page for a special look
at the next novel in
Janet Chapman's
Midnight Bay series

Coming soon from Pocket Books

"I'm going to be sick." Maddy clutched her stomach.

Eve laughed, pushing her hands out of the way to finish buttoning Maddy's blouse. "That's just your hormones doing a happy dance."

"I can't believe I let you badger me into asking William on a date. When he said yes, I nearly threw up, and I couldn't do a damn thing right the rest of the day." She gave a nervous laugh. "I think I put Mem's dentures to soak in ginger ale, and I know I sent Hiram home from the assisted-living center without any socks."

"It's August—he probably wasn't even wearing socks."

"But Hiram's not a day camper; he lives there! Oh, what have I gotten myself into? It's been so long since I've been on a date that I've forgotten what to do!" Eve laughed.

"You think this is funny?"

"I think this is payback," Eve teased. "Are you forgetting helping *me* dress for my first date with Kenzie? I have about as much sympathy now as you had for me that night. Come on," she said, pulling Maddy over to her old vanity.

"I'm sorry. I know you're just trying to help," Maddy said.

"Because I love you. It's killing me to see you running around with a huge smile on your face all the time, when you're barely holding it together inside. When was the last time you did something just for yourself? The only new outfit I've seen you buy in the last six months is a new set of scrubs for work."

"Oh, please," Maddy said, rolling her eyes. "I do not have martyr's syndrome; I just don't have time to lie around with cucumbers on my eyes, sipping mint juleps."

Eve led her toward the hall. "As of tonight, everything changes. You are going on a date with a handsome man, and you're going to forget about everything except having fun."

Maddy tried resisting. "Slow down, dammit; I'm not ready to have fun with William! You said yourself that he's too much man for me. He's going to eat me up!"

At the bottom of the stairs, Eve wagged her finger at her. "Honest to God, if you're wearing your panties when you get home tonight, I will never speak to you again." She unbuttoned the top two buttons of Maddy's blouse. "The minute you get to the restaurant, order a drink and chug it down to relax yourself," she continued. "But only *one* drink." Eve spread Maddy's collar to expose some cleavage, then grabbed her hand to lead her toward the kitchen. "And you do the driving to-night."

"I can't drive if I'm drinking."

"*One* drink. But even if you drank an entire fifth you'd still be safer than letting William drive."

As they entered the kitchen, William stood up from the table.

"I picked these for you, the prettiest lass around." He held out a fistful of . . . goldenrod from off the side of the road?

Maddy reached for them, but Eve plucked them out of her hand. "Okay, you two," she said, herding them toward the door. "I'll put these in a vase. 'Bye. Have fun."

William stopped on the porch and turned to Maddy. "When I was with Trace this afternoon, he told me that every Wednesday there's something called ladies' night at the bars in Ellsworth. Would ye prefer to go there instead of the restaurant?"

"No!" Maddy and Eve yelped.

"I'm quite hungry," Maddy said more demurely.

William started to take her arm, but Eve took hold of *his* arm and stopped him, her eyebrows raised. William sighed heavily, reached into his pants pocket, and took out his truck keys.

He handed them to Maddy. "I thought you might like to drive this evening," he said, smiling tightly. "So I can concentrate on learning the road signs. I've been told there's also a set of traffic lights in Oak Harbor."

The knot in Maddy's belly suddenly eased, and she all

but skipped down the stairs to his shiny new, fire-engine red pickup truck. "Okay," she said, climbing into the driver's seat. "But it's your job to watch for moose."

William hated feeling out of his element. And Kenzie's list of dating rules had confused him more than they helped. Why did this century have so many blasted rules?

In his homeland, when a man found a lass who was willing, they got straight to business. And if they both felt they'd had a good time, they continued on together until one or both of them found someone they fancied more. Permanent unions were political, not for love.

Love was a woman's notion, anyway, invented to make her feel secure enough to have bairns. Whereas in this century, people got married and never had children, often staying together even though the woman was barren.

After explaining modern courtship, Kenzie had handed William a box of little packets. William had ripped open one of the packets, unrolled the little disk, and stared at the thin tube in confusion. When he realized what it was and exactly how he was supposed to use it, he'd started cursing.

Kenzie had walked out of the barn with a laughing warning that Eve would run William through with a sword if he knocked up her best friend.

Now William looked out the windshield, trying to remember the things Mabel had suggested he talk to Maddy about. "They've set the foundation for my house," he said, grabbing the door handle when she brought the truck up to speed rather quickly.

"Already?" she asked. "So did you set it in the sheltered cove like Samuel suggested, or up on the bluff where Elbridge thought it should go?"

"I wished to place it far out on the point, where it would be surrounded by water on three sides, and every room would have a good view, but the men persuaded me that nor'easters would likely sweep it away. And they said it would cost a small fortune to heat, and that I'd constantly be washing the salt spray off the windows."

"So where are you building it?"

"High up on the bluff where Elbridge suggested. Everyone seemed happy with the decision."

"What style of house are you building? A New England cape, or a more modern design?"

"It's going to be more of an Irish keep."

"You mean, like a castle?"

"Nay, it won't be that big. It will have only eight bedrooms."

"Eight!" She glanced over at him. "It's going to take a year to build a house that size."

William finally let go of the door handle. Maddy appeared to be quite a good driver. She sped down the winding road much as he liked to do, but she didn't let the tires stray onto the gravel. He must need more practice, because when he moved the steering wheel only a wee bit, the damn truck seemed to bolt for the ditch.

"Robbie MacBain found a good local carpenter for

me," he told her, "and the gentleman agreed to hire more men so I can be moved in by next spring. Was that a stop sign?" he asked, looking over his right shoulder as a signpost went flying by.

"No, it said 'yield.' It was a triangle, not a hexagon."

He relaxed and faced front again. "I have a question to ask ye, Maddy. Is it common practice for a woman to ask a man out on a date?" She didn't answer, and her cheeks turned a soft pink.

"I only ask because Hiram made a comment about how young women today are always chasing after anything in pants."

She slowed the truck abruptly, bringing it to a full stop beside a red sign that said "stop," then turned right and shot off again.

"Hiram then went on to say the affliction seems to be contagious, as the older women at the assisted-living center have started being quite forward. So, is a lass asking out a man common practice or not?"

"Hiram is ninety-one years old," she finally said. "When he started dating, women had just won the right to vote."

"So is that a yes?"

He heard her sigh. "It's a sometimes. Sometimes women ask men out, because if we have to wait for them to ask *us* out, it might never happen."

"I was going to ask you out," he said softly. "I knew that if I wanted to spend some time alone with you, I should ask ye to go on a date."

She slowed the truck again and blinked at him. "You were?" Her gaze drifted down to his forearm, exposed by his rolled-up cuff, then her cheeks darkened and her breath hitched.

She snapped her gaze back to the road and resumed speed.

William suddenly decided modern society could take all its blasted rules and shove them. "I was thinking that after dinner we might drive to Dragon Cove so I can show you my house."

Maddy glanced over at him, her gaze straying to his arm again before she looked back at the road. "I . . . I think I'd like that."

And that's when William knew that no matter what century it was, some things would never, ever change.

William found that he quite liked the concept of dating; he couldn't remember spending a more entertaining and enlightening meal with a lovelier woman. And a rather talkative one too. The more Maddy drank, the more she talked, and the more she talked, the more enchanted William became. She'd even admitted that Eve had said she could only have one drink to calm her nerves—a little tidbit she'd divulged after finishing her third Long Island Iced Tea.

William had taken a sip at her insistence, and decided it wasn't like any tea he'd ever tasted; the fumes alone could have brought down a bear. When he'd asked why she felt the need to calm her nerves, Maddy had explained that dating was like riding a horse, and that when a person repeatedly fell off, they sometimes needed a little liquid courage to climb back on again. Then she'd gone on to say she was limiting herself to only three drinks tonight, as four seemed to be her tipping point for outright stupidity.

When she'd obviously lost count and ordered her fourth drink, William had followed the waiter to the bar and he'd instructed him to cut out the liquor. He was glad Maddy was comfortable enough to let her guard down with him, but he preferred his women consciously willing.

He'd limited himself to two drinks of warm straight whisky, unwilling to let his own guard down as long as Maddy was in his care.

All in all, he felt the evening was a success. In fact, he even got to drive. Maddy had handed him the keys as they'd stood up to leave, saying she certainly wasn't drunk, but maybe it would be better if he drove.

It was his first experience driving at night, and once he left the town of Oak Harbor and was traveling a dark road, the headlights were more of a hindrance than a help. He tried to turn them off, but no matter which button he pushed, he couldn't make them go out. Total darkness would have allowed his eyes to adjust, whereas the headlamps only shone a few hundred paces in front of the truck, so he had to go very slow for fear that something would suddenly appear in front of him.

Maddy complimented him several times on the drive

back to Midnight Bay, and said he should be able to get his license very soon.

William decided the more time he spent with the lass, the more he liked her.

He slowly made his way down the dirt road going into his land, then stopped at the edge of the cove and shut off the engine. And *still* the lights didn't go out.

"Are the blasted lights going to stay on all night?" he muttered.

Maddy giggled. "They're on a timer; they'll go out in a minute or two. They stay on so you can walk to the house without tripping over anything." She giggled again. "I haven't been down this road since high school. We used to come here to drink and go parking."

"How does one 'go parking'? If you're parked, you aren't going anywhere."

The dash lights let him see her surprise. "You've never been *parking*?"

"I believe we're parking right now, are we not?"

Her expression went from surprised to somewhat . . . intense.

The headlights suddenly went out, plunging them into darkness, and Maddy giggled again. "We're certainly not going to be able to park in this truck with the stupid console between us." There was enough moonlight that William could see her smiling as her fingers feathered over his forearm. "But I guess that's why they make backseats," she said huskily.

He glanced over his shoulder and would have laughed

if he hadn't known she was serious. Full-grown men and women made love in backseats? He'd get a leg cramp just trying to undress her.

"Come on," he said, opening his door. "Let's head up to the bluff so I can show you my building site. Stay there; I'll walk around and get you, so ye don't trip and fall."

On her side of the truck, he took hold of her hand as she slid out, then laced his fingers through hers. "Are ye cold, lass?" he asked when she hugged herself with her free arm. "Here, I'll give ye my shirt," he said, letting go of her to unbutton it.

"No! You should leave it on," she said, her voice sounding husky as she stopped him by grabbing both his wrists.

William heard her breath hitch, and suddenly her hands were gone from him.

William unbuttoned his shirt, pulled the tails out of his pants and shrugged it off, and then wrapped it around her shoulders.

"Ohmigod," he heard her whisper on an indrawn breath, which was quickly followed by a strangled giggle.

"Slide your arms in the sleeves," he told her. As soon as she did, he took her hand and led her up the new road the crew had carved through the trees. "Can ye see well enough?" he asked, wrapping an arm around her waist and tucking her against his side when they reached the uneven ground of the building site.

She stumbled anyway, and William immediately steadied her. When she leaned against him, her eyes wide, he cupped her face in his palms, tilted her head, and covered her mouth with his just as her soft, sweet lips parted in surprise.

He felt her breath hitch, and as she leaned into him more forcefully, he smiled. He knew exactly what the lass wanted, and he was all too glad to make her happy.